HEAVY PRAISE [P9-DGS-298]
EVA WYLIE,
AND *MONKEY WRENCH*

"Fast-paced and first-rate. . . . [by] the excellent British writer."
—Chicago Tribune

"Slam-bang . . . Eva Wylie plows through with brute strength and rough honesty."
—New York Times Book Review

"Eva Wylie tells her tale in the honest voice of a woman used to making her way in spite of the odds. . . . One always feels that Eva is going to make it."
—Associated Press

"Eva is one of the funniest narrators in recent fiction. . . . MONKEY WRENCH is as well-packed as Eva's wrestling costume."
—Sunday Times (London)

"A startlingly original new series . . . hilarious and occasionally painful. . . . You can't slide your eyes away."
—Minneapolis Star Tribune

"Cheeky, vulgar, side-splitting . . . ribald."
—Buffalo News

"Like Miss Marple and Lord Peter Wimsey, Eva Wylie is a character of such convincing reality. . . . The pace is breathless and jittery, much like the London Lassassin herself, who is a singular treasure."
—Publishers Weekly (starred review)

more . . .

MONKEY WRENCH

BY LIZA CODY

Monkey Wrench
Bucket Nut
Backhand
Rift
Stalker
Under Contract
Headcase
Bad Company
Dupe

LIZA CODY

MONKEY WRENCH

THE MYSTERIOUS PRESS

Published by Warner Books

A Time Warner Company

First published in the United Knigdom by Chatto & Windus Ltd. in 1994

MYSTERIOUS PRESS EDITION

Cover illustration by Rick Lovell

The Mysterious Press name and logo are registered trademarks of Warner Books, Inc.

 Mysterious Press books are published by
Warner Books, Inc.
1271 Avenue of the Americas
New York, NY 10020

Visit our web site at
http://pathfinder.com/twep

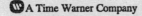 A Time Warner Company

Printed in the United States of America

Originally published in hardcover by The Mysterious Press.
First Printed in Paperback: October, 1996

10 9 8 7 6 5 4 3 2 1

Chapter 1

I only wanted a bunch of bananas. I was on my way to the shop to buy them when I saw a bunch of kids circling and yowling like hyenas. They chanted,

> Dirty Dawn
> Stinks like a prawn.
> She lost her bra
> In a punter's car
> And she don't know where her knickers are.

Dawn is trouble. She's a mess and a waste of space. She's always on the piss. I crossed over to the other side of the road. If she saw me she'd expect me to get rid of the kids and wheel her home in a barrow. I ducked into Hanif's shop instead.

I took my time behind the shelves. If I stayed there long enough Dawn would pull herself together and shamble off without my help. Helping people always ends in tears. And helping drunks is a total waste of time. They're never grateful, they don't pay their debts and they've got rotten memories. What's the point in being nice to someone who can't remember how nice you've been? Tell me that. The only point in doing someone a favour is if they remember and do you a favour back.

Besides, angry wasps are better-natured than the kids in this part of London. Take a tip from me—if you like a quiet life don't *ever* get yourself outnumbered by kids. I was a kid once myself so I know how evil they can be once they get into a pack. Normal rules don't apply to a pack, and a little kid who wouldn't do hokey-cokey on his own becomes Conan the Barbarian in a bunch. Come to think of it, that's true of grown-ups as well.

I know about crowds. I should, I'm a wrestler.

That's right. Me. I'm Eva Wylie, the London Lassassin. Maybe you heard of me, maybe you haven't, but I'm getting myself a reputation as one of the meanest, toughest villains in the business. So don't you tell *me* about crowds—just shut your mouth and give your ears a chance. You think all you have to do is cram a load of people together and what you got is a crowd? Wrong. A crowd is *not* just a lot of people. It's an animal. It's an animal which roars. It can be stroked quiet. It can be goaded. It can be tweaked and revved up. It can be kind, but mostly it's cruel. People who wouldn't dare insult me eyeball to eyeball if they met me on the street call me dreadful names when they know all they have to do is duck back into the body of a crowd.

I don't care. I can take it. It's what I get paid for.

I do not get paid for taking on a bunch of nasty, dirty-minded kids. And besides, I don't owe Dawn anything. The opposite, in fact.

I used to know Dawn's little sister, Crystal—we dossed together sometimes and went on the same collection routes. That was in the days before my luck turned, when I was still on the streets. And before Crystal's luck turned and she got a stall on the market. At the time it was Dawn who was doing all right, and Crystal and me who were hanging on by half a fingernail.

Here's what happened. It was one hard cold night, so cold that the damp in your coat freezes and your chilblains split, and Crystal and me had made a nest in a condemned house in Hammersmith. We thought it was safe and we'd just settled when we got roused by a family of crusties and their dogs. Eight crusties and three dogs.

I might have managed some of the crusties because even in those days I was a big girl who could be a bit useful. But eight of them! And three dogs. I could do it now—they wouldn't know what hit 'em. But then, I hadn't realised my full potential. And besides, Crystal was such a little thing—knee-high to a piss-pot, she was. And we hadn't managed to scrounge any supper so we weren't at our best.

Anyway, the crusties tossed us out and there we were back on the street with nowhere to go. And Crystal says, "Maybe we could go over to Paddington and see if my sister will lend us a bit of floor."

I was dead surprised. I never knew she had a sister, and as we slogged along the empty streets to Paddington I wondered why, if her sister had a room, Crystal was always so down and out.

I found out why when we got there.

"Piss off, Crystal," Dawn said. It was the first thing she said when she opened the door. Looking past her, I saw a warm room, all painted pink. But Dawn barred the door.

"If you think I'm letting you in here," Dawn said, "you've got another think coming. You smell like the corporation tip, and who's that you got with you—the Incredible Hulk?"

"That's Eva," Crystal said.

"Well, she can piss off too," Dawn said. She was all made up with pink cheeks and black eye shadow at three in the morning. Which meant only one thing to me. And I wasn't wrong.

"You're costing me money," Dawn said. "Stood here on my landing like this was some dosshouse."

"Just a warm-up, Dawn," Crystal said. "We won't stop long. It's perishing outside."

I hated to see her beg. She was only little but she had grit.

"I know your warm-ups," Dawn said. "Last time you was in here I scratched for days. I had to douse me bed with flea spray. Now sling yer hook." And she slammed the door in our faces, but not before I saw a huge box of chocolates spread out on her bed, and comics, and heated hair rollers. Everything a whore needs to occupy her mind between sessions.

And there we were, out in the grinding cold.

"So much for family feeling," I said. Because *my* sister would never've chucked us out. If I'd known where to find her. *My* sister would've had us in for a cup of tea and a kip on her bed. She'd of given us a whole handful of chocolates, and a bath.

"Well, where *is* your sister then?" Crystal said. Because she could be quite spiteful when she was hungry, and she knew I hadn't seen her for years. I was looking, but I never found her.

So that was the first time I saw Dawn and I haven't forgotten. Forgiving and forgetting's for those who can afford it. Not me. I can hold a grudge forever if I want to.

But it wasn't worthwhile holding a grudge against Dawn. She was her own worst enemy. She had no guts. Crystal had all the guts in that family. So now Crystal has a place to live and a bric-a-brac stall in the Mandala Street Market, but Dawn stands on street corners and gets in blokes' cars. And then she pisses all her takings away in the pub. How stupid can you get?

She only moved down here, south of the river, so she could leech off Crystal. She used to have a bloke to look after her, but he went the way all blokes go when they're through with a woman—onwards and upwards. And Dawn went the way all gutless women go when there's no one to look after them—backwards and downwards.

That's what happens when you depend on other people. Take it from me. You got to depend on yourself in this world. Crystal did. I did. We made our own luck.

I paid for the bunch of bananas and went on. Dawn was still there. The kids had got her down and one of them was trying to lift her skirt with a stick.

"Dawn's a whore," they were screeching, "she's so poor, she does it up against the lavvy door."

I turned away to go home, when all of a sudden Crystal burst out from the alleyway opposite. She grabbed the stick and started laying about her like a homicidal midget. She's not much bigger than a ten-year-old kid herself, but she cleared a space round Dawn in no time at all. She looked so funny I just stood there splitting my sides.

Big mistake. She saw me.

"Eva," she yelled. "Give me a hand."

"Get stuffed," I yelled back. "I got work to do."

But then one of the kids pointed and said to his mates, "Ain't that Bucket Nut?"

Bucket Nut is one of the more civil things I get called when I'm fighting. And I was so chuffed the kid recognised me I strolled over, all casual like. I took my jacket off as I went so everyone could see the size of my arms. I'm proud of my arms. A lot of time and trouble went into them. I'm not so proud of my belly but I wasn't going to show it off to anyone, was I? Not in the middle of the road, I wasn't. Not without getting paid.

"Give us a hand, Eva," Crystal said again.

"You really Bucket Nut?" one of the kids asked.

"What you think?" I said. "And watch yer mouth or I'll show yer."

"My dad says wrestling's all an act."

"Yeah?" I said, taking just one pace forwards. I could tell the kid was impressed. He took two paces backwards.

I was chuffed to buggery. This time last year no one knew me. Now I get recognised in the street. It goes to show I'm on my way.

"My dad says wrestlers are about as much use as jelly door-knockers," the kid said. "When it comes to real fighting . . ."

"Tell you what," I said, "you give me your dad's name and address, if you know it, and I'll see what he says when I push you through his letter box."

Crystal said, "Why don't you stop posing and help me?"

She'd got Dawn sat up and she'd wiped her off a bit, but it would've taken an engine hoist to get her on her feet. She didn't have any bones in her legs. I've seen my ma in that state, and there's only one thing for it—the good old-fashioned fireman's lift. Which is what I did. Not for Dawn, mark you. She could go rotten in the road for all I cared. But Crystal and me have a history. We aren't mates—we never were, exactly, but we were in the same boat once or twice, and if she never did me any favors, she never did me any damage either. And that's as close as I get to having friends.

Crystal's room looked a lot like her stall. She didn't have furniture, it was more like her stockroom with a mattress in the middle. We laid Dawn out to snore and then Crystal went back to the market, and I went off to the yard.

That's where I live—a breaker's yard. And if you think that's funny, ask yourself, do *you* get paid to live where you live? If you're the one with a landlord or a mortgage don't you sneer at me. I get my accommodation free. It goes with the job. Because that's the other thing I do besides the wrestling—I mind the yard at night. So if you fancy a few spares or plant, and if you don't fancy paying for it, it's me and my dogs you have to deal with. You won't find it easy, let me tell you. Me and Ramses and Lineker have practically a clean sheet where thieving is concerned. We may not be pretty, but we're bleeding effective, and between us we can pack a lot of muscle and make a lot of noise.

So that night, after all the men had gone home, I locked up the yard, as always, and I let out the dogs, and we did a tour of the property. I'm supposed to be there all night, but sometimes there are other things to do. It depends who pays best. But so long as I'm back in time to feed the dogs and open up, who's to know?

Tonight I was going to see The Enemy. She thinks she's so sharp and in control and she's just waiting to catch me at it.

At what? Who bleeding knows? There are some people like that, and they're all polizei of one breed or another.

That's right, The Enemy is a lady cop. She says she isn't anymore, but I say, once a copper always a copper. You can't clean it off like shit on your shoes.

The sign on the door says "Lee–Schiller." Lee is The Enemy, Mr. Schiller is her partner. He's an old geezer, and the secretary is an old bird. The Enemy runs a day-care center for wrinklies. Which is why she needs me for stuff that can't be done by someone in a walking frame.

I opened the door and a bell rang. The secretary-bird was at her desk writing things in a big book.

She said, "Hello Eva, come for your money?"

"What you think?" I said.

She gave me an envelope. I tore it open and counted the dosh. It was all there.

"Got anything else for me?" I asked.

"Anna's out at the moment," she said. As if I didn't know. If she's in, The Enemy pops up whenever she hears that door bell ring. Nosy cow—always got to know what's happening. Even when it doesn't concern her. Typical polizei.

"If there is anything new she knows where to find you," the old secretary-bird said. Which narked me off. That's why I go to see The Enemy regular. I don't much like her "knowing where to find me." If there's one thing you should know about me, it's this—Eva Wylie was not put on this earth to make life easy for the polizei.

And The Enemy wasn't making life easy for me. No extra work, no extra scratch. Well, sod her.

Chapter 2

The very next day I heard that Dawn was dead.

I got up as usual about 3 P.M. and had my breakfast of tea, bananas and bread and jam. Then I went down Sam's Gym for the weights and the shower. Sam's Gym is where the mob from Deeds Promotions hang out. Some of us train properly—like Harsh and me. The others just mong about flexing their dangly bits and gossiping. Either way that's where I go to keep myself big and strong, and to pick up word of where I'm fighting next. I also pick up my purse from my last fight.

There aren't many people in this world who pay you cash on the nail the way they ought. You do the business but you have to wait for the readies. The boss-class have got it all sorted to their own advantage. I mean, the folk who watch me fight got to pay or they don't get in. That's dosh in the cash box. So how come I got to wait for mine? Eh? Tell me that. How come Mr. Deeds of Deeds Promotions, who does bugger all but sit on his fat arse all day, gets his first? And me, who takes all the bruises and abuses, gets mine last?

"Go on, count it," he said, like he was doing me a favour. "It's all there, but you go on and count it anyway. You always do."

And I did. I'd be a fool not to. In that last fight, I was with a woman called Gypsy Jo and when I took her down by the knees in the last round she got one leg out of my grip and hammered my elbow with her boot. My elbow's been sore for days, and if Mr. Deeds thinks a sore elbow's not worth a few quid he's a bigger twat than even his wife thinks he is.

"You have swelling there," Harsh said. He was getting paid too. "Treat it with hot and cold. Rest it."

"I'll work it off," I said, because Mr. Deeds was listening.

"You on the injured list?" he said. Arse like an elephant, ears like a rabbit, brain like a dust ball.

"Not me," I said. If I'm injured he won't find a bout for me. No bout, no purse.

Harsh said, "Then you will hurt yourself more than Gypsy Jo did."

I didn't know whether to be chuffed or choked. It's brilliant when Harsh takes an interest, but like as not, when he does, he says something I don't want to hear. He was wearing grey sweat bottoms and an old black singlet, and his deltoids were shining wet from the exercise.

"There was someone here looking for you," he said.

"Who?"

"She didn't say. A kid."

"When?"

"Earlier."

"I don't want no strangers in here," Mr. Deeds said. He thinks if people know what we do when we train they won't believe in the fights anymore.

"She came to the entrance," Harsh said. "I saw her there." He's the soul of patience, is Harsh. It wasn't any of Mr. Deeds' business earwigging other people's conversations.

"She was very cold," Harsh said, "so she came in only for a minute. She said, 'Tell Eva . . .' "

"Over here," I said, jerking my chin. Harsh may be a lovely wrestler but he's as thick as potato pie when it comes to keeping his lip buttoned in front of someone who doesn't like me.

"What did she say?" I asked, when we were alone by the window.

"She said, 'Tell Eva that Dawn's dead.' She wants to see you."

That was the message. Harsh don't know anything else.

Dawn was dead. No how or why or where. No reason why Crystal wanted to see me.

That was the mystery—what would Crystal want with me?

Dawn being dead wasn't much of a puzzle. You knew something bad would happen to Dawn every time you looked at her. She did sex for money and she wasn't choosy. You could see her pissed any hour of the day or night. Out of her skull. She couldn't look after herself. And if you can't look after yourself you're done. Simple as that.

"I'm sorry," Harsh said. "Was Dawn a friend of yours?"

"No, she bleeding wasn't," I said. "She was just around— near where I live."

"All the same," Harsh said.

"All the same nothing," I said, and I went off and warmed up. Then I started on the machines. I could imagine Dawn sprawled out on a hospital meat tray. For some reason I thought she drowned. What did it matter how she went? She was half fucking dead when she was alive. Fucked. Fucked up. Dead drunk. Dead.

I was on that machine which works your inner thighs. You pull a roller with one ankle so your leg snaps closed. And that's how I was counting the repetitions—fucked, fucked up, dead drunk, dead, five, six, seven, eight. And so on, nice and rhythmical. Change legs, start again on the other side. I thought I'd give my legs and abdominals a real working over. Give me elbow a rest. Like Harsh said.

You think I'm a cold-hearted bitch, do you? Or maybe you don't. Maybe you think I'm pretending to be a cold-hearted bitch to protect my image. Because the London Lassassin is a hard nut. She don't care if you're smaller or injured. She'll smash your nose into the canvas whatever you are. And if the London Lassassin's a stony-hearted bastard, Eva Wylie's got to pretend to be one too. While, in fact, deep down inside she's soft and warm and cuddly.

Don't kid yourself. I do not give a wet fart for Dawn. What did Dawn ever do for me except kick me out into the cold one night. Who was the stony-hearted bitch then? Her with her chocolates and heated rollers, that's who. Did she give a wet fart about me? She did not. She was young and pretty, and as fresh as you could be, leading the sort of life she led. That was her luck. But she never shared it, not even with her own kid sister.

She used to be young and pretty. When I saw her yesterday she was sort of bloated and shapeless. A blob on the pavement. Now she was a blob on a meat tray.

When I go, I want to go with a bang. I don't want to be a blob everyone screwed and nobody knows. By the time I go, everyone'll know my name. I'll be someone. See if I'm not!

So don't you talk to me about Dawn. I don't want to know.

Which is why I didn't go looking for Crystal. What does Crystal mean to me anyway? I sort of knew her when we were both down and out—a time I'm not too keen on remembering—and we both live in the same square mile in South London. Big deal. So do two million other erks. I don't owe any of them dropsy either.

Later that night Crystal came to see me. I was sitting on the steps of my Static eating cold spaghetti hoops out of the tin. Lineker was nosing round even though he knows he doesn't get scraps from me. He's fed when he's done his job and not one minute before. Why should he be different from any other working stiff? He's not a bleeding pet.

All of a sudden we heard Ramses from the gate.

"Ro-ro-ro," went Ramses. He barks like a bass guitar on full amp.

Lineker pricked up his ears and that was about all—which really narked me off.

"Lineker," I said, "you're a greedy, lazy know-nothing. And if I wasn't so soft you'd be living on a tin of cat food—fifty tins of cat food, seeing as you're so big."

He didn't like my tone of voice. Which was the first piece of sense he'd shown that night. I was serious. Lineker always takes the flabby way, and I don't like it.

He ran off, going, "Yak-yak," and showing his big white fangs like he meant it. What a poser that dog is.

I picked up a wrench and a torch and went too. There's a sign on the fence which says, "Armour Protection." The sign's pretty faded and I don't know who Armour Protection were, or if they ever existed, but that's what I call myself and Ramses and Lineker. It's a good hard name.

When I got to the gate, Ramses was standing with his shoulders up and his head thrust out and Lineker was running up and down the wire. He was still yak-yak-yakking, but Ramses had this steady phlegmy roar going in the back of his throat. It's a lovely scary sound. Sometimes, when you're up close you can't tell the difference between him and a 1000 cc Harley.

I whacked the metal gate with my wrench and yelled, "Who's there?" I thought it was kids, but it was Crystal.

She said, "Eva, it's me. Can you come out a minute?"

"No," I said. "I'm on duty."

"Then can you do something about the dogs and let me in?"

"They're on duty too," I said. It was embarrassing talking to someone with a sister on a meat tray and I wanted to get back to my spaghetti hoops. Besides, Crystal had someone with her, and if you think I'm letting strangers into my yard you're even stupider than I thought.

"Didn't that bloke give you my message?"

"What bloke?"

"At the gym," she said. "I gave him a message."

"Oh, the gym," I said. "I didn't go in today. I went to see my ma."

Which, as you well know, was a total pork pie. I *should* have gone to see my ma. I *thought* about going to see my ma, but I didn't want to hear her troubles any more than I wanted to hear Crystal's.

"You've not heard, then?" Crystal said. "Dawn's dead."

"Shit," I said. I was trying to sound sympathetic. A sister's a sister after all even if she does shag for shillings.

"They beat her up in the alley behind the Full Moon," Crystal said. So Dawn didn't drown. I don't know what made me think she did. Perhaps it was that bloated look.

"We left her safe in bed," I said. I didn't want to be associated. "She was all right when we left her."

"She must've got thirsty or something," Crystal said. "She was gone when I got back from the market. She never come home all night. They came and told me in the morning. I had to identify her. Eva?"

"What?"

"I hardly knew her, Eva. They marked her up so bad."

There's not a lot you can say to that.

"Shut up, Ramses," I growled. Ramses gave me his I-eat-babies look.

The stranger hadn't opened her trap so far, but now she said, "I was in the Full Moon last night. I think she went out with two men."

"Stupid mare," I said.

"She was drunk."

"Same difference."

"Look, Crys," the stranger said, "I thought you told me she was sympathetic."

"I never," Crystal said. "I told you she could help. I never said she was sympathetic."

"What sort of crap is this?" I asked.

"Some women," Crystal said. "They do business out of the Full Moon on and off. They want to learn how to do karate or something."

"Ha ha," I said. "Those slags?"

"Ha ha, yes," the stranger said. "Us 'slags.' "

Crystal said, "See, Eva, Dawn wasn't the first round here."

"And she won't be the last," the stranger said, "unless we organise."

"You lot *organise*?" I had to laugh. "What you going to do, set up a slags' neighborhood watch?" I was falling about, it was so funny.

The stranger drew herself up as tall as she could, which wasn't very tall, and said, "We were going to start by getting you to learn us self-defence. But if you ain't interested we'll take our money elsewhere."

I stopped laughing. I said to Crystal, "Is she serious? And what's it got to do with you, anyway?"

"Nothing really," Crystal said. "Only I had to go to the Full Moon. See, Eva, the police don't tell you anything. And when it's, y'know, someone like poor Dawnie they don't really care. They think, y'know, she was asking for it. So I had to go to the Full Moon to find out if anyone seen her."

"And some of 'us slags' was in there," the stranger said. "Having a confab. Because there was that kid from Leeds last year. And then another one in March. And now Dawn. That's three of us dead."

"I can count," I said.

"The cops can't," the stranger said. "Three 'slags' do not equal one 'respectable' woman. We won't get no protection there. So we got to look after ourselves."

"Yes," Crystal said. "When they were talking about it I was wishing and wishing Dawn could of known how to look after herself. She was always getting knocked about. So I thought, y'know, you and your wrestling. You could teach them self-defence."

I was gawping at them through the gate. I didn't know what to say, it was such a silly idea. Me, teach *them?*

"They've got money," Crystal said. "They can pay."

Well, of *course* they got money. I just couldn't see them parting with it for anything sensible. And another thing, women who earn their living on their backs, believe it or not, aren't very physical.

"Well?" the stranger said.

"Shut up. I'm thinking about it."

"Don't take all night."

"Who the fuck are you anyway?" I said.

"You can call me Bella," she said. "And if you must know, I got a little boy and a grandfather to support, and I can't make much of a job of it hanging around outside your gate while you scratch your great thick head."

"Yeah, t'rific," I said, grinning at her. "Well, off you go then. Go on. Go and get your fanny warmed up and while you're at it get *your* thick head bashed in."

"You in then?" Bella said. "Never mind. Look, I'll make it easy for you, 'cos I can see thinking don't come natural. If you're in, come to the Full Moon dinner time tomorrow. If you're out, get knotted. All right?"

And she turned round and walked off looking exactly like what she was. And I thought, how can I teach someone who can hardly walk in that little skirt and those shoes how to fight?

"Self-defence?" I said to Crystal. "She can't hardly walk. What's the point me learning her how to punch and kick, if she dresses like that?"

Both Crystal and me watched Bella teetering from the light of one street lamp to the next until she disappeared round the corner into the bottom of Mandala Street.

Crystal sighed. She was wearing jeans and a T-shirt. Sensible, like me. But then Crystal wouldn't attract no horny punters either. She's got a face like a monkey and she doesn't wear make-up.

She said, "Eva, can I come in? I've only got my room to go to, and it still smells like Dawn."

Well, I couldn't really tell her to fuck off, could I? Call me a sentimental fool, but I couldn't just walk off and leave her looking pitiful by the gate.

"You got to promise not to cry," I said, unlocking one of the padlocks. "I can't abide people crying."

"I'm not crying," she said. "I'm angry."

Which made it all right. So I let her in and took her to the Static for a brew.

Crystal is no more of a crier than me. But she did want to talk. I don't mind that too much. I like stories.

"You never took to Dawn," she said, when we'd got our hands wrapped around a couple of mugs of tea.

"She never took to me," I reminded her. "If she'd of let us in that night it'd be a different story."

"You always remember the bad bits," she said.

Well, I'd be a fool not to, wouldn't I? If you forget about the bad bits how you going to avoid them in the future? Besides, I never did know any good bits about Dawn.

"Dawn wasn't always like that," she went on, dipping her upper lip in her tea. "Except she was always the pretty one. I used to think she was lucky, but when we got more grown up I reckoned she wasn't. Everyone wants things off you if you're pretty. Being pretty makes you a mark."

Crystal knows about marks. That's what makes her such a shrewd trader down the market. I never thought about it before—mark, market. Geddit?

She didn't notice me sniggering, and she went on, "Even when she was very young, y'know, eleven or twelve, there'd be blokes coming up to Dawn, saying things like, 'Hey, gorgeous. Fancy a drink, want to come dancing?' Stuff like that. And she used to go to pubs and things before she was old enough. And she thought the blokes were giving her a good time. She didn't know they never *give* anything. There's always a price. The first time she came home crying with blood on her legs and she said someone hurt her. That's when she realised about the price. But, see, she didn't learn from it 'cos she kept falling in love. She believed in love. She said it made her feel real.

"There was this bloke. We used to see him on our way home from school sometimes. On the days we actually went to school. He had a big red car and he used to wear very flash suits. He collected the money from the arcade. That's where we used to go after school—to the arcade. And I could tell he had his eye on Dawn. Because, even then, I used to try to watch out for her. She really needed a minder.

"This flash bloke, he'd say to me, 'Shove off, titch, you're in the way. Three's a crowd.'

"And I'd say, 'I'll tell our mum. I know your sort.'

"And he'd say, 'You know bugger all.' And then he'd say to Dawn, ' 'Course, if you *want* your kid sister tagging along why don't you go down the playground with the boys.'

"And then she'd say, 'Shove off, Crystal.' And if *she* said shove off, I had to shove off.

"One time when I got really worried I did tell our mum. And she went and told her husband. And he gave Dawn and me the strap and locked us in our room at night. But Dawn was in love so she climbed out the window. And she wouldn't talk to me for weeks. Which is why, when she started missing her monthlies, she never told me. And by the time she did she was already three months gone."

"I never knew Dawn had a baby," I said.

"She didn't," Crystal said. "She lost it. Well, she had it, but it was born blue and we couldn't save it. See, what happened was, she told me about being up the spout and we decided to go and talk to this flash bloke together. She thought he loved her too. She thought he couldn't wait to get married, and the only thing stopping him was her being underage.

"But the first thing he said was, 'How do I know it's mine?' And the second thing he said was, 'Get married? I think my wife might have something to say about that.' Turns out he has a wife and a couple of kids not much younger than Dawn.

"Then he says, 'Here's some money for an abortion, but if you come round me whining again, the next time you look in the mirror you'll think you're looking at a butcher's window.'

"That's what he said, word for word. That's the type Dawn fell in love with.

"There wasn't much I could do. Of course I slashed his tires with a carpet knife, and I lobbed a brick through the windscreen."

"'Course you did," I said. Crystal's like me. She has a lot of self-respect.

"But he didn't change his mind," said Crystal. "And by the time Dawn plucked up enough courage to go to the doctor, and by the time the tests were done she was nearly five months gone, and no one would touch her. And then our mum noticed, and her husband threw Dawn out."

"I suppose you went too," I said, "to look after her." Because if it had been *my* sister, I'd've done the exact same thing. Except my sister wouldn't get into trouble that way. She's much too smart, and she isn't interested in men.

"Yeah," Crystal said. "We came to London and hit the streets, and then one night Dawnie had these pains, and along came a little baby, all black and blue, like she'd been thumped, and we couldn't make it breathe, so we buried it in the garden of one of those houses on Kipling Road before they knocked them all down.

"It was my fault really. I hadn't got the hang of things and I could never seem to scrounge enough to feed Dawn proper. It was just as well, though, about the baby. I'd never've managed with three of us, and Dawn would've got taken in care for sure. She never could've stood for social workers and things.

"Anyway, it cured her of love, and the next bloke she met she made him pay. 'Crystal,' she said, 'it's no different from doing it for love, but you eat better.'

"And then, because she was still young and pretty, another bloke she met set her up in that room in Paddington. And he took care of her. And even though she gave him two-thirds of what she made she still lived better than she ever did before. Or since, for that matter."

"You said you wouldn't cry," I said.

"I'm not," she said. "I'm just bloody angry."

So I lent her a T-shirt to blow her nose on.

Chapter 3

I said I like stories, but I didn't like that one much. For one thing, I've heard it too many times before. Change the names, change the dialogue, and I bet you've heard it too.

Crystal dropped off to sleep on my couch so I went out to do my rounds with Ramses and Lineker.

"Good thing you're not female," I said to Lineker. "You're just the type who'd fall pregnant to a married bloke." He was sleek and beautiful and dozy, and if he didn't have Ramses and me to keep him up to the mark, people would take advantage right, left and centre.

I heard a lot of girls' stories when I was young. If you spend much time in reform schools and what they call "places of safety" you hear just about everything bad that can happen to girls. And let me tell you, this love thing is fucking lethal. Because what's love for the girls is just a poke for the blokes, only the girls don't want to admit it. I'm glad I've got more moral fibre.

I bet you think I don't know what I'm talking about. You take one look at me and you think, no one ever fancied her. So what does she know about sex?

Well, that just goes to show how ignorant you are.

I tried it once and I didn't like it. So there.

Actually, I didn't try it. Someone did it to me. But I still didn't like it. And, tell you the truth, nor did he. 'Specially after I threw his trousers in the furnace. Because that's where it happened—in the boiler room of one of those "special" schools they kept sending me to. I used to bunk off lessons to the boiler room because it was the warmest place in the building, and one afternoon the maintenance man caught me there. He said he wouldn't dob on me if I let him have a little feel. Ha ha. Well, he lost his trousers and I found out where a lot of the other girls got their sweets and cigarettes.

Place of safety? Don't make me laugh!

'Course, what you don't hear about in special schools is the girls who get to marry the flash-suited bloke in the big red car. I mean, someone married him, right? Or he wouldn't've had a wife and kids. And maybe she thought she'd got it all. Maybe they'd go out together of a Saturday and choose wallpaper for the spare bedroom. Maybe she never knew about little Dawnie and her blue baby. Or maybe she did. Maybe she divorced him and cleaned him out. But maybe she's still with him, cooking his tea at night and watching what he wants to watch on telly, because she can't get at his money and she'd rather be miserable than poor.

Whoever has the pennies has the power, I always say. Which is why I intend to earn as many dolly-drops as I can. And when I'm rich and famous I won't have to be polite to bobble-heads ever again.

When I got tired of watching Lineker chase rats I went back to the Static. Crystal had woken up and put the kettle on. Her little monkey face was a picture of woe, and I thought it was about time she went home. She was making a dent in my cheerful disposition.

But she said, "I wish I knew who did it, Eva. There was more than one of them. The girls said Eva went out with two blokes, and she had punch marks and boot marks all over."

"If I do decide to teach self-defence," I said, "one of the first things I'll say is, 'Never take on two at a time.' That's so dumb."

"Dawn wasn't very clever," Crystal said.

"Still, she was rat-arsed," I said, trying to be kind. "Could be she was seeing double and didn't know the difference."

"She didn't have any money on her," Crystal said. "So the bastards robbed her too."

"Maybe she drank it."

"No," Crystal said. "The girls say she bought her last drink out of a ten-pound note."

"That's another thing," I said. "Always hide your stash. No point reeling round with tenners in your pocket, putting temptation in people's way."

"I don't think it was about money," Crystal said. "She didn't have much. And y'know, she didn't *look* like she had any, either. Not in the last year, anyhow. She looked, well, like no one cared."

"I know," I said. "I saw her." She'd been like something you see in the gutter. No self-respect.

"But I cared," Crystal said. "She was my Dawnie. But I couldn't stop her boozing, and I couldn't stop her, y'know, going with blokes. Never could. Not even when we was young. And now, no one cares even less. The cops don't care. They aren't even looking for who killed her. They say it goes with the job, for someone like Dawn."

"They would," I said. I wouldn't want anyone to catch me agreeing with the polizei, but they had a point.

"So Eva," Crystal said. "If I find out who did it, will you help me kill them? Or something?"

What a question! Me. Kill someone over Dawn? Crystal had to be bonkers. When I thought about it I realised she *was* bonkers. And if it was *my* sister on a meat tray with boot marks all over I might be bonkers too. But I wasn't going to put myself out over Dawn. No way.

"Okay," I said. "You find 'em, I'll kick 'em."

Well, I had to, didn't I? Crystal was demented, right? Always agree with a demented woman, because if you try to reason with her you'll end up as demented as she is. In fact you'll end up agreeing with her. So why not save yourself the bother of becoming demented and agree straight off?

Just for once in my life I'd said the right thing because Crystal finished her tea and dropped off to sleep again, although even in sleep she looked forlorn.

But she was in my way. I had to creep around in case she woke up with any more thoughts which would need a total brain bypass to understand.

I got through the night one way or another, and then I penned the dogs and went to bed.

'Course I had to dream about it, didn't I? Other people's griefs are infectious. You catch 'em like a case of the snivels. Or maybe *you* don't. Maybe I'm just sensitive. Yeah. That's it. But in dreams it all comes out churned up. Because while I don't give a squashed turd about Crystal's sister I do give one about mine. And in this dream I had a baby. Only it wasn't a baby, it was my sister, Simone, and she was all black and blue. And she was dead. But the horrible part was that she kept sitting up and pushing her black and blue face into mine saying things like, "You shouldn't have let them do it. You should have looked after me." And I'd say, "Do what? You're only a baby." And, "I can't have a baby. You're my sister." And I wanted it to stop. I wanted to get away. But I couldn't move.

I was really cheesed off, I can tell you. And it was all Crystal's fault.

I was even more cheesed off when she woke me up at one o'clock. I hadn't had enough kip.

"You're in a putrid mood, Eva," she said. "You better buck yourself up. We're going down the Full Moon."

"Drink piss," I said. "I'm not going nowhere." I turned over and dragged my sleeping bag up round my ears. I'd forgotten, see. And anyway, I never said I would. I just said I'd think about it.

"It's not like you to turn down a paying gig," Crystal said. "Some of those women are loaded."

I shut my eyes and said nothing.

"Don't matter," Crystal said. "There's loads of blokes who know kung-fu and all that stuff. Bella could get one of them. Easy. One of the big blokes from your gym. They'd prob'ly know more about it than you do anyway."

I was halfway up Mandala Street, with Crystal trotting along behind, before I remembered what she was like. Find your mark and milk it. That should be written on her tombstone. And she'll have a tombstone sooner than she expects if she thinks she can twist me round her finger like she does with one of her punters up the market. Conniving little cow.

We went all the way up Mandala Street, through the market, to the pub. As we went, people called out to Crystal, "Sorry for your trouble, Littl'un," and "Give us the word about the funeral, Crys, I'll let you have some flowers." Stuff like that. Everyone knew Crystal. No one said a dicky-bird to me, even though I get my name on posters.

The Full Moon was packed with everybody except Bella and her mates. Frigging typical. Those slags are so unreliable they can't be bothered to turn up and learn something that might save their skins. I'd taken the trouble to show up so why couldn't they?

Crystal went scurrying off to round them up, and I ordered meat pie and chips for my breakfast. Harsh says I ought to eat more vegetables. Well, chips is potato, right? And potato is vegetable. I don't know why Harsh is so hard on chips.

Harsh also says I should drink fruit juice so I had a lager and lime instead of straight bitter, even though lager and lime is a poncy sort of drink. I was feeling quite virtuous. Having fruit and veg for breakfast meant I could eat what I liked for the rest of the day.

"You come then," Bella said, when she showed up.

"Quicker than you did," I said.

"This here's Eva Wylie," Bella said to the two women behind her.

"And this here's Stef and Mandy," she said to me.

Crystal said, "Kath and Lynn are down the dole office. They'll come when they can."

So I looked at Stef, Mandy and Bella, and, know what? Not one of them looked as if she'd be as good as a chocolate frying pan. Bella was only two inches taller than Crystal, Stef was a skinny little zombie and Mandy would have to go on a diet to fit in a circus tent. If they had one functioning muscle between the three of them I'd die of shock.

"Poop on a pogo-stick," I said.

"What?" said Crystal.

"The state of them," I said. "They don't look very fit, do they?" I was trying to be polite.

"Fit fer what?" Mandy said. "We don't got to look like you, I hope."

"I wouldn't do much business if I looked like her," Stef said. "Hey, Bella, we aint going to end up like her, are we?"

"I don't like muscly women," podge-ball Mandy said.

"It ain't feminine," said Stef.

"A fine way to talk to your fairy fucking godmother," I said. I stood up. As far as I was concerned they could all get their arses booted from here to Cardiff and back. It was their own stupid doing.

"If you think trolloping around like a kicking waiting to happen is fucking feminine," I said, "good bleeding luck to you. You'll get exactly what you deserve."

"Don't you fucking shout at us," Bella screamed. "I thought you'd understand. But you're no better than a man— the way you go on about what we do."

"And you're no better than a man—the way you go on about my looks," I said. "I know I'm no oil-painting, but nobody lays a finger on me 'less I'm paid for it."

"No one'd want to," said Mandy.

"Shut up, shut up, shut up," bellowed Crystal. For a gnome she had a healthy pair of lungs. "Shut up and sit down, all of yer."

Would you believe it? We all shut up and sat down. That Crystal. She looked like a mouse going nuclear. If they turned off the lights she'd glow in the dark.

"What's the matter with you all?" she said. "Yer all mental. Dawnie died yesterday. Just a couple of yards away. And yesterday you was all in here going, 'What'll we do? What'll we do? There's a bleeding ripper about. There's none of us safe.' Now look at you! Don't none of you care about Dawn? Don't none of you care about yourselves? If you'd been down the morgue, like me, and seen her all broken up, you'd care all right. You'd be frightened for more than twenty-four hours."

"I'm frightened all the time," Bella said. Which showed she had a brain or two hidden behind all that paint and hair. I'd be frightened too if I was her size and walked around in a skirt no bigger than a hair band. It wasn't a skirt, it was a piece of string tying her thighs together so she couldn't run away.

"Don't say it, Eva," Crystal said, like she could read my mind. "Don't say nothing at all. Just shut up and listen to what's been happening here. Bella, you been around longest, you tell her. Tell her what you was talking about yesterday."

"We were talking about three dead women," Bella said. "They all worked round here. They all used this pub. We think there's someone out to get us."

"Or two of 'em together," Mandy said. "Dawn left here with two blokes."

"You said you didn't see them," Crystal said. "You told the cops you didn't see."

"Well, we saw them," Bella said. "But we didn't see them. It was just another two blodgers who followed Dawn out. I wasn't paying any attention. I only pay attention to the ones who pay attention to me. Sorry Crys."

"None of us saw," Stef said. "I wish we had, 'cos now there's two killers out there and we don't know who."

"They may not be out there," Mandy said. "They may be in here."

"Looking at us," Stef said.

"Wondering which next," Mandy said.

"Change pubs," I said.

They looked at me like I was stupid. But while they'd been nattering on, scaring themselves silly, I'd been watching the drinkers watching them. Normally I just see a load of people, faces. But this time I saw a load of men. There's nothing like sitting in a busy pub with a bunch of business girls to make you see the men, and only the men.

"This pub has advantages," Bella said.

"What advantages?"

"The market," Bella said. "Lots of people use the market and drink here."

"It's open all day," Mandy said. "We got working hours to suit ourselves."

"The landlord don't give us no aggro," Stef said.

"We live round here," said Bella. "The kids know where to find us, and we can keep an eye on the kids."

"You're all right," Stef said. "You've got your granddad to babysit. The law went and took my Trevor."

"Her boyfriend," Bella said. "Living off immoral earnings, they said."

"They just locked up my babysitter," said Stef. "It's not fair."

"Shit," I said. "You *all* got kids?" And here was me thinking my ma was a slut.

"Some of us," Bella said. "What you think? If you're on the game you didn't ought to have kids?"

"She didn't say nothing," Crystal said. "Don't start. Stick to the point. The point is you need protection. Right?"

"How can anyone protect them," I said to Crystal. "They got to be alone to do the business. They got to protect themselves."

"Show her the alley and the car park," Crystal said. "She don't know what's involved."

"You show her," Bella said. "She don't want to keep company with us 'slags.' She thinks she's too good for us."

What a laugh! Have you noticed—it's the people who despise you who accuse you of thinking you're too good for them? Go on, check it out next time it happens and you'll see I'm right.

Those slags despised *me!* And all because I'm big and strong and not feminine enough for them. And I make an honest living. Well, nearly honest. Too good for them! I'll say I'm too good!

"What's everyone drinking?" Crystal said quickly. "C'mon Eva, we'll get a round in. I'm buying."

So we went to the bar. Which was a good thing because I couldn't get away from that table fast enough. They were all such losers. They just couldn't wait to climb on that meat tray and join Dawn. I fucking hate women who parade themselves around like they're saying, "Here I am, come and have me, and if you fancy a bit of rough stuff you can do that too. Nothing I can do about it except whine." It gives us all a bad name.

I'm not like that. Never have been. Never will be. And I'm glad.

"It's a job," Crystal said. "It's only a job, Eva."

We were at the bar, waiting to be served.

"It's not the job," I said, although it was. "It's the attitude."

"You mustn't judge," she said. "I never judged Dawnie. I thought, one time, Dawn might save up and be a beautician. She was clever with her face. And she could've had her own salon, y'know. When she was earning a lot. But she wasn't no good with money. She'd make it, and then she'd spend it. She never put anything by. It's no good wishing people are what they're not. Y'know, like clever or careful or strong."

"You can learn," I said.

"No you can't," Crystal said. "Well, you can learn some things. But I can't learn to be tall or pretty. You can't learn to be Einstein, and Dawn couldn't learn to be a career woman to suit me. People are what they are."

And then it was our turn. The landlord said, "What's it to be, Crystal?" And Crystal was about to give our order when the landlord's wife came up and said, "This one's on the house, Crystal. We were really sorry about your sister."

Crystal said, "Thanks, but it's my round and there are five of us."

The landlady looked over to where Bella, Stef and Mandy were sitting. She said, "Oh well, just this once. I expect the girls are really shaken up."

And she poured drinks for everybody, even me. I couldn't help noticing how much credit Crystal had everywhere. Maybe no one else knew her like I did. I knew her when she was a little thief and a scrounger. She probably still is, for all I know. Where else would she come by all that junk she sells on her stall?

But, see, that's how she survived when she was cold and hungry and never had a pot to piss in—thieving and scrounging and knowing the right mark to milk.

And I survived by being big and learning to be strong.

And Dawn? Well, Dawn didn't survive, did she, so I can't hold her up as an example, can I?

What I mean is, thinking makes my teeth ache. And toothache reminds me why I need gelt.

"Where you going?" Crystal said.

"Dunno," I said. "I'm not going nowhere."

I hate it when someone interrupts me thinking.

"What's it all about?" the landlady said. "Council of war or what?"

"Eva here's going to do self-defence classes," Crystal said. Which was a liberty.

"Now that's a good idea," the landlady said.

"That's a fucking awful idea," the landlord said. "Women learning how to beat up men! I don't think I like that at all."

"You don't learn how to beat up men," Crystal said. "You learn how to stop them beating *you* up."

"I never took you for butch, Crystal," the landlord said. "Your legs aren't hairy enough and you're far too small."

"Well, I think it's a good idea," the landlady said. "The things that go on round here. A woman isn't safe walking to the news-agent and back. Put me down for a couple of lessons, Crystal."

"What do you want self-defence for?" the landlord said. "You've got me to defend you."

"Not all the time, I haven't," she said. "And besides, who's going to defend me against you when you turn nasty?"

"That's enough!" the landlord said. He pointed at Bella, Mandy and Stef, sitting at the table waiting for their drinks. "*That's* who you'd be doing your lessons with, and I'm not having it. My wife isn't going to socialize with that sort. Maybe they should learn to take better care of themselves—I don't know and I don't care. They aren't my responsibility. But my wife is, and I'm not having my reputation ruined by you and your damn fool fads."

The funny thing was, I could have grabbed the front of his shirt, hauled him across the bar, landed him a couple of easy ones on his knobbly little chin, had a sip of my drink, decked his wife and robbed his till—all in the time it took him to jibber out that load of gob-vomit. Him? He couldn't defend a duck from a stale crust of bread! His precious reputation was kumquats as far as I was concerned.

"Eva!" Crystal said. "Take the drinks over, and shut up."

It's a good thing for that poxy landlord I'm into self-control and mental discipline.

I took the drinks over to our table, but I didn't shut up.

"I don't give shit for your opinion," I told Bella. "I don't give shit for your job, and I don't give shit for you. But if you want to learn how to look after yourself, and if the money's right, I'll show you what's what. Take it or leave it."

Chapter 4

We left the Full Moon and stood on the pavement outside. It was a busy road with traffic groaning and growling non-stop.

"What do you mean I can't learn to be Einstein," I asked Crystal. "I can be whatever suits me. Who's this Einstein anyway?"

"No one," Crystal said. "I just meant some things you can't change. Y'know, like you couldn't learn to wear size 5 shoes, no matter how hard you tried."

"Oh, right," I said. I thought she was getting at me. But she wasn't.

"Yeah," Bella said. "Einstein was a bloke with small feet and a big . . ."

"Shut up!" said Crystal.

"I don't give squat how big his tackle was," I said. "What we doing stood here on this corner like paper sellers?"

"This is a good corner," Mandy said. "The cars slow down 'cos of the traffic lights, see. So if you're stood here the drivers can give you the once-over, and they're not going so fast they can't stop and have a word if they feel like it."

"That's the drill, is it?" I said. "You stand here waiting for drivers?" What a way to make a living!

"Sometimes," Mandy said. "Sometimes you meet someone in the pub, or walking around outside."

"Is this where Dawn got clobbered?" I asked.

"Have a little respect," Bella said. "Don't you ever watch your big mouth?"

"It's all right," Crystal said. "She don't mean nothing. No, Eva, it wasn't here. I'll show you."

"I'll show her," Bella said to Crystal. "You don't have to come."

" 'S all right," Crystal said. "I want to see too."

"Well, anyway," Bella said. "What happens is this—you're in the pub, right? And a bloke comes over, and then you get up, and usually he'll follow you out." She started walking, and the rest of us followed.

"Then there's this alleyway by the side of the pub," she said. She turned down the alley.

It was narrow. There was the pub on one side and the next line of shops on the other. There wasn't any lighting I could see.

"Sometimes they can't wait," Bella said, "and they want to do the business standing here. Otherwise . . ." and she carried on walking about twenty paces. "Otherwise you turn into the car park here."

I said, "Is this where . . ."

"Yeah," said Bella.

The alley went on past the break in the wall. It was dark even in daylight. It was a really horrible place, and even if I hadn't known it was where Dawn was scrubbed it would've given me the squits. Two people could walk side by side down the alley but only by bumping arms and shoulders. We'd walked along it single file—first Bella, then Crystal, then me, and behind me Mandy and Stef.

All the time I was walking along I was looking down the back of Crystal's neck. She's only got a thin neck holding up her little monkey head, and I could imagine someone hooking an arm round that thin stalk and snapping her head back, crack. She wouldn't stand a chance.

"But usually," Stef said, "you turn into here."

If you went through the break in the wall you found yourself in a sort of car park. There were three vans and a lorry there, all unloading goods into the back doors of the shops. There were lots of cars too.

"It's a private car park and loading area in the daytime," Stef said. "But at night, all sorts come here."

"If you get in a car at the front of the pub," Mandy said, "like as not you'd show the driver how to get in here. It's quiet, see."

"The police don't come by hardly ever," Stef said.

"And it's only a few steps back to the pub," Mandy said.

"Dump on a dead dog," I said. "This car park's crap, but that alley's frigging deadly. You couldn't find a riskier place if you searched for a year."

I turned round, and there was Crystal, still in the alley, looking like she'd grown roots. She's so dumb. She should've known she wouldn't like it.

"You're not going to fucking *cry,* are you?" I said.

"Shut up!" said Bella. She went back to Crystal and led her by the hand back up the alley to the main road.

The rest of us followed.

"You're a stony-hearted bitch," Mandy said, from behind me.

Which showed how much she knew. I was only trying to help, but some people haven't the brains to be grateful.

All the same, I didn't like her walking behind me up the alley. I don't like people walking behind me in places where you can't swing your fists.

Of course if she turned nasty I could deal with her. Easy-peasy lemon squeezy. She was too much of a lard lump to do any mischief. A cow in a field would have more mettle than her.

No. It was the place—walls on both sides and not enough room to turn round without grazing your elbows. It gave me the spooks. It made my teeth feel like sandpaper.

I didn't like Mandy behind me, so I whipped round. Sudden. Her cow-eyes blinked at me, all fearful. I got one hand under her wobbly jaw and pushed her back against the wall.

"Who you calling a stony-hearted bitch?" I said.

Her head sort of shrank into her neck, and her neck shrank into her shoulder.

"Don't," she said. "Don't." She was wobbling all over. And the worst part was that as she shrank down she was strangling herself on my hand. She was fluttering and gobbling like a twelve-stone turkey. Disgusting.

"You're disgusting," I said. And I let her go.

All the time, Stef just stood there. She didn't even let out a squeak.

"You're disgusting too," I said. I was so put out I nearly bopped her.

"Is that what you do?" I said.

"What?" Mandy said.

"Nothing," I said. "Absolutely fucking nothing? When someone grabs you by the neck? You just go, 'don't, don't?' "

"I was frightened," she said.

"You was frightened," I said. "That's when you got to *do* something. When you're frightened. Don't you understand? If you're *not* frightened, okay, do nothing. If you're frightened, for Christ's sake, do something. Shit!"

I was so narked I had to get away from them. The people I fight fight back. They don't go wobbly and strangle themselves. If someone whipped round and caught *me* by the throat I'd . . .

As I came out on the main road I began to feel better. I know what I'd do if someone had me by the throat. Well, I'd better know, hadn't I? It happens twice a week in the season.

But how was I going to explain it to Margarine Mandy? The woman was a cringe on two legs.

What puzzled me most, though, was how a woman her size could do sex in a car. It didn't seem physically possible. So that was two puzzles—how had she lived so long, and how did she do it in a motor? Which narked me off all over again, so I thought I'd go back to the Full Moon and have a drink.

I turned in that direction and saw Crystal talking to a bloke just outside the door, and the polizei sensors in my brain went off—beep-beep-peeep! So I cantered away in the opposite direction. Never talk to the polizei unless they sit on your legs and make you. No good will ever come of it.

I borrowed a van and went to the gym instead.

Mr. Deeds was lolling by the window smoking one of his filthy brown whiffs.

He said, "I'm arranging a programme for Lewinsham a week today. You available?"

'Course I was. When wasn't I?

"Only I thought you was whingeing about your elbow. I thought maybe you weren't fit."

What a bim! He only says that sort of bolly 'cos he knows it winds me up. But I wasn't going to give him the satisfaction.

"I'm always fit," I said.

"You never know with females," he said. "I never could trust anyone who bleeds for five days and doesn't die." And he started coughing. Choking on his joke and his smoke. He could choke his lungs out and I'd use them for a trampoline— the foul-mouthed bim. Women's stuff is horrible enough without the likes of Mr. Deeds poking fun. I went away to change.

I was totally brassed off with the women's stuff, if you must know. What with Crystal and Dawn, Bella and Stef. And wondering how Mandy could do it in a motor. The only stuff that's interesting is *my* stuff. You can stuff the rest.

And I had a fight next Friday—either against Gypsy Jo again or Stella Bombshell. One or the other. I wish there was more variety but there isn't. There just aren't enough women wrestlers, so you meet the same ones over and over. I fought a woman from up north once, and she was magic, but you don't get that quality in the London area. Maybe one day when I'm famous I'll go and fight in America. I'd find some good strong opposition over there. I've seen it on TV.

All the same, a fight is something to look forward to. I got to have it. Up there, under the lights, strutting, working the crowd. That's what I want—doing what I'm good at where everyone can see me do it. How many of you suckers can say the same? Eh? Tell me that. How many of you can stand in that cage of light and yell at hundreds of faces—"Shut yer face, you rumbums, I'm up here in the light and you're down there in the dark!" Go on. How many? That's what I call job satisfaction.

The only two actually working in the gym that afternoon were Phil Julio and California Carl. Let me tell you about Carl. He's been to California as many times as I've met the Prince of Wales, but he reads the body building mags. And he thinks they grow the best muscles in America. He thinks if he calls himself California, he'll get some of the credit. That's how clever he is.

He was doing barbell bicep curls with the heavy weights. Arms is his favorite muscle group, and I have to admit, although the man is a champion heavyweight wanker, his arms are a picture.

As a fighter he's about as supple as a garden shed, because his real love is his own body which he exhibits whenever he can in Boy Beautiful contests all across the southern counties.

He's a peroxide blond and he spends a fortune microwaving his skin under sun lamps. He shaves everything. Shaves! I tell a lie. He uses those evil-smelling creams which rot the hair out of its follicles.

Also he does anabolics, anabollox I call them, and he's touchier than a wild sow with a sore snout.

The women love him.

The other blokes, the ones with dirty minds like Gruff Gordon and Pete Carver, think maybe he's a woofter, because often he brings a friend almost as pretty as he is to train with. But I reckon the only one he fancies is himself.

But he does work. You got to say that for him. He works.

And he's having an influence on Flying Phil. Flying Phil used to be an idle sod, half of a father and son tag team, who did a quarter of the work his dad did. But now he streaks his hair and he's gone in for muscle definition and he's angling for a solo career.

He'd better watch out. If he keeps on bulking up like he's doing now he'll get too heavy for the aerial work and he won't be Flying Phil anymore.

I warmed up on the mat the way Harsh taught me. Phil was working on his lats—pulling down weights behind his head, so I went over for a word.

"What would you do," I said, "if a bunch of women asked you to learn 'em self-defence?"

"Shut up, I'm counting," he said. But even though he's born again as far as work is concerned it doesn't take much to get Phil to skive off.

"Self-defence?" he said. "Women? Do me a favor, Eva. I'd never teach women self-defence. They're hard enough to pull as it is."

Chapter 5

The next day, at about four thirty in the afternoon, all those women came to the gym. I was so narked I almost toppled over in the middle of a squat. A boiling saucepan couldn't have felt hotter than my face.

They were all there—Crystal, Bella, Mandy, Stef and the other two, Kath and Lynn. And they were all wearing day-glo shell suits and leggings and lip gloss. I could've died.

"Ay-ay!" Gruff Gordon said. "Quim alert, quim alert."

And everyone stopped what they were doing except California Carl who was polishing his washboard abdominals in front of the mirror.

"Where's Eva?" Bella said, standing there, fists on hips, chin up. Even stood like that she did not look serious. Her hair was like a mound of blackberries.

"You don't want Eva," Pete Carver said, moving in.

"You want a real man," Gruff said. Those two go in team-handed like polizei.

"I'd rather have haemorrhoids," Bella said.

"She fancies me," Gruff said.

"Eva!" bellowed Mr. Deeds. "What the fuck's going on?" His eyeballs were whizzing around in their sockets, which is a bad sign.

I put my weights down and stayed squatting. I wanted to keep out of the firing zone, but I wasn't born lucky.

"Eva's going to learn us self-defence," Crystal said. She was the only one who looked even close to human. But the blokes must've been blinded by the day-glo and blusher so they didn't even see her.

One of the women, Kath as it turned out, had a chest you could've balanced teacups on. Gruff Gordon couldn't keep his eyes off it. And she couldn't keep her hands off California.

"Nice arse," she said. She had a voice a track-side bookie would've been proud of, so we all heard.

"Don't touch, bitch," California said. And we all heard that too. It didn't sound friendly.

"Ooh," she said. "Spank me."

They had all been drinking, except maybe Crystal. She said, "Eva, when do we start?"

And the one they called Lynn began to do little kicks and punches in the air—Pinocchio taking the piss out of kung-fu.

"Ha!" she squealed. "Ah so! Ha!"

At the same time Flying Phil said, "Self-defence. That's what it's all about, Mr. Deeds." It'd taken awhile but the penny dropped. "Eva's going to teach this herd of scut self-defence."

Harsh said, "How interesting." And steam started to fizz out of Mr. Deeds' ears.

He said, "If this is one of your fucking stupid jokes, Eva Wylie . . ."

And I sort of stopped hearing. The rest happened like I was watching TV.

What it looked like was Bella doing a deal with Pete Carver for an upright against the wall. And while that was going down, Stef started to roll a smoko. Gruff Gordon grabbed Kath. Kath grabbed California. California missed Kath with a right armed hay-maker, and Gruff caught it between his pecs.

Mandy, escaping to the door, tripped over a barbell and took Mr. Deeds down on to the mat—two suet puddings with arms and legs.

Gruff head-butted California.

Harsh strolled away to the showers.

My meter ran out. The gym was full of freaks and retards, and California was spitting bloody phlegm at Lynn. I did what I'd wanted to do ever since I met him—I sank a putt into Gruff Gordon's belly.

I don't know why. I just wanted to. I was very exact about it. The target was just under his ribs. I aimed, fired off my right fist, and jabbed the bull's-eye. Woof! If I'd done the same thing to California Carl I'd have broken my hand, but that's because he's got a gut like a door. Gruff Gordon has a belly like a laundry bag and my knuckles sank right in. If I'd put more behind it I'd have tickled his kidneys—his abs were that spongy.

A shirt couldn't have folded faster. It was ever so satisfying.

Gruff Gordon doesn't think women should go in the ring. He's always on at Mr. Deeds to kick me off the programme. Gruff Gordon, who thinks a woman's place is on her back on the kitchen table with her skirt over her head, folded like a shirt and hit the floor retching.

It was lovely. And if you ever get the chance to wallop someone who has pissed you around for as long as Gruff Gordon has pissed me, you'll agree. With knobs on.

"What you done that for?" Flying Phil asked, all amazed. "What's Gruff done to you?"

I was still a bit over-excited and I couldn't be bothered to talk so I shouldered him out of the way and went.

Next thing I knew I was driving up to my ma's block of flats and my hair was wet. I don't remember having a shower but I must have because my hair was wet. I don't remember changing but I must have because I was wearing jeans and a sweat shirt. I don't remember borrowing a car but I must have because I was driving a yellow Ford Cortina with a little blue doll dangling from the mirror. I don't remember leaving the gym but I must have because I wasn't there anymore.

I hate that. It's weird. You're in one place, and then you're in another. And there's space in between which is empty. I hate the empty space. I'm in charge, right? But who's in charge when I can't remember?

Also, I do not want to see my ma. I used to see her regular, but last year she let me down and she ain't been forgiven yet. She doesn't believe in family feeling like I do. She could bring us all together but she won't. She never did. So I'll go and see her when she has a change of heart, but not before.

I used to think that because she had a hard life herself she couldn't look after my sister and me the way she wanted to. But last year I decided she never wanted to—she'd rather see us in Council care than make a home for us herself. Making a home was too much like hard work for our ma.

So I'm buggered if I know what I was doing, driving up to her block of flats. It was the last place I wanted to be. Also, if you must know, I was totally cheesed off with people. And if you're cheesed off with people the last person you want to see is my ma.

So I turned round and went home to Ramses and Lineker. They may not like me much but at least I know where I am with them. And they do what I tell them, if I shout loud enough, which is more than you can say for friggin' people. Like those five slags and Crystal when they tottered into my gym all tiddly and turned the place arse over elbow. Not understanding or caring how my gym works.

"Right," I shouted at Ramses. "You sit there and shut up." And I fetched his brush and started to shine him up. I worked on his coat starting at the neck, brushing his hair up the wrong way, inspecting the parting of bluish skin, searching for scabs and fleas. Then, starting at the tail, if he'd had a tail, I brushed all the hair flat again, bit by bit, along all his hard muscles. Afterwards I washed his face and ears with a wet cloth getting into all the folds and crannies of his massive ugly head, feeling that stony scar around his neck, and feeling, all the while, his stony little eyes on me. He sat absolutely still, but he watched me, and while I was searching him for fleas, he was searching me for weakness. He's waiting, always waiting, for a time when I'm not ready for him.

He'll die waiting, because I'm always fucking ready.

And then Lineker, slimmer, faster, with his long lean snout and his short hard coat which shines up like the paint work on a brand new motor. "Keep still, shark face," I growled, because he's not like Ramses. He's got a smaller head and a smaller brain and he doesn't concentrate like Ramses does. But he polishes up lovely.

They are the tools of my trade, those two, and anyone'll tell you, you got to keep the tools of your trade in good nick. Ramses and Lineker are in fighting nick. And so am I.

"But only as long as you stay ready," Ramses said, in my head, watching me with his stony little eyes.

Now, the thing about elbows is that when they are hurt they really hurt. My elbow had swollen up again. It must have been the weights. I hadn't noticed at the time, but now I did.

In the Static I put some water on to heat. First, I made tea because you have to get your priorities right in this life. Then I sat down, resting my elbow in a bowl of hot water, and studied the bruising where Gypsy Jo hammered on me with her feet.

"Hot water," Harsh says. "You want all the veins and capillaries to open wide. You want increased circulation. You want your blood to feed an injury. You want your blood to take away the poisons."

Which made me think about Dawn who was kicked to death. It'd take more than a bowl of hot water to tweak up her circulation now.

One time, my ma took a bit of a kicking, and she had black and blue all up her legs. So she limped away to the off-licence for a couple of bottles to ease her pain and soothe her freaky boyfriend. Only when she got home the boyfriend had scarpered so she sat down and eased her pain all by herself. But while she drank she smoked, and while she smoked she drank. Things being how they are with smoking and drinking, the time soon came when she nodded off and dropped her ciggy down the side of the sofa, where it continued to smoulder. The ciggy smouldered, and then the sofa smouldered, and the cushion smouldered. And very soon my ma's frock started to smoulder too.

How do I know this? Well, I smelled it. That's how. From inside the cupboard under the stairs, which is where my ma used to put my sister and me whenever she wanted to fuck or fight or both. She put us in the cupboard under the stairs and turned the key in the lock and did whatever it was she didn't want us to see.

It was dark in the cupboard. They don't build windows in cupboards. We didn't know what time it was. We'd been in there a long time. Simone was asleep. She always used to sleep after she'd been frightened. She was frightened because even though we couldn't see what our ma didn't want us to see we could hear everything. And we heard every one of those black and blue bruises on ma's legs.

You think you can't *hear* a bruise? Well, believe me, you can.

I smelled smoke. I wasn't very old at the time and I hadn't learned much, but I'd learned enough to know that smoke meant fire. I woke Simone up and we started to scream and cry and bang on the cupboard door.

Nobody heard us. Ma did not wake up, and we began to choke and gag on the smoke. We were too small to break the door and too weak to make a hole in the stairs above. So we did what small weak people do—we screamed and cried and wet ourselves. And still Ma did not wake up. Well, she couldn't, could she? She was sotted out of her brain-box, and even before that, she'd forgotten all about us.

So you see, there might have been no Eva, no Armour Protection, no London Lassassin, and all because of a few bruises. If you think bruises can't kill, you're wrong. I know better. And so does Dawn.

I looked at my bruised elbow and I thought about having a tattoo—a green and red dragon swarming down my arm. Or up my arm. Which way should it go? If its head was up it would look as if it was crawling on to my shoulder which would be fine if I was bare-shouldered. But if I were wearing a shirt it would look as if it was crawling up my sleeve. A dragon with its head at the wrist end of my arm would look as if it was trying to get off. I thought about rats leaving a sinking ship. Rats. I've never seen tattoo rats on anyone, but maybe rats were righter for the London Lassassin than dragons.

I imagined fighting. Me in my black costume with three rats tattooed on my left arm. Just the left one. It would be classier than tattoos on both arms. Three rats—one on the deltoid, one on the bicep and one on the forearm. The three rats would all be facing in different directions and that would solve the problem about whether they were coming or going.

I get these ideas sometimes. I'm a lot more creative than people think.

By that time the water was cold and I was hungry. But I'd forgotten to go shopping again. I'd like to invent a pill you could buy in packs of twenty which you could take when you forgot to go shopping. The pill would swell up in your belly to the size of a full meal and you wouldn't feel hungry for twelve hours. That's the trouble with food—you've got to buy a lot to feel full. And when you feel full, like as not, you've eaten too much. And when you've eaten too much you get fat. And when you get fat you stretch your black costume in all

the wrong places and the crowd calls you names on top of all
the other names they call you. So if they already call you
Bucket Nut, for instance, and they add "fat butt," you can
wind up being called "Fat Butt Bucket Nut." Which isn't very
nice. But I'm a big girl, and if I don't eat lots I get hungry.
Which isn't very nice either.

Rat tattoos would distract attention. Everyone would look
at the rats and forget about the size of my arse. Although, actually, it isn't my arse which bothers me. It's my abs. Big Gut
Bucket Nut.

Life can be a frigging awful problem sometimes.

But sitting on your arse with your elbow in a bowl of cold
water doesn't solve any problems, so I dried off and went out.
I took a torch and one of those big Bonio things I give the
dogs as treats, and I went off to inspect the fence.

Which turned out to be a mistake.

Crystal popped up like a gremlin from behind a parked car
and said, "Where you been, Eva? I've been waiting hours."

"Fuck off, gnome," I said. "Ain't you caused enough trouble for one day?"

"We shouldn't of come to the gym," she said, scratching
her curly mop. "I saw that, soon as we fetched up there."

"Fucking right," I said. "The deal's off."

"What we need is premises," she said, like I'd never
opened my mouth. "So I've found us premises," she said,
"and I want you to come and see."

"Got turds in your ears?" I said. "The deal's off."

"What you doing, eating dog biscuits?" she asked.

"I'm not," I said, swallowing. "It's training. This dog does
what I say, I give him a Bonio. See?" I threw the other half to
Lineker who had been following me round like I was a bitch
in heat.

"I really fancy a pizza," Crystal said. "Double cheese and
pepperoni. Want one? My treat."

"Where's the others?" I said, suspicious.

"There's a cock fight in the car park," she said.

"What?"

"Y'know, bloke hens," she said. "Men from the market and the Full Moon, they fight cocks sometimes."

We walked up Mandala Street. There's nothing so dead as a market street at night. All the stalls were gone to their lockups and the gutters were ankle deep in lettuce leaves and wet paper bags. It's so quiet you notice it. Everyone shouts in a market, but at night there's just the smell of dead cauliflowers.

"Where you going?" Crystal said. She'd stopped by a door and I'd walked on.

"The pizza place."

"In a minute," she said. "I told you."

"Oh no," I said. "The deal's off. I told *you*."

"It's right here," she said.

"It" was a broken down shop with a boarded up window and a "To Let" sign which looked as if it'd been there since before the Beatles.

"Want a look?" she said.

"Fuck off," I said. "I'm hungry."

"Me too," said Crystal. "Only I ought to inspect the site."

"Well you inspect it," I said. "I'm off."

"Only I sort of lost the key," she said. "It won't take a tick if you, y'know, open up for me. I'll stand you the biggest pizza ever."

I went back and looked at the door. I tested it with my shoulder.

"It's locked," I said.

"Yes," she said. "I lost the key."

"You got a key?" I said. "It's your place?"

"We need premises," she said. "I thought this'd do."

It looked as if there had been squatters inside, and the place had been cleared and battened down afterwards. It looked as if someone had tried to get in again but failed.

I heaved with my shoulder. Nothing budged.

"You better find that key," I said. "I can't shift this."

"Got a crowbar," she said, and she rooted in a plastic bag which I had taken for rubbish left in the doorway.

It was a good stout lock. Even with the crowbar I had to shove with all my weight before the door tore open. It was a bit like the old days when Crystal and me needed a place to kip. The mouldy smell was the same too, and the cold. These places feel like cellars even on a warm night.

"Takes you back," I said, and went inside.

Crystal came behind me, and that was the same too. Whenever we were together I always used to go first. Just in case. And whenever we had to talk our way out—Crystal went first. She had a good mouth on her, even in those days.

"Plenty of space," Crystal said, waving her torch around. The circle of light boogied around the walls and empty corners.

"I'll get some carpet in," she said. "And a bit of mattress or something like you got at your gym. See, it's much better here. It's nearer where the girls and me live. And you too."

"Count me out," I said. "I *told* you."

"And it's private," she said. "None of those stupid blokes poking their noses in and telling you what's what. Making you feel like a carrot. You'd be in charge here, Eva. Your own private gym. And we wouldn't have to pay anyone but you, see. That fat geezer, up your gym, he said we'd have to pay entrance money or we couldn't go there. Mean git. Whereas here. Well, see, if we don't have to pay entrance money you could charge more for your classes, couldn't you?"

"How much?" I said.

"It's up to you," she said. "Charge what you like. You're in control. I'll collect the money for you if you don't want to be bothered."

"Fuck off," I said. "I'll collect me own money."

But I had a thought. "What about the rent?" I said. "Who pays the rent?"

"Rent?" Crystal said. "Leave all that to me. It's the least I can do. If only I'd thought of it before poor Dawnie . . ."

"And light," I said, before she could get sniffly again. "I don't want to take that boarding down. I don't fancy people in the market seeing in."

"Yeah," she said. "Nor me neither. I'll figure something out about the light. Ain't you hungry yet? I'm starving."

"What about the door?" I said. "It's broken."

"Almost forgot," she said. "I brought a padlock. Just temporary, like."

She'd come prepared, I'll say that for her. She held the torch while I rigged the padlock, and then we went for the pizza.

She stood me for two deep pan, twelve-inch, double cheese and ham pizzas.

"Do you remember?" she said, with her mouth full. "When we was up the West End one time? And all we could snaffle was cold pizza out of the bin?"

"No," I said. But I did. And let me tell you, hot pizza, with the cheese all soft and supple beats the shit out of cold pizza, half eaten with stuff set in it like bricks in mortar.

Crystal, when she's feeling sentimental, like about the old days and dead Dawn, is a bit of a soft touch. Which is why I was feeling quite pleased with myself. I mean, she's supposed to be such a sharp operator but she'd coughed up rent-free premises and two twelve-inch pizzas all in one night. *Now* tell me who's the operator?

Chapter 6

"Where's the dirty Half Dozen?" Gruff Gordon said. He rolled in whiffing of bitter as usual when I was just about finished and ready for my shower. "Where's all that lovely hot buttered twat?"

"Eva's mucky mates," Pete Carver said. "I thought it was my birthday—all those prezzies just waiting to be unwrapped. What you got for us today, Eva?"

"A snootful of knucks," I said, backing off.

"That reminds me," Gruff Gordon said. His hairy eyebrows scrunched down, and his shoulders went up to keep his ears company.

I beat it to the ladies' shower. I'd thought I was too early for them. I thought I'd have done my work, washed and been long gone before they shambled in from the boozer. But those two heavyweight tossers never do nothing to suit me.

Their idea of a chat-up line would be, "Lay down and spread 'em." But I reckoned Bella's Babes could look after themselves in that department. And it wasn't because I couldn't look after myself—punching Gruff in the lunchbox was a pleasure I was willing to pay for. And I would if I knew anything about him. I wasn't scared of him. And I wasn't scared of Pete. I just didn't want to see them. That's all.

For your information, in case you think I'm telling lies and I really beat it to the ladies' shower because I'd made a belly-button sandwich out of Gruff Gordon and I was scared he'd return the favour—I'll tell you—those two blubber boys don't scare me one tiny bit. But I hate them, really loathe them with a capital L, and I'll tell you for why. They are chip-mongers, chip-chip-chipping away at everything important. That's why.

I am a self-made woman. I was nothing before I took myself in hand. Zero. I'm strong because I made myself strong. I got a career ahead of me because I made it happen. I hung around on the edge of the wrestling scene until Mr. Deeds got so fed up with me he gave me a go. And once I'd got my foot in the door I wouldn't take it out. I've got jobs. I've got a home. I've got dogs I trained myself. I done all that, *and* I'm getting a reputation. I'm going to be famous. I'm going to be top of the bill one day.

What I hate is Pete Carver and Gruff Gordon chip-chip-chipping with their smelly yellow teeth, trying to make me small and weak again. Miserable, mean-minded snot-bags who can't bear to see someone succeeding.

That's why I beat it to the ladies' shower. Got it?

And if I want to teach Crystal, Bella, Stef, Mandy, Kath and Lynn how to defend themselves, I sodding well will. So there. Stick that somewhere. Sideways. You won't stop me by taking the piss out of me. Or them.

But I didn't really know how. Which is why I asked Harsh for advice. Harsh knows things. He uses his head for more than stopping footballs.

I caught up with him on his way to the tube station.

"These women, Harsh," I said. I was walking backwards because Harsh didn't stop. "These women," I said, "they want to learn self-defence but they're just a pile of parts. They can't even walk straight. It'd take fifty years to get them fit. And they ain't very bright either."

"Well, Eva," Harsh said, "first you should ask yourself why you wish to spend your time in this way. Second, why do the women wish to learn. And third, what do they wish to do with such skills as you are able to impart."

I wished he would stand still. He is a very clever bloke who has been to college and all that. He can think and talk and walk all at the same time.

"Do not walk backwards, Eva," he said.

"Why?" I said.

"We are arriving at the station stairs," he said. "I do not wish to carry you up them after you have fallen down them."

"Oh."

"Speaking spiritually, also, it is better to know where you are going and to approach problems from the correct angle."

"Yeah, right," I said. "These women . . ."

"And I wonder," Harsh went on, "if the fact that you have been walking backwards is symptomatic. Have you considered, Eva, that you might be approaching the problem from the wrong angle? Why, for instance, are you asking me for advice of this nature? Wouldn't it be better to ask a woman what it is that women wish to know?"

He started down the tube station stairs, sort of gliding, weight perfectly distributed. I notice the way people move, and it's always a pleasure to notice Harsh. But I had to gallop to keep up.

"Yeah, but Harsh . . ." I said.

He was buying a ticket from the machine and I had to decide what to do. Between you and me, paying good money for a little piece of cardboard is against my religion. And another thing, if you must know, I hate traveling underground. It makes my teeth ache and my scalp sweat.

I planted myself between Harsh and the barrier. "These slags are useless," I said. "How'm I going to teach them to fight?"

"This is precisely what I mean," Harsh said. He stepped neatly round me. "You cannot teach them to fight. They probably do not want to learn. You think you should teach them because it is what you yourself know how to do."

He went through the barrier and glided towards the escalator.

I took a deep breath and vaulted the barrier.

"But Harsh," I said when I'd caught up, "what else is there?"

"What else but fighting?" He laughed. I do admire his teeth, I really do. One day, when I've saved up enough money, I'm going to get mine done so they look just like his.

He stood on the escalator. It was moving, but at least he was standing still. I went after him.

He said, "Most women do not want to learn to fight. This is the advantage men take."

"Well then what can I do? If they don't want to fight and they're too lazy to get fit and they go in strangers' cars and down dark alleys, what the hell am I supposed to do about it?"

"Nothing," he said. "You have no respect for the problem so you will never solve it."

"Respect it?" I said. I would have been really narked if anyone but Harsh said stuff like that.

"An act of imagination," Harsh said. "Think of one of these women and put yourself in her place. Then think what she needs. She, Eva. Not you."

The escalator slid Harsh softly on to the ground, but it tried to trip me up.

"Me?" I said. "Think like a slag?"

"Please don't shout, Eva," he said. "No, maybe it isn't possible. If it were possible you wouldn't use rude words about it."

"It's a rude job," I told him. He doesn't know about these things.

The trouble with Harsh is that he's far too high-minded. A couple of rounds with Bella would change his tune. I couldn't imagine that either.

He stood on the platform with his sports bag slung neatly over his shoulder. Every thing he does looks right. He taught me just about everything important about training and diet and personal hygiene and mental discipline. It's not because he's a teacher. It's because he's so perfect that I copy him. Or I ask him. He doesn't make fun of me not knowing stuff. He doesn't say, "Don't you know that, Eva? I thought everyone knew that," in that superior tone of voice which makes you wish you never asked.

All right, so I don't know everything. Who does? But being ignorant of a few things doesn't make me stupid. Does it? Well, *does* it? It'd better not, because if it did, everyone would be stupid.

Most people make you feel stupid when you're only ignorant. But Harsh doesn't. Maybe it's because he comes from foreign parts. Maybe where he comes from the people are politer about ignorance than they are here.

So I don't mind asking Harsh stuff. And, if he has time he always answers. But he doesn't always understand the problem. And I don't always understand the answer. Apart from that, we get along perfect.

We stood on the platform in the gritty wind, and after a bit he said, "Have you thought about personal alarms, Eva?"

"No." I thought about it. Trust Harsh to see things sideways.

I said, "You mean go mechanical? Alarms, mace, flicks and knucks?" It was a good idea.

"No," he said, "I did not mean flicks and knucks. Those things are weapons. If you can't teach someone to fight, then most certainly you should not give them weapons."

"What then?" My skull was prickling. I could hear the rumble in the tunnel, and the lines were singing. The train was coming. Harsh would get on. I did not want to get on with him.

"Eva," he said, "the first line of defence is to be prepared for attack: to know your weaknesses and to make sure they are not exploited. A woman in isolation is in a position of great weakness, therefore . . ."

But the train burst out of the tunnel, crashing and roaring, and I couldn't hear what he said. It stopped. The doors opened. Harsh got on saying, "And that is what you should address."

"What?" I yelled. "Harsh, what am I supposed to address?"

The doors closed and the train carried Harsh away underground.

"Shit!" I said. "Fuck and daggers. I know they're 'in a position of great weakness.' I *know* that. That's why I fucking asked."

Harsh had said something brilliant and I hadn't heard. Now his secret had gone down the tunnel. Typical.

That's the story of my life—the important bits go down the tube. I hate the tube. It's like a human sewer. Everyone is squashed in together and flushed off underground. There you are, cramped, sweating, with tons of bricks and earth and worms on top of you. And you can't get out. I mean—what if there was a fire or a flood? What if the tunnel collapsed? Sewers collapse all the time round here, so why should tunnels be any different?

I'm prepared for a lot of things. Do you know that I carry a survival kit? I've got stuff for purifying water, making a fire, sawing through wood or metal. I've got stock-cubes for making soup, candles for light. I've got a blade and a bola for hunting or defence. All these things are in a small biscuit tin. It used to be a tobacco tin, but I had to expand. I carry the tin in my kit bag.

I got the idea from the SAS survival manual. Which is a book you should get if you want to be prepared. At the back

there is a bit about disasters like tornados, volcanos and nuclear explosions, so it's a very useful book. But even the SAS
can't tell you what to do if you're in a tube and the tunnel col-
lapses. That is a disaster they've left out of their survival manual. And it is a disaster I mean to avoid by never travelling on
underground trains. Because even if you're as well prepared
as I am, there's not a lot you can do with a ton of bricks on
your bonce.

I felt better back in the open air, but as I was walking along
I met Flying Phil coming the other way. I would've walked
past, but he said, "Hey, Eva, stop a minute, will you? I've had
an idea."

So I stopped.

He said, "Look Eva, never mind self-defence for those
girls. It won't work. What you want to get into is portable
phones. Geddit? Each girl has a portable phone, right? So if
she gets in trouble she can call for help, see?"

"Oh right," I said. "First, remember the number, then dial
it, and while she's doing that there's a maniac mashing up her
skull."

"And she could use the phone for making appointments
with guys as well. One phone, two functions. Clever, huh?
You should tell the girls about it. Get rich and save your life
all in one go."

"Why don't you get rich and get stuffed all in one go?"

"I've got this mate, see," Phil said. "Got a load of phones.
Special price, Eva, seeing it's you."

"Ain't you listening?" I said.

'Course he wasn't. A bloke who wants to sell you something don't listen to nothing. I walked off.

"Think about it," Phil shouted. "You'll thank me."

Thank him! I'd thank him to keep his hooter out of my
business. I'd thank him to clean his lug-holes out with a
plunger, except it'd probably suck out his one and only brain
cell too.

Why can't people leave me alone?

I don't like people. They always want something. They always let you down. I forget about people when I can, but it's hard. They're always around, buzzing like flies on turds. Sometimes I'd like to get a ginormous fly-swatter and smash the lot—just to clear a bit of space round my head so I can think.

I like dogs better than I like people. Dogs don't talk. They don't say things you can't understand. They don't try to sell you portable phones. They don't chip-chip-chip away at your confidence. You teach a dog what to do and he gets on and does it. He doesn't stand there arguing, making you feel like a class A futtock.

On the down side, though, a dog can't make you a bacon sandwich.

I really fancied a bacon sandwich after all that training and aggravation, but I didn't have any bacon in the Static. And even if I did it wouldn't have been much use because I didn't have any bread either.

I let the dogs out, and they barged through the gate the way they always do. Ramses first. Lineker tried to get in the lead, but Ramses has a better sense of position and won't be budged. Ramses knows his place. He is top dog when it's a contest between him and Lineker, but I am top dog when it's between him and me. Simple. Life's so simple for a dog—do your job, get fed, go to sleep. Nobody expects anything more. I wish I was a dog sometimes. Especially now when I'm narked and hungry. I've got everyone on my back, and no bacon.

"Lucky for some," I said. The dogs were snuffling around, bumping into my legs, making sure I was who I used to be.

"You always got me to look out for you and feed you," I said. "Who've I got?"

"What's the matter?" Ramses sneered in my head. "Going soft are you?"

"Try me," I said. "Go on, try me."

He gave me the eye for a couple of seconds and then he turned his back and went off to inspect the gate. That Ramses! If he can't face me down he ignores me.

"If you could make a bacon sarnie you'd be perfect," I yelled after him. But he just walked away. So I decided to go to the caff on Mandala Street. They make an ace bacon sarnie there. What they do is fry the bacon crisp, and then they fry the bread on one side in the bacon fat. That way the bread is squishy on the outside but it's hot and crisp and salty on the inside next to the hot crisp bacon. Magic.

It made my mouth water just thinking about it, and by the time I got to the caff I was so hungry I asked for three.

After the second one I felt better. I was just about to crunch into the third when The Enemy walked in.

This is what she does—she walks in as if she knows I'm here all along, like I've got a collar on, and she stands for a minute looking round, making sure everyone's behaving proper. And then she comes over to where I'm sitting like we've got an appointment or something, which we haven't. She comes over like she owns the place, head up, shoulders back, eyes open. Typical polizei.

"Want another tea?" she said. No "How-do, what a surprise seeing you here." No "Mind if I join you?" Nothing like that. Just "Want another tea?"

"If you're buying," I said. And I got my laughing-gear round the third sandwich. Even The Enemy, "I'm-in-charge" Anna Lee, can't spoil a good bacon sarnie.

"Doing anything tonight?" she said.

"Who's asking?" I said. See, she never comes straight out with stuff. She doesn't say, "I've got a job for you tonight, Eva, are you free?" She always asks her bloody questions first, like it's an interrogation. Polizei always do that. They ask you a question and they don't tell you why they want to know. You got to guess. And you got to hope to buggery you guessed right.

The bloke behind the counter brought the tea, and she grabbed her mug with both hands. That's another thing she always does. She laces her fingers round the mug like she's freezing—which might make sense on a cold night out in the open, but it just looks stupid in a stuffy caff on Mandala Street.

"Why are you so prickly tonight?" she asked.

"Why are you so nosy?"

"Do you want a job?"

"Why? You got one?"

She sighed and stared at me over her tea mug. I was getting under her skin. I grinned.

She said, "Why don't you ever answer a simple question straight?"

"Why don't *you?*"

"What question?"

"Have you got a job for me?"

"Isn't that why I'm here?" she said. She looked as if she was grinding her teeth. Then she took a deep breath. She said, "Eva, I've got a job for you tonight if you aren't already busy."

I won! I won. I won. I won.

I stuffed the last bit of bacon sarnie in my trap and chewed slowly. She waited. She tapped a fingernail on the rim of her mug. I swallowed. I washed it down with a good swig of tea. I wiped my lips. I was feeling great.

"All right," I said, like I was thinking it over. "What's the score?"

"Eva, one—Anna Lee, nil," she said. "But it isn't even half-time yet, so watch it."

I had to stop myself laughing. She may be a copper, but she does get the picture. Sometimes. If you wait long enough. It made me feel even better. I won, and she knew I won. There's not much point winning if The Enemy doesn't know she lost, is there?

She said, "I had a bloke in the office this morning. He manages the estate agency just down the road."

"Yeah?"

"He's got a lot of property on his books which he can't sell or let at the moment. Naturally. Trade's very slow in the property market."

"So?"

"Well, with property standing empty, and Agency boards up advertising the fact, there has been a lot of vandalism and break-ins. There are some squatters, apparently, but I'm not going to do anything about that."

"Why?"

"I run a security firm," she said. "It isn't the heavy mob. We don't go round chucking people out. My job's to stop people getting in."

"I don't mind," I said. "I'd take the dogs. Squatters is a piece of piss to us."

"I'm sure," she said. "But all the same, that's up to the owners of the property, not the agent. I told him that, and he understands. And anyway, I don't want to throw people out on the street when they've got nowhere else to live."

"So what you want me for?"

"There are three properties—a house, a flat and a shop, right here—a stone's throw from your yard. I thought I could take you round and have a look-see. I've got some stuff in the car in case we need to do any emergency repairs or replace locks or bolts. And then, I thought, since you are more or less on the spot, you could keep an eye on them overnight. Until we can work out something permanent."

"That's it, is it?" I said. I was glad she was spelling it out. I like to know what I'm getting paid for. I forgot to ask once, and it got me into a lot of kak.

"That's it," she said.

"What if I find someone breaking in?" I said. "Can I chuck

them out? Or d'you want me to pat their heads and help move the furniture?"

"Chuck 'em as far as you like," she said. "I've been assured there's no one actually squatting at present, although all three places have been interfered with. We've just got to secure them and keep them secure. Okay?"

Chapter 7

We left the caff and walked up Mandala Street. About halfway up, The Enemy stopped. She said, "This one here. Look. Someone broke in. You can see where the door was forced."

I looked. There were the marks where the crowbar bit the doorframe.

How did I know it was a crowbar? I knew it was a crowbar because last night I was on the other end of it. It was the same door I forced for Crystal. Her "premises." The place she said she was renting.

Renting! Ha-fuckin'-ha.

Bloody Crystal—always getting me to do her dirty work.

It was a good thing The Enemy couldn't see my face. If Crystal had been in kicking range I'd have booted her into the Balls Pond Road and back. What a nerve that little sow's got.

But the funny thing was the padlock I'd put on had been wrenched off. And it couldn't have been Crystal who did it. Crystal wouldn't pull it off, because Crystal had a key. Like me.

"Someone's in there," The Enemy said.

"Who?" I said. I turned the handle and gave the door a push. But the door didn't budge. It was locked from the inside. Can you believe that? The cheek some people have!

"Odd," The Enemy said. "It wasn't like than an hour ago. There was a padlock on. We'd better see what's happening."

She raised her hand like she was going to knock on the door. Knock? I'd show her knock.

"I'll do it," I said, and I charged the door with my shoulder. The wood shrieked and I went flying inside. I only just saved myself from landing on my nose by going into a forward roll. That's one good thing about wrestling—the first thing you learn is how to fall without breaking your hooter. I'm very good at falling over.

So I rolled and bounced back up on my toes. Behind me, The Enemy was saying something feeble like, "Don't do that." But I took no notice. Who was she to talk? It wasn't her gym, was it? It was mine. *Mine.* And I didn't give any grubby squatter leave to park his arse in it, did I? Well, *did* I?

So I bounced back up on my toes.

There was a bloke crouched in the corner. He had a sleeping bag round his shoulders. He was on top of a pile of newspaper and he had a little gas camping stove alight in front of him. He was brewing up. All his clobber was strewn around. Untidy sod.

"What?" he said. He looked scared out of his wits which made me stone chuffed.

"What you doing in here?" I said. "This here's private property."

The Enemy pushed past. "Eva!" she said. "Calm down."

"Out me way," I said. "I got a job to do."

"I . . . I . . ." said the bloke.

"Pack up and clear out," I said, "or I'll pack you up and clear you out, and you won't like it."

"Eva! Shut up and stop jumping around."

"I'll pack him up and clear him out," I said. "He's got no right in here!"

"Shut up shouting!" The Enemy yelled. "He's just a kid."

"It's my bitch," the kid said.

"Who you calling a bitch?"

"*My* bitch," the kid said. "Queenie. She's in the family way and I think it's her time."

"Queenie?" The Enemy got her torch out and turned it on. The light skipped on to a dark pile by the wall. The pile growled.

"That's Queenie," the kid said. "I was making her a cup of tea. She likes a cup of tea when she's stressed. I wish I had some sugar for it. She likes her tea sweet."

The dark thing by the wall was a big old German shepherd. She was lying on her side. She only growled the once. Otherwise she just lay there panting.

"Ain't she too old to have puppies?" I said.

"She *is* getting on a bit," the kid said. "I don't know how it happened, and now I'm worried about her."

"Sweet tea?" The Enemy said. "You give your dog sweet tea?"

"She likes it," the kid said. "It's her blood sugar. I think it's low. You're not going to kick us out, are you?"

"Flaming Nora," The Enemy said.

"'Course she won't chuck you out," I said. "I won't let her."

"Flaming *Nora!*" The Enemy said again. "Make up your mind."

"I have," I said. "He's staying. So's Queenie. So up yours."

"Okay." The Enemy fumbled in her pocket and came up with a fiver. "Go and get him some sugar then. And anything else that might help. You know dogs, Eva."

I took the money. That bleeding Enemy. You never know where you are with her. First she wants to kick that poor little sod and his dog out in the street, and next she's buying the dog sugar for her tea. She just ain't stable—that's what's wrong with her. Her mental attitude's all up the bleeding spout.

So I trotted off to Hanif's, which is open all hours, and as I went I hummed to myself, "Anna Lee, The Enemy, she wanted to shit, then she wanted to pee. She changed her mind at half past three."

I was feeling pretty pleased with myself, having got my own way again. All you need is willpower. You can even make things rhyme with willpower.

"Hee-hee-hee, Anna Lee," I sang to myself, and then Crystal came up behind me and grabbed my elbow.

"Fuckin' *ow!*" I said, because my elbow was all bruised.

"Sorry," Crystal said. "What's happening, Eva? I looked out me window and there you was busting into the Premises."

Which reminded me.

"Those bleeding premises," I said. "I thought that was supposed to be my gym. I thought you said you was renting."

"I never," she said. "I said you would have it rent free."

"Me and everyone else," I said. "It's a bleeding squat now."

"How?"

"There's a kid and his dog in there."

"Can't you get them out?" Crystal asked. "And who's that other woman you're with?"

"That's Anna Lee of Lee-Schiller Security."

"Who's that when it's at home?"

"Security," I said. "Like me. Taking care of empty property."

"Oh shit," she said.

"Yeah. Your '*premises*.' My gym."

"Does she know?"

"You think I'm stupid or what?"

"What she going to do, then?" Crystal said. "Turf this kid out?"

"Over my dead body," I said. "His dog's just about to drop her litter."

"Puppies?" Crystal said, her little monkey-face all screwed up. "You mean this Lee person's letting this kid stop in our premises for a load of puppies?"

"She ain't," I said. "But I am. That bitch didn't ought to be moved."

"Lee?"

"No, stupid. The fucking dog."

"Oh," said Crystal. Honestly, she gets on my nerves.

I went on, and Crystal scurried along behind me.

At Hanif's I bought sugar, eggs and milk. They're all good for sick dogs. You got to separate the eggs though. You don't want to give a dog white of egg, only the yolk. I got some more tea bags too because Queenie looked like she was going to have a long night of it.

Crystal tagged along on the way back too. She said, "What we going to do?"

"What you mean—*we*?"

"Us," she said. "You. Me. Bella and the girls."

"Don't you lump me in with that lot," I said. Which shut her up.

Back at the Premises, The Enemy had rigged the light a bit better, and the kid's pan of water was boiling. I dumped the shopping down and said, "This lot's for Queenie. Not for you."

"I know," the kid said. "Thanks."

"Well," I said. "You can have the egg whites, I suppose. Queenie don't want them. She gets the yolks, mind."

"Yes," he said. "You're very kind." He was a bit bloody polite for a squatter. I didn't trust him.

"Whip an egg yolk up in the milk and let her drink it," I told him.

He was squatting over his stove, making the tea in a plastic bowl. He spooned some sugar in. I stood there making sure he didn't nick any for himself.

The Enemy stopped looking at the kid and saw Crystal.

"Friend of Eva's," Crystal said, before she was asked. She's clever that way, is Crystal. She'll *seem* all open and honest but she won't even tell her own name.

"Haven't I seen you round here?" The Enemy said.

"Prob'ly." Crystal grinned her monkey grin. "I'm local."

"The market," The Enemy said. "You've got a stall, right?"

That's double-dyed polizei, that is. Everything slotted in place.

"That Queenie don't look too clever," I said, to put her off.

She sighed. "The kid's none too well either." She nudged me aside and said in a whisper, "He *says* his name's Justin Ventura. Yeah, I know. He says he's from Hampshire. He says he came to London to get a job and stay with friends."

"Oh yeah?"

"Mmm. And he says he'll be going home when his dog's better. He only looks about fifteen, but he says he's eighteen."

I said bugger-all to that.

Of *course* he said he was eighteen.

Everyone says they're eighteen. Especially to strangers. I said I was eighteen ever since my thirteenth birthday. I said it so long I couldn't remember how old I really was. Even now I have trouble remembering my age. You've got to be eighteen or you'll have social workers swarming all over you.

I looked at so-called Justin Ventura. He was thin and he looked like he didn't have any blood in his veins. He had fair curly hair, quite long, and a cold sore on his bottom lip. He was pretty.

The Enemy was probably right—he didn't look as if he'd shaved more than twice in his life, but it was too dark to see properly.

Queenie didn't seem to have the strength to get up and drink, so Justin held the bowl in one hand and helped support her head with the other. She lapped up about half the bowl and then flopped down exhausted. Her tail flapped once against the concrete floor, and she never took her eyes off of Justin's face.

"Poor thing," Crystal said. She knelt down next to Justin, but he said, "Please don't come too close. I don't mean to be rude, but she might get upset if she doesn't know you."

Crystal moved away. She doesn't know sweet FA about dogs.

Justin said, "May I finish her tea? She won't drink any more now, and I'll make her some fresh when she's ready."

He couldn't be all bad, could he? I don't know many blokes who'd give their dogs first slurp at the tea.

"Frigging Ada," The Enemy said. "He's not going to drink from the same bowl, is he?"

But he did. He didn't seem to have a cup for himself.

Then something happened. Well, no, it didn't happen. Nothing happens, but everything changes. Suddenly things look long ago and far away. As if you're stuck to the ceiling like a fly, and you look down on something you saw at the movies ages ago. Does that happen to you? It's creepy. I hate it.

Crystal got weepy. That's what started it. Bloody monkey face. What's she got to snivel about? So, there was Crystal, and The Enemy, and the kid drinking tea out of Queenie's bowl, and Queenie panting on the floor, never taking her eyes off of the kid's face. And they all sort of glided away like Harsh on the escalator, going down. Going down. Until that corner of the Premises was small enough to put on a telly screen, all black and white from the torchlight in the dark.

And you know the creepiest thing of all? I wasn't there. I couldn't see me at all. Me. The biggest, strongest one there. Because I *am* big and strong. I'm so big and strong that when I'm there I'm really there. I *am*.

But when this creepy thing, which happens but doesn't happen, happens, I'm not there. Well, I'm there but I'm not there.

And I fucking loathe it. I loathe being a tiny fly on the ceiling. So I walked out.

I just turned round and walked out. Well, wouldn't you? You don't have to put up with being not there if you don't want to. Just go away and be somewhere else. That's what I do.

Another bit of advice for free—if you want to prove you really exist, kick something. Go on. Try it. Pick something that won't hurt your foot, haul back and plant your toe—smack bang flick.

A market at night is a really good place to have a kick. There are loads of old boxes and crates and veggies. I was just having a lovely whack at a heap of dead broccoli when The Enemy came out of the Premises saying, "Oh, there you are, Eva." And I was glad she said my name.

"Let's go on," she said. Which reminded me we had a couple of other places to go. We walked on up Mandala Street, past the Full Moon and onto the main road. I thought she was going to talk about Justin and Crystal and how they'd need checking up on, but she never. She started in on me instead. Which was worse.

She said, "When are you going to get yourself sorted out, Eva?"

"What you mean?" I said. "I am bleeding sorted out. I'm doing very nice, thank you."

"I mean, when are you going to get things on a proper footing? For instance, it's quite difficult to employ you when I keep having to pay you out of petty cash. I have to fiddle the records and it's driving the bookkeeper spare."

"That's your problem," I said, narked.

"And why don't you do the decent thing and get a driving licence? You'd be much more useful to me if you were a kosher driver."

"I don't live my life to be useful to you," I said.

"True," she said, and started laughing. "But one of these days you're going to be nicked for taking and driving away. Without a licence. And then where will you be?"

I said nothing. I was stone choked. I mean, how does she know I haven't got a licence? Well, I'll tell you. She knows because she's been checking up on me. That's how.

I could've killed her. But she didn't notice. She said, "If you had a licence I could help you get a cheap motor to fix up."

What right had she? Interfering mare. Besides, there's no
cheaper motors than the ones I borrow.

"What's wrong?" she said. "Is it the forms? I could help
you fill in the forms."

I stopped walking. I could hardly speak I was so rampa-
geous.

I said, "Why don't you keep your beak out of my bird-
seed?"

Fill in forms? Name, address, date of birth, place of birth,
name of father, name of mother, distinguishing features, con-
victions, religion, employment, who, what, where, which,
why, when? Oh yeah, there's a lump of stuff they'd want to
know about me. And some of it I don't know myself. But it's
all my sodding business. No one else's. My business does not
fetch up on official government computers. No chance. You
can build the Tower of London out of ice cream and eat it with
chopsticks before I'll tell official government computers my
business.

Oh no. You can stuff your forms. I don't tell nobody nothing. If I ever get into trouble it's because I've said too much.
That's why I keep my mouth shut.

Even a fish'd never get caught if it kept its mouth shut.

Chapter 8

Next day I went to the gym early. I was still trying to avoid Gruff Gordon and Pete Carver, and it was messing up my timetable. I don't like getting up early. I'm a big girl and I need my eight hours kip. What I like is going to bed at seven in the morning, getting up at three in the afternoon and no dreams in between, thank you very much.

If I wake up when I shouldn't, I want to hear the blokes in the yard. I want to hear the crane or the crusher. I want to hear loud stuff happening. What I don't want is to wake up and hear nothing—like you folk do when you wake up at night. I bet that's why people get married—so they can hear something when they wake up in the night. I can't think of another reason.

I hate waking up in the dark. You can't see nothing, and you can't hear nothing. So how do you know you haven't woke up dead? Tell me that? If you wake up in the night, and you've had a queer dream you don't like, in those seconds before you decide you're real and the dream wasn't, how do you know you ain't dead? If you can't see and you can't hear.

But, see, I'm smart. I never have that problem, do I? It's light any time I wake up in my eight hours. I can always see. And I can hear the blokes and the machinery in the yard. Except on a Sunday.

California was the only one in when I got to the gym, but I reckon he just about lives there. He was raising weights on his ankles. He must've been at it for hours because his rectus femoris and his sartorius were writhing like ferrets under his wet skin.

He stopped when I came in. Which was a first. Carl never stops for nothing.

He said, "Listen. Your body's sacred. This here gym is its temple. You've got to keep it clean."

"You keep it clean," I said. "I don't come here to mop up."

"Don't get clever with me," he said. "You know what I'm talking about."

"Buggered if I do," I said, because I didn't. What's more, Carl barely ever talks to me.

"Bringing prostitutes in here," he said.

I didn't like the look of his eyes. They seemed to be boiling. Give him half a chance, I thought, and he'll work himself up into a 'roid rage. Which is what happens to blokes when they're taking the anabollox.

"I didn't bring them in," I said. "It's not my fault."

"They came to see you."

"So what?"

"You keep them out," he said, "or you'll be sorry."

"You keep out of my business or *you'll* be sorry."

He stared at me out of his boiling eyes. I thought he was going to do something nasty and I got ready. But he decided not to lose his temper.

"Nobody here's serious," he said.

"I'm serious," I said. "Harsh is serious."

"Kid's stuff," he said. "Come here. I want to show you something."

"What?"

He got up and led the way to the men's changing room. I'd never been in the men's so I followed. And, believe me, it whiffed. I don't know what it is about a blokes' locker room, but it's like the zoo. It doesn't half make your eyes water.

"What?" I said again. Because I wanted to get out. I didn't fancy being in the men's room with Carl when his eyes were boiling.

"Tell me what you think of that." He pointed. And there, on the bench, was a big square fish tank. There was no water in it, but it had a lid, and its own light. And inside was a bloody great snake.

"Crap in a car park!" I said. "It's a snake."

"Brilliant," he said. "It's a python. Gruff and Pete brought it in yesterday."

"What for?"

"Little game they've got planned."

"What?"

"What do pythons eat for breakfast?" he asked.

"Dunno. What?"

"Look." He crouched down and pulled some small plastic boxes out from under the bench. Inside those were six twitchy, whiskery brown mice.

"Mice?" I said.

"Go to the top of the class," Carl said. "That's what pythons eat. Look closer."

I looked. Each little box had a name written on the lid. There was a mouse called Bella. There was one called Mandy. There was Stef, Kath, Lynn, and Crystal.

"One missing," Carl said. He reached further under the bench, feeling around, and came up with one more box. It was Eva. Eva was a red-eyed albino. She was bigger than all the others, and, shit, was she ugly! The others were sweet and furry, but Eva looked like a freak.

"Funny joke, huh?" Carl said. "You laughing, Eva? You want to know what happens?"

"No," I said. I made for the door. He got between me and it. He had a body like a god and his eyes were boiling.

"You know what happens when Percy the Python gets hungry, Eva?" he said. "We don't just feed him, do we? No, Eva, we don't. We have a little game. We release all the mice into the tank. And we take bets. Which one gets swallowed first? Which one goes next? Get the picture? The big bet goes on which mouse survives longest."

"Gimme that fucking mouse," I said, "and let me out of here."

But he held the white mouse above his head and didn't budge an inch.

"You know the funny thing, Eva?" he said. "You know what really makes us bust our guts laughing? See, Percy the Python eats mice whole. He opens his mouth and swallows them whole. And you know what, Eva, you can see a lump in the snake. And the best bit, Eva? The lump squeaks. You can hear the mouse squeaking from inside Percy. Ain't that a laugh?"

I had enough. So I aimed a real up-and-under at his godlike jock strap. But he swung aside and I kicked the door instead.

"That python," Carl said, while I was hopping around. "Sometimes he's called Percy. Sometimes he's called Roger, and sometimes he's called Dick. Geddit, Eva, geddit?"

"No I sodding don't get it," I said. I wrenched the door open and hopped outside. "But why don't you take your limp Percy-Roger-Dick and screw yourself?"

"Don't get all upset," Carl said. "I just thought you'd like to know the effect your little friends had. Just in case you were thinking of inviting them around again."

"Know what, Carl," I yelled. "Your body may be sacred, but your brain's two hundred percent sicko. And a beansprout'd have better muscles than you if you didn't pump yourself full of hot air and anabollox."

He didn't have an answer to that. But you know what he did? He took the white mouse called Eva out of its box. He held her in his fist so that just her little head poked out. And he raised her up to his lips.

He said, "I bet you think this Eva-mouse will last longest. Eh? Because it's biggest. Eh? Well, Eva-mouse may be big, but it's all show. Eva-mouse is slow. Retarded. Eva-mouse will get swallowed first."

And you know what he did?

He bit her head off.

I couldn't believe it. He bit her little white head off, and he spat it out on the floor.

One minute there she was with her garnet eyes flickering, and the next she was staring up at me from the floor. And her eyes were just the same color as her blood.

I couldn't believe it. What kind of sicko-psycho does a thing like that?

I couldn't even kick him because I'd already hurt my foot. I looked round for something to hit him with, but where we were standing everything had been nailed to the floor.

"What you got to say to that?" he said. He wiped his mouth with the back of his hand and spat again.

"I didn't know you was that hungry," I said. It's a good thing I'm into mental discipline. "If I'd known you was that hungry," I said, "I'd of brought you a septic tank to suck on."

Mental discipline is what saved California Carl's nuts. That and the fact that everything was nailed down. And also my teeth were hurting.

But he better watch out. I burn slow. And I don't forget.

"Going?" he said. "So soon? What's the matter, Eva— can't you take a joke? That's the trouble with you girls. No sense of humour."

I don't forget and I won't forget. Not about Gruff and Pete and their python. Nor about the mice. Nor about California Carl. Especially California Carl.

On my way out I met Mr. Deeds coming in.

"Oy! Where's the fire?" he said. "You could've knocked me over. Still, I'm glad you're here. I want to talk to you about masks."

"What?"

"Masks, Eva. What you put over your head when you don't want anyone to see your face."

"I know what a mask is. I ain't pig ignorant."

"Very popular," he said. "Kendo Nagasaki, the Rasputin Brothers. It's the air of mystery. What I want to know, Eva, is have you ever seen a woman fight in a mask?"

"What woman?"

"No woman," Mr. Deeds said. "Have you ever *seen* one? Only me and some of the boys were talking dinner time. And we reckoned a mask might suit *you* Eva."

"What mask?"

"I don't know," he said, sounding cross. Which made two of us. "I don't know what mask. That'd be up to you. The Woman in the Iron Mask. Could be a splash, Eva. Think about it."

Some of the boys and Mr. Deeds. Talking about me at dinner time. Masks.

"Where you going, Eva?" Mr. Deeds shouted. "I ain't finished."

"Dentist," I said. "I got a toothache."

Mr. Deeds is the guv'nor. He is Mr. Money Bags. He pays me my purse. I can't sit on his head and chop his legs off at the knees. I can't stuff his head in a bag like he wants to stuff mine. And cut off his light and air.

I've seen those masks, and I wouldn't be caught dead in one. You can't see proper. You can't hear proper. You can't breathe or talk.

Wear a mask? I'd rather disembowel myself with a rusty spoon.

One day, I'm going to be so freaky famous, no one, not Mr. Deeds, not California Carl, not Gruff, not Pete, *no one* will have the nerve to piss me around.

Chapter 9

I don't like running. In fact, I despise running. Running don't do nothing but hurt your knees and puff you out.

The gym was enemy city that day. But I am a big girl and I need exercise, so I ran all the way from the gym back to Mandala Street. Which is most of two miles.

I did not jog. Jogging is for recreationals. I ran. Get the difference? Good. Not many do.

It was mizzling and cold enough to make your nose drip. I ran, but I didn't enjoy it. It was turning out to be the sort of day I don't enjoy.

By the time I got to Mandala Street it seemed my whole life was like that—just one mega screw-up after another. Beginning with birth. If you don't believe me, ask my ma. She'll tell you. Why shouldn't she tell you? She tells me often enough.

My ma wishes I'd never been born. More than that, she wishes I'd never been got. She says she was sick for the whole nine months and when that was over I came out the wrong way round. The doctor had to haul me out by the feet. She says I ripped her from stem to stern and I've been nothing but trouble ever since.

My ma has been ashamed of me since day one. She says no one at the hospital had ever seen such an ugly baby. She says my sister Simone cried when she took me home. She says Simone cried and asked for a pretty doll instead. I bet she's lying. Simone'd never say a stupid thing like that. She's a lying cow, my ma.

She says she doesn't know who my dad is. I used to want to know who he was when I was a kid but I don't care anymore. Why should I? But she should know. You don't go round having daughters by any old bim you meet, do you? I bet she knows, and she's lying as usual. Like she does about Simone. She just wants to keep us all apart.

That's the sort of thing you think about when you're running. Running doesn't occupy the mind like weight-training does. Running gives you the hump.

I had the hump by the time I got to Mandala Street.

Crystal was not on her stall so I went to the Premises. She was coming out just as I got there.

She said, "Oh Eva, I was going to fetch you. Queenie's in a bad way."

I went in.

Everyone was there. I was all amazed because the place had changed so much. The shop floor had been swept out and there was a light. In the back room I found fat Mandy, Kath with the bosoms, a little boy, and a plumber.

Kath said, "Cup of tea, Eva. Milk and sugar?"

"Yeah," I said, blinking. They were boiling water in an electric kettle. The plumber was on the floor with his head under the sink.

Kath said, "This is Stef's kid, Marlon."

A bigger kid came in saying, "I wanna biscuit." He stopped when he saw me. He stood for a minute with his mouth open. "Hey!" he said. "You're Bucket Nut, ain'cha?"

"Don't be so fucking rude," Mandy said. "This is Eva."

"Who're you?" I said.

"Stu," Mandy said. "He's Kath's eldest."

"Can I have your autograph?" Stu said. "You're nearly famous, aren't you?"

"Less of the 'nearly' " I said.

"Stop strutting, Eva," Crystal said. "Queenie and Justin's upstairs."

"What the fuck's happening?" I said. "Everyone's here, and it ain't exactly discreet."

"You heard of squatters' rights?" she said.

"No," I said. "When you and me was roughing it, squatters had rights like donkeys had feathers."

"Well," she said, leading the way upstairs, "I thought, 'The more the merrier.' Like, the more of us there are in here, the more 'in' we are, the harder it'll be to get us out. And it's ever so damp downstairs, so we had to get Justin and Queenie up to a smaller room we could keep warm. And we needed power and water so Kath brought her feller. He's quite handy. And some of the market people helped too."

"You told them?" I said. "Shit, Crystal, they'll dob on us."

"They're mates of mine," she said. "Mates don't dob on mates."

Crystal didn't used to have any mates at all. When me and Crystal teamed up, even her own sister wouldn't take her in.

There were two bedrooms and a bathroom upstairs.

"We thought the front room was best for Justin," Crystal said.

Who the fuck was "we?" That's what I wanted to know. It was supposed to be my premises, my gym. It was supposed to be Crystal and me.

I was going to ask, but she opened the bedroom door. Inside was Bella, Stef and Justin. There was a big mattress on the floor and Justin was in bed. Last night he only had a sleeping bag. Now there were sheets and pillows and he looked warm and comfy. He was eating soup out of a china bowl. Stef was holding the bowl.

"You landed on your feet," I said.

"I've been incredibly lucky," he said. He looked at me out of swimming pool eyes.

"He ain't well," Stef said. "Eat yer soup, Justin. You got to keep your strength up."

"It's Queenie," Justin said. "It's Queenie who isn't well."

Queenie lay at the end of the mattress. She looked half dead and barely breathing. There were two little fur balls cuddled into her stomach.

I squatted down to look. I didn't touch her or the little fur balls. You got to be careful of dogs who just had puppies. They don't like strangers butting in.

Justin was right to be worried.

Bella said, "I don't think she's got any milk."

Queenie looked sunk in on herself, like a dusty old fur coat someone threw on the floor. She had a nasty discharge and it smelled bad.

Crystal said, "We thought you'd know what to do."

"She's not right, is she?" Justin said.

"Her babies are okay though, aren't they?" Crystal said.

"There was too much blood," Justin said. "There shouldn't be. With dogs, I mean. She tried too hard, poor thing."

"Eat yer soup," Stef said.

"What you think?" Bella said. She was leaning against the window with her arms folded.

"I think Justin's right," I said. "This ain't normal."

"Poor old girl," Justin said. He leaned forward and stroked her head very gently.

I watched carefully. Queenie's eyelid flickered and the muscles at the base of her spine twitched. She wanted to wag her tail but she wasn't strong enough.

Ain't that amazing? The poor old bitch was dying but she was still grateful Justin stroked her.

"What you going to do?" Bella said from the window.

"Get a vet," I said. "She's too far gone for home nursing."

"I haven't got any money," Justin said. "You'll never get a vet to come here."

"Wanna bet?" I said. I stood up.

"Eat yer soup before it gets cold," Stef said. "Eva'll look after Queenie."

"Keep her warm," I said, "and try and get some water down her."

"She won't drink her tea," Justin said sadly.

"Try and get some water in her mouth," I said. "She looks as if she's drying up."

"She can't hold her head up."

"Use an eye dropper or something," I said. Honestly, I have to think of everything. Justin had no right to give up on Queenie. Not when she was using her last bit of strength to show she loved him.

Bella peeled herself off of the window.

"I'll get something from the chemist," she said. "What about a douche bag? Will that do?"

"How would I know?" I said. I went downstairs with Crystal and Bella.

"You just want to drip some water in her mouth and down her throat," I said. "You don't want to choke her."

"Okay," Bella said. "What about a gravy baster."

"Jesus!" I said. Because I never seen a gravy baster. I never seen a douche bag either. Bella was just saying it to make me feel ignorant.

"Only an eye dropper seems awfully small," Bella said. "And Queenie's a big dog. Suppose she bites it and ends up with broken glass in her mouth?"

"Don't you go near her," I said. "Whatever you get, you let Justin do the business. Right?"

"Right," she said. "I don't like big dogs anyway."

Which showed what sort of woman *she* was.

"Where you going?" Crystal said.

"Phone."

"Who?"

"Vet."

"Oh," she said. "Yeah. You know, we could do with a phone." And she got that look in her eye which meant some poor bugger from the phone company had better watch out.

And I thought about Flying Phil.

"Portables," I said.

"What?"

"Portable phones. I was thinking, like, for the girls anyway. And personal alarms." Because Harsh was right really. Those scrubbers had about as much idea of self-defence as those whiskery little mice. And you know what was going to happen to those whiskery little mice, don't you? They was going to get eaten alive. If the best they could do was squeak, they better learn to squeak loud. Very loud.

"Lord love us all," Bella said.

"What?" Crystal said.

"Old Bucket Nut's been thinking."

"Shut up, Bella, Eva's got a point."

"No, I mean it," Bella said. "I'm touched. I could've sworn she never gave us 'slags' another thought."

"A lot you know," I said, and I went off up Mandala Street before she could ask what else I'd been thinking about. Which was that there was too many people in the Premises. Too much going down. It made my brain feel all creased and crumpled.

There is only one public phone box in Mandala Street, and there was a queue outside of it. I don't like phone boxes. They're like stood up coffins. I didn't fancy waiting in a queue to stand in a coffin. Besides, that coffin's what the boys piss in when it's cold.

So I decided to visit the vet in person. I thought I'd give him the full force of my charm and personality. Which is best done in person. Because, in spite of what I told Justin, that vet's a lazy sod and if there was a way of ducking a housecall he'd find it. If Ramses or Lineker ever needed him, we went to him. He never came out to us.

It wasn't far, and when I got there he was just sitting down to his tea.

He said, "No. The best thing is for the owner to bring the dog in. There's less trauma to the animal that way."

"Less trauma to you, more like."

"I *beg* your pardon!"

I stuck my fists on my hips and ruffled up my muscles like I do before a fight. I said, "The owner's sick too. He ain't got no transport. The dog can't walk. I told you. There's two new-born puppies."

"I'm just about to have my supper," he whined. "I'll put you on my visiting list for the morning."

"I'll wait," I said. And I stood there with my foot in the door. I could smell roast beef. And so could he. It's lucky I'm such a patient person.

"You'll have to go now," he said. "I'll come in the morning."

"Now."

"In the morning."

"Now."

"Oh hell!" he said. "I'll get a locum."

"Get what you like," I said. "But come *now*."

"Please don't raise your voice to me," he said. "What I'm going to do for you is to ring one of my colleagues who may be available. Now, be so kind as to let me close the door."

I've heard that one before. I leaned on the door until he stepped back. I walked in.

What a bim. Did he really think I was going to let him shut me out? Me? Wait around till he'd filled his fat belly, smoked his pipe and picked fluff out of his tummy button? Not sodding likely. I may be patient but I'm not that patient.

I stood over him while he got his scrubbed little fingers round the phone. He was very polite to whoever he was talking to. He even called me a lady. But he turned his back while he was talking so I couldn't see what he was calling me with his face.

When he finished talking and put the phone down his face said nothing, but his mouth said, "Stop looming over me, Eva. It's all arranged. Mrs. Gibbs will meet you in Mandala Street in an hour's time. Will that suit? I do hope that will suit."

"Yeah," I said. "But she better be good or I'm coming back." And I went out. The roast beef was making my mouth water, but the vet didn't look like he wanted me to stay and eat some.

I bought a couple of burgers on the way back and ate them while I walked.

Sometimes you got to force people to do things you need done. You got to twist their arms and tweak their noses till they do their jobs. Makes you wonder why they got their jobs in the first place, doesn't it? I mean, why did that bim want to be a vet if he couldn't get off his fat arse to see a dying dog? For money. That's why. When you're an expert at something like sick animals you can make a lot of dosh. Because people with sick animals will pay a lot of dosh. So the vet gets rich and then he can do what he likes. He doesn't have to care and he doesn't have to turf out to see a poor dying old bitch if he doesn't want to. If he wants to eat roast beef instead, he'll eat roast beef instead, and sod anyone who needs him.

I despise needing a rich person who's an expert. I always try to find someone poor. But you won't find a poor vet. Or a poor doctor or a dentist or a lawyer however hard you try.

If that vet's father was a syphilitic goat, his mother was a dung beetle.

I decided to go back to the gym and rescue the mice.

But by the time I decided, I was back in Mandala Street. What with thinking about vets and all, I'd lost track, and there I was back in Mandala Street with Crystal swinging off my sleeve like the lunatic monkey she was.

"What's up, Eva?" she was saying. "What's the matter? Where you going? Couldn't you find the vet?"

"Leave off dragging my arm," I said. "I'm going to rescue some mice."

"Don't shout, Eva," she said. "Where's the vet? What mice?"

"Let go my arm!"

"You're all of a tiz-woz, Eva," she said. "Have a beer and calm down."

"You got beer in there?"

"While you was gone Kath's Billy brought us in an old fridge and fixed it up. We got a few pints to celebrate."

"Celebrate what?" I said.

"Your premises," she said. "Grand opening. We got mats and everything, Eva. Wait till you see. Come and have a beer."

"Oh well," I said. "Just the one." And I followed her into the Premises.

They weren't proper mats. They were old horsehair mattresses. But they'd do. The only trouble was they were all rolled up on the shop floor and they had people lolling around on them. There was Bella, Mandy and Stef with her little Marlon. And there was Lynn and Kath with the bosoms, and Kath's Billy and little Stu. Which was a lot of people in a small shop.

They were all talking and laughing and drinking beer out of plastic mugs and jam jars. Bob Marley was singing "Is It Love?" from a blast box and there was this sweet smell of smoko.

"Piss in the port," I said to Crystal, "this is nothing but a whore's parlour." And everyone cracked up cackling and kicking their heels although it wasn't funny at all. Some gym!

"It's a celebration," Crystal said, and she fetched me a beer out of the back kitchen.

I couldn't think what I was doing drinking beer with a party of trollops, and suddenly it felt like the bone had gone out of

my legs. So I had a big slurp and sat down on the floor till my
strength came back.

"Ain't the vet coming?" Stef said.

"She's coming," I said.

"She better hurry," Bella said.

"If that dog dies," Stef said, "Justin'll just break his heart."

"He's sweet," Mandy said.

"Lay off," Stef said. "He's not your type."

"Lay off yourself."

"What mice, Eva?" Crystal shouted over the racket. She
thought she was stopping a fight starting between Stef and
Mandy, see. But she made a mistake. Tarts don't go for mice.
I could of told her that. My ma goes spare if she sees a
whisker. Not that my ma's a tart. She's not a professional. She
just has a lot of temporary fellers and she can't stand mice.

At the word "mice" they all went berserkers.

"Mice? Mice, yeugh! Where? We got mice in here? Where?
I hate fucking mice!"

And Kath's little Stu ran around among them going, "Eek,
eek. I'm a mouse. Eek-eek."

I had to laugh. And I felt a lot better.

"Shut up laughing, Eva," Crystal said. "There's no mice in
here, is there?"

"How do you know?" I said, "Eek-eek-eek."

"You're winding us up," Crystal said. "*She's winding us up*.
THERE'S NO MICE IN HERE!" And she got things quieted
down. Which was a pity.

Everyone sat down again except Kath's Billy who'd never
got up, and Kath's Stu who kept on running in circles going,
"Eeek!" until Kath smacked his ear and made him cry.

They were so fucking silly, I told them about the whiskery
little brown mice called Crystal, Bella, Stef, Mandy, Lynn and
Kath. And I told them about Percy the Python and how Percy
swallowed mice alive. And I told them about the game and the
betting. I even told them about the white mouse and how Cal-

ifornia Carl bit her head off. I did *not* say her name was Eva.
I kept that choice piece of news to myself. It still made me
feel weird.

"That's disgusting," Bella said. "That's fucking disgusting."

"No more disgusting than cockfighting," Lynn said.

"Cockfighting's disgusting too," Bella said.

"You know what's really disgusting?" Lynn said.

"What?"

"What the boys used to do when I was a kid."

"What?"

"I was brought up in a little place in Kent," Lynn said. "In
the country. And in the country all the boys can get hold of air
rifles."

"So?"

"Well, what the boys used to do in the summer was to catch
frogs. They'd catch these frogs, see, and then when they
caught a frog they'd stick a straw up its arse."

"What sort of straw?"

"Any old straw—a cocktail straw."

"Why?"

"Shut up and listen," Lynn said. "They'd stick a straw up
the frog's arse and blow it up."

"What you mean?" Bella said. "Blow it up? Blow what
up?"

"The frog. Like a balloon," Lynn said. "Till it was all
stretched fat and round and it couldn't use its little legs. Then
they bunged up the end of the straw with mud to stop the air
escaping. And then they pushed it out on the pond. The frog
couldn't swim or dive 'cos it was like a balloon, see. So it just
floated out. Out on the pond."

"And then?"

"And then they shot at it with the air guns," Lynn said. "Till
someone hit it and it sort of exploded."

"You're right," Bella said. "That's really disgusting."

"What a way to die," Crystal said. She looked all upset.

And then the vet came.

I'd just about decided I didn't much like Lynn's story. Or Lynn. Or the celebration. And I ought to go and see to Ramses and Lineker. And then Mrs. Gibbs turned up.

She was small and pasty-faced and she had big round spectacles. She didn't look much like a vet to me, but she carried a vet's bag and she said, "Where's the patient?"

Everyone shut up when she walked in, like they do when a stranger comes. And that made Mrs. Gibbs shuffle from foot to foot and look at the cracked walls.

She said, "I was supposed to meet a Miss Wylie here."

She looked pretty harmless, so I said, "That's me." And Crystal and I showed her upstairs.

Crystal turned on the light and woke Justin up. He was still pretty even though his face was sweaty and yellow from the light bulb.

"The vet's come to see Queenie," Crystal told him.

He sat up and said, "She won't take her away, will she?"

But the vet said nothing. She was looking at Queenie and listening to her heart. She wasn't interested in Justin.

Crystal said, "Drink some water, Justin. I'll get you something to eat in a minute." And she arranged his pillows.

Mrs. Gibbs said, "I'm going to have to take this dog in."

"You can't," Justin said. "She's my dog, and she gets really unhappy when we're apart."

"She needs a Caesarean," Mrs. Gibbs said. "There's at least one more pup inside. She can't deliver it herself."

"But she'll be really upset."

"It's better than being really dead," I said.

"Is it?" Justin said. "I think it's better to be dead than to lose the people you love."

"You'll have to decide," Mrs. Gibbs said. "I can't perform a Caesarean here. This place is filthy."

"We could clean it up," Crystal said. She looked doubtful.

Mrs. Gibbs said nothing.

Justin said, "It isn't one of those Roman Catholic things, where you save the puppy but lose Queenie?"

"I rather think the puppy's beyond saving," Mrs. Gibbs said.

"Maybe Queenie's just resting," Justin said. "She'll do it naturally if we give her time. Can't you just give her an injection?"

Well, he was very young. But he should've had more of a sense of responsibility to his dog. I looked at Crystal, and Crystal looked at me.

She said, "Shut up, Eva." Which wasn't fair, because I hadn't said a dicky-bird.

Mrs. Gibbs said, "Your dog will have a better chance if we can operate."

"I hate hospitals," Justin said. "They're horrible. All that noise and pain. They smell. Nobody listens. They just do things to you in hospital. Without asking. As if you're not a real person."

"It's a small animal clinic," Mrs. Gibbs said. I didn't understand what Justin was talking about so I couldn't blame her.

Suddenly, he cheered up. "I can't pay," he said. "I haven't got any money."

"We'd never refuse to treat a distressed animal," Mrs. Gibbs said. Her eyes blinked behind her round spectacles.

Crystal said, "We'll have a whip-round. We can pay."

Justin looked at her like she was a traitor.

"Shut up, Eva," Crystal said. And I *still* hadn't opened my trap.

"Justin," she said, "you got to let the vet look after Queenie. She's too old to have babies. You said so yourself. She can't look after herself and she can't look after her babies."

And that reminded me that Crystal had buried Dawn's blue baby, so she knew what she was talking about.

She said, "Stop jumping around, Eva. You're upsetting him."

She said, "Justin, you got to let Queenie go. You know you must."

"You're wasting time," I said. I couldn't help myself.

Justin said something and then he hid under the bed clothes.

"What?" Crystal knelt by the bed. Justin said something else.

"Take her," Crystal said. "Quick. Before he changes his mind."

So we took Queenie, wrapped in a blanket, out to Mrs. Gibbs's Volvo. We took the puppies too.

At the last minute Crystal came down and got in the car too.

"Justin says I got to stay with her," she said. But she didn't look as if she wanted to. Her little monkey face was all creased up and misery-looking. A whole day spent getting other people to jump around the way she wanted them to must've tired her out. Stupid monkey. Maybe that'd teach her to leave folk alone.

I left Stef and Mandy squabbling about who was going to give Justin his supper. Honestly! You'd think they'd be cheesed off servicing blokes by now.

I was cheesed off with *them*. I can tell you. Cheesed and totally choked.

Chapter 10

I'm glad both my dogs are blokes. What goes wrong with them goes wrong with skin, muscle and bone. They don't have horrible female problems—which all happen deep inside, in secret places you can't get at without an operation. They don't come on heat and act weird and wimpy. They aren't in any danger of being put up the spout and having puppies they can't deliver.

No, Ramses and Lineker are dogs you can count on. They're nasty all the time.

They're lowdown bad animals, and that's the way I like 'em. Give me a shit-faced mean bloke dog any day of the week. I can handle that. I don't have to make allowances. I don't have to say, "Poor baby, it's her time of the month," or stuff like that. I don't have to understand stuff or watch out for stuff or protect them from stuff. If something bad gets done, nine times out of ten, it's Ramses and Lineker doing it. It doesn't get done to them.

I did my rounds in the cold and dark. I checked the fence for holes, the chains for weak links. I tested all the locks, doors and windows. I looked in the used cars. I shone my torch in the stacks, heaps and piles. I made sure none of the silly sods who work there by day had left keys in any of the machinery.

Ramses and Lineker prowled behind me, sticking their snouts in this and that. They started up rats. They growled at passing traffic and snarled at passing people. They glared at me with killer eyes.

"That's the way to do it," I said. And I went out to have a look at the other two properties The Enemy had given me to watch.

It started to rain as I walked along—a slow fat rain—and the streets emptied. Which suited me. I'd had enough of company that day, and I began to feel more normal.

You can only be yourself by yourself. That's what I always say. You can't be yourself with a monkey wrench like Crystal hanging on to you and squeezing your brain. Because that's what she does—make no mistake—she gets a grip, like a monkey wrench, and then, try as you will, you can't shake her off.

I mean, look at the dung she got me into the last few days. She's got me tied up with trollops. She got me breaking and entering. She got me fucked up at Sam's gym. She got me in trouble with my vet. Me. Who only wants to be myself by myself. Who only wants a quiet life with a few fights to get my jollies.

The first property I looked at was fine. It was a flat in a block with outside walkways. We'd boarded up the windows, The Enemy and me. And there it was—untouched, tighter than a fish's arse—which is watertight. No bugger had tampered with it. No pitiful little bastard with a pregnant bitch had wormed his way in. It was all sweet and dandy.

I went on to the next, and the rain rained heavier. The gutters ran with garbage and water and swirled around blocked drains. The street smelled like an overflowing sewer. It was good to be out alone.

The next property was a little house in a row of little houses. I could smell trouble almost before I turned the corner just like I could smell the drains.

First off, I could see the door was open a crack. And then I saw a light. Torch light.

I thought maybe I should go back for one of the dogs. Ramses. He'd appreciate the practice. We got things all sewn up at the yard so he doesn't get much chance to do what he's trained for.

Then I thought, why wait? I mean, suppose I go back for Ramses but when we get back the dregs are gone. That'd waste my time and his time. And I'd've missed all the action. Because that's my job too—to be all pumped up and greased for action.

I took off my kit bag and rummaged in it for the torches. You don't know about the torches? Well, I'll tell you. The one I hold in my left hand is for light. Spot the target, see. But the one I hold in my right is my lethal weapon, the torture torch. It's one of those big long jobbies that hold six batteries. Only it ain't got batteries in it. Oh no. It's specially fitted with something a lot heavier. It's covered with black rubber so it's ever so comfy to hold, and it's designed to bounce a treat off any bugger's bonce who gets in my way.

And here's the clever bit—a torch isn't an offensive weapon. If I get rousted by the polizei I'm not carrying, am I? It's just a torch, innit? So long as they don't look too close.

I checked to see my high-tops were laced tight—it's about the uncoolest thing in the world to run into heavy action and trip over your shoe laces. Straight up. If you want to be cool, check for trailing laces.

Because, see, even if all you're doing is rousting a couple of twitchy sweaty junkies, what you want is authority. I'm in charge of that house, right? And it ain't going to turn into some creepy shooting gallery or flop house while I'm in charge. So I got to have cool. I got to go in fast and mean, and clear the ground before them vein-poppers know what hit 'em.

Then I took a few deep breaths to store up oxygen. See, there's no point being cool, fast or mean if you run out of puff.

Then I was ready. I crossed the road, sprinting. I hit the door with my shoulder. I burst inside. I pointed the light. I yelled, "Outside, fart faces! Out, out, out!" I swung the torture torch and crashed it against an inside door.

Big noise. Big shock. Job over, right?

Wrong.

I kicked the inside door open and hurtled into the room.

There were two of them. One leaped aside and went down in a crouch.

"Move!" I yelled. "Outside while you still can."

I charged the one who hadn't moved.

I was right there. Torture torch up. Blood pumping.

And then I saw this face. White with fright. Gob hanging open. Crystal.

And quick as a flash, I thought, without thinking, if I gave her a little knock—just a little one on the nut—I could get her out of my life. Just one little whack could get me free of monkey face. Not forever. Twenty-four hours would do. Just a day without her and her stupid ideas and maybe I could get my life back in one piece.

I was right there. Torch up. Blood pumping ready. All it would take was one tiny bang on the bean.

"EVA!" roared The Enemy. "STOP!"

So I stopped. Well, I had to, didn't I? I couldn't very well bean Crystal, *knowing* it was Crystal. Could I? Not if someone saw me know it was Crystal. Especially if that someone was The Enemy.

"Oh it's you," I said. "I thought you was junkies. You might have warned me."

"*I* might have warned *you?*" The Enemy shouted. "My fucking car's parked right outside. How much warning do you need?"

"Don't you shout at me," I said. "I'm just doing my job. If you had been junkies, I'd be a bleeding hero."

"Well, we're not junkies, and you're a bleeding head-banger."

"What's *she* doing here?"

Crystal still looked like she was going to lay an egg. At least I'd shut her up for a while.

The Enemy wiped the palms of her hands on her denims. I'd made her sweat and that felt good.

She said, "Look, Eva, I'm really glad to know you're on the job." She'd forced her voice down to sound calm and in control. I grinned.

She said, "But would you mind, next time, looking before you leap? I don't want any accidents."

"If you say so," I said. Next time, I'd give her wet knickers, and it wouldn't be any accident.

"You probably didn't notice," she said, "but there are two new locks on the front door, and I put security shutters on the windows. That should be enough to deter anyone. But I'd still like you to come by once a night, for a week, anyway. Okay?"

They always talk too much when they've had a fright.

I said, "You letting *her* move into this one too?"

"Who?"

"Crystal. Old Monkey Wrench here."

"What're you talking about?" The Enemy said, looking peeved. "If you're talking about the property on Mandala Street, there was already a squatter in residence when we turned up. That makes it the owner's problem. Not mine."

"Did you tell the owner?"

"No. But I told the agent. It's the agent I'm working for."

Crystal stuck her tuppence worth in at last. She said, "Who's the owner?"

The Enemy looked from me to Crystal and back again. "I don't know," she said. "Why?"

"Just wondered," Crystal said. And *I* wondered who she was planning to get her jaws locked onto next. And I wondered what she'd been nattering about to The Enemy. And what The Enemy would do if she got too curious.

Actually, The Enemy and Crystal seemed made for each other—a marriage made in Hell.

"What're you grinning at, Eva?" The Enemy said.

"Nothing," I said. "I'm off now. Can't stop around all night socializing. Not like some."

And I left because I was winning but it felt like things was going to go the other way. I mean, I made The Enemy sweat and roar. Which was good, right? But then there was midget monkey under my feet again. Which was bad. And it made me think. What did The Enemy want with Crystal? Was she going to get Crystal to spy on me?

Crystal knows stuff. She knew me when I was ducking and diving. Before I learned mental discipline and cool. She knew me when I was a grungey kid and I didn't care wibbly-dibbly about health and hygiene. She knew me when I was on the run and I hadn't realised me full potential.

And that's who you got to watch out for—people who knew you before you realised your full potential. They're dangerous, see. Because they never truly believe you are what you are now. And they tell stories about you as you were then.

There are plenty of things I wouldn't want Crystal to natter about to The Enemy.

I was just thinking about some of the stuff I wouldn't want Crystal to tell The Enemy when she came puffing up behind me. Crystal, I mean.

"Wait, Eva," she puffed. "Wait for me."

So I walked faster and her little legs went like pistons trying to keep up.

"What she want with you?" I said.

"Who?"

"The lady copper."

"Her?" Crystal puffed. "Anna?"

I stopped, and she crashed into the back of me.

"Anna?" I said. "*Anna?* You want to watch her, Gremlin. She's the law. There's stuff she didn't ought to know."

And suddenly I cheered up. Because if there were a few little naughties I didn't want Crystal telling on me, just think how much I had on her!

Like, I know for a fact that her whole business was started with stolen property. Everyone says so. I seen her myself. She was a dab-hand dipper. If it wasn't chained to you or stuck down with glue, if it wasn't nailed to the fucking floor, Crystal would have it in her pocket.

She'd go out begging. Well, truth to tell, *we'd* go out begging. You know the deal—"Got any spare change, mister?"— "Got the price of a cuppa, missus?" Only, me being the size I was, even as a kid, I wasn't much good at it.

"Get a proper job," they'd say to me. "Get a job down the mines." Or the building site. The worst one was, "What's the matter, you run *away* from the circus?"

But Crystal—well, being little did her no harm at all. She'd stick her hand out and bob up and down like a cork in a basin—all curly mop and freckles—and they'd say, "Ah, the poor wee article."

She was specially good in the rain. And she had this system in car parks—mostly with women. She'd pick a mark with bags to carry, and she'd offer to help. The skill was in picking the right mark—someone in a bit of a fuss. Someone well-dressed but not too dandified. She said the best marks were women carrying books. For some reason, she said, if they read books they were a soft touch. Don't ask me why. But Crystal was hardly ever wrong. For herself. Me, I couldn't screw a penny piece out of someone carrying a whole library shelf.

So Crystal would pick her mark. "Help with your bags, missus?" she'd say. And she *would* help. Ever so eager, she was. She'd help with the bags, and help herself at the same time. She always got a few coins for her trouble, and the mark'd drive off and never find out till later she was missing her purse, her umbrella or a few tins of baked beans.

But being little wasn't all a bed of roses. Getting the goodies came easy for Crystal. But keeping hold of them was a lot harder. There's no point having a pocket full of loose change and valuables if someone's going to bash you and take it off you when you boogie round the next corner. Which is where I came in. I only took my share. And I never bashed her. So she knew I was honest.

Well, I was her protection, wasn't I? And you got to pay for protection. It's only right.

A leopard does *not* change its spots. So don't you tell me Crystal's changed hers. If you think she came by all that bric-a-brac she sells off her stall honestly, you're even stupider than you look. Crystal and her connections! They're all a bunch of thieves down Mandala Street Market.

It was still pouring down and we were stood there getting soaked which was just as well because I hadn't had my shower. But a hot shower and cold rain aren't the same thing, so I found a nice little Vauxhall Astra and drove us home. The heater worked a treat so we warmed up in no time, although the windows got too steamy to see out of and I nearly hit a lamppost at the end of Mandala Street.

Crystal didn't say much while I was driving but when we stopped she said, "You was going to kill me back there, wasn't you?"

"What?" I said.

"Back there," she said. "In that house. If Miss Lee hadn't stopped you. You was going to smash my head in."

"Take a pill," I said. "'I thought you was junkies."

"Yeah, but you was going to beat crap out of me."

"I wasn't."

"You was."

"I was only trying to scare you," I said. "I thought you was junkies and it's my job to scare you off."

"Doesn't matter," she said.

"*Wasn't* going to hurt you."

"All right. Don't yell at me. Fancy a tea, or something?"

"It's too late," I said. "The caff's closed."

"Your place?"

"Forget it."

"Only I can't seem to get to sleep these days," she said. "Every time I close my eyes I see Dawn with her face all black and blue."

"That's your problem," I said. "I can sleep perfect."

"It's funny really," Crystal said. "Dawn, I mean. It's not really a dream. It's just when I close my eyes. You know, they kicked her teeth out. She didn't have hardly any teeth in her mouth when I saw her in the morgue. Her mouth was all sunk in like an old lady's mouth."

"What you telling me for? You know I can't stand teeth."

"Oh, well," she said. "I thought, seeing as you're a night animal, y'know, we might stay up and talk."

"I got work to do," I said. "If you want someone to talk to, bend Justin's ear. He'll be lonely now Queenie's at the clinic."

"That's true," she said. She got out of the car and wandered off up Mandala Street looking pitiful.

I know her tricks. If she wants me to feel sorry for her she'll have to do better than that. I'm fed up being her mark. Besides, she made my teeth ache.

Chapter 11

The next day Crystal looked better and I felt worse. She'd swapped pitches with a greengrocer and stuck her stall slap bang outside the Premises. I couldn't believe it when I saw what she'd done. Now she could catch me coming and going. I couldn't turn round without her seeing. If I burped she'd ask me what I had for dinner.

But what choice did I have? I ask you. I was all cocked up at Sam's Gym, and I had to have somewhere to work.

Today was Thursday. Tomorrow was Friday. Friday night was fight night. I had to get ready. I had to get sharp and hard. And that wasn't easy because I had no equipment except a skipping rope.

Skipping rope may look candy-arsed, but it's cheap and it's great for footwork and stamina and concentration. I used to think it was only good for girls in a playground, but Harsh showed me different. To skip rope properly you need speed and coordination. You need to be on your toes, and being on your toes keeps your ankles supple and tough.

If you want to be a wrestler you need to avoid ankle injuries. That's why you strap up and wear boots for support. Turn your ankle, tear ligaments, get a tiny little sprain and you could be out of the ring for weeks. Take my advice—keep your ankles in good nick and they'll look after you.

The only other piece of equipment I had was me. My own strength, my own weight. You can get a lot done raising your own dead weight. Of course I would've been better off with a chin bar or some parallels, but I did what I could with the door frame.

It wasn't much fun. I like all that shiny steel and the clang-clunk of the weights. I like the bright lights and the mirrors. I like the central heating and hot showers.

In that shop front in the Premises there was barely enough headroom to swing the rope. It was damp and the concrete floor was hard on the feet. The mattress smelled mouldy.

They've got sprung floors at Sam's Gym and the mats are covered in bright red and blue plastic. It choked me off just thinking about it. Those bastards over there had everything and they'd left me with nothing. Them and their fucking python.

Still, it's no use crying about what you can't have. I know that for true. In fact it's best not to *want* what you can't have. So I worked up a fair old head of steam with just me own weight and a skipping rope.

I was doing press-ups when the girls straggled in. It looked like they'd come by appointment, only no one had bothered to tell me.

They were all wearing their day-glo fun-run gear and I was glad that this time there was no one serious around to cop an eyeful. They stood around watching, so I did a few reps on one arm only—just so they knew to respect me. I can only do it with me right arm. Me left's probably strong enough, but I can never seem to get the balance right.

"Are you going to fanny around in your pretty colours?" I said as I got to my feet, "or are you here to work?"

"What d'you want us to do?" Lynn said. Which was a good question. Buggered if I knew.

"Warm up," I said. I could show them warming up without having to think, which would leave my brain free to figure out what to do next.

They made a ragged circle round me and stood there waiting.

"Jesus in a jump-suit," I said, looking at them. "They can't even *stand* without looking clapped out."

"You just going to lip off?" Bella said. "Or are you going to learn us something?"

"Shit. I'll have to start at the beginning," I said. I ignored Bella. I mean, what can you do with two-inch purple fingernails?

"Feet apart," I said. "Not that far apart, Mandy. You're not going to do the splits. Backs straight. Don't stick your bums out. Now, flex your knees a little. A *little,* I said. I'm not teaching you to curtsy."

I almost started to laugh. They stood there like puddings. Puddings. Sort of wobbly and stodgy. And at that moment, I have to admit, I wondered if my mental discipline was up to the job.

I bit the inside of my cheek. "Right," I said. "We'll start at the top with necks. Roll your heads around on your necks. One, two, three . . ."

They couldn't even get that right.

"Shit," I said. "Just do what I do, all right? You got to feel the muscle from your head to your shoulders stretch. One, two, three, four, five, six, seven, eight. Now the other way, one, two . . ."

I did necks. I got them wheeling their arms. I did waist rotation and hip rotation. They seemed quite good at hip rotation. But we came unstuck on legs.

All I wanted was for them to stand on one leg and pull the other knee up to their chests. You'd think I was training 'em on a high wire. They all hopped around and fell over giggling. All except Mandy. I was quite surprised about fat Mandy. I expected her to be the uselessest of the lot, but she was the only one who kept her balance.

"Get the fuck up," I said. "Backs against the wall."

"I can do that all right," Lynn said, flopping.

"Shut up," I said. "You're using the wall for balance."

"I know, dear," Kath said. "You don't have to tell *me* what a wall's for."

I could feel my brain beginning to barbecue.

"Mandy," I said, "show 'em."

So Mandy showed them. And she could do the next stretch, which was also on one leg. That went better, and only Kath with the bosoms fell over.

I didn't want to push my luck, so I gave up on the stretching and got them running on the spot. For about five seconds.

"Phew!" Bella said. "Are we finished? I'm knackered."

I looked at them, gob struck. They were all pink and sweaty. The mascara was running. They were huffing and puffing like they'd done a five-mile run. Not a five-second jog where they'd scarcely moved their feet.

"Can't we do it to music?" Stef said. "It's so boring."

"I'll get a tape," Mandy said. "We could do it all like a routine, couldn't we, Eva?"

"Could we?" I said.

"Yeah," she said. "I'll show you." And out she went—useless fat Mandy—full of go-go-go.

"Don't look so surprised," Bella said. "Mandy did the London Marathon once."

"She never!"

"She did."

"Mandy?"

"Yeah, Mandy," Bella said. "We weren't all just born to be 'slags,' you know. Some of us done other things. I know you can't believe it, but there was life before we met you."

"But," I said, "the London Marathon." It couldn't be true. Not fat Mandy.

"What happened?" I said.

"She got older and fatter," Bella said. She had a nasty grin on her pan. "Women do, you know. They get old and fat and turn into 'slags.' You wait and see."

"Shut up, Bella," Stef said. "Tell her proper."

"She ain't interested in Mandy," Bella said. "She ain't interested in any of us. She's just amazed she got one of us wrong."

"Tell me, then," Lynn said. "I ain't heard about Mandy."

"Well, she took up running 'cos of her asthma," Bella started. "Don't ask me why, but she said running's good for breathing."

"Running's terrible for breathing," Lynn said. And she lit a cigarette.

"Shut up and listen. She took up running, and she got really good at it. Joined a club and everything. And one year she qualified for the London Marathon. They gave her a gold medal for finishing. That's what you get when you finish—a medal and a Mars bar. Something like that.

"They put her picture in the local paper so she was quite a celebrity."

And then Mandy herself walked in with a blaster and a handful of tapes. I stared at her, but I just couldn't see it. She looked like her shell suit was stuffed to bursting with foam rubber and her legs were pillows. She couldn't run a bath now.

Stef said, "Bella was just telling us about the London Marathon and you getting your mug-shot in the paper."

"Oh that!" Mandy said. And she went all pink.

"Why did you give up?" Lynn asked. "What happened?"

"Dunno, really," Mandy said.

"She met a fella and got married," Bella said. "Go on, Mandy, tell us."

"Yeah, this fella," Mandy said. "Robin. He ran too, you know. We was in the same club. He was gorgeous, and ever such a good mover. But he never finished the London Marathon.

"Well, one night Robin was out training with some of his mates and he got hit by a bloke on a bike. And he broke his leg. And that was that, really, because, even when it mended, one leg was shorter than the other."

"You can't run with one leg shorter than the other," Bella said, nodding like she knew all about running.

"But even before the accident," Mandy went on, "he'd got really weird. Like, I was working in Woolworth's then, and he'd come in sometimes six times in one day. At first I thought it was ever so romantic, but then he'd ask all these funny questions about the customers."

"The men," Bella said.

"Right. He'd ask if they looked at me, if they touched me. I thought he was joking, and I'd say, 'Oh yeah, he got me behind stationery and took me bra off.' But it wasn't no joke.

"And then he wouldn't let me run in shorts. Even in summer."

"I had a boyfriend like that," Stef said. "I couldn't even undo the top button of my shirt without he went crazy."

"But the worst bit was after the accident. He let me go out training, but he had this schedule for me. He had a map of all the places I was allowed to go and he had a route all worked out. And he had a list of all the phone boxes on the route. And he used to ring the numbers. He had it all worked out. He'd sit by the phone at home with a stop watch. So, like, after twelve minutes I was supposed to be at the phone box on the corner of Dover Road, and if I didn't answer the phone, he'd get in the car and haul me back home."

"What if there was someone else in the phone box when he wanted to ring?" Lynn asked.

"I had to wait," Mandy said. "Because if I wasn't where I ought to be, *when* I ought to be, there was hell to pay. He got a bit quick with his knuckles after the accident."

"I know what I'd've done," I said. "I'd've sealed him in one of his fucking phone boxes and buried it under a ton of wet goat shit."

Lynn said, "What did you do, Mandy?"

"Nothing." Which was typical.

"I just kept running," Mandy went on. "And I tried to get to the phones on time. But he kept shortening the times, see. He said it was to help me with my speed.

"And then one day I sort of broke down. What happened was, I got to the first phone on time. Just. But I was late to the second. Only there was someone there already, so I didn't know if Robin had already rung, or if he'd tried to ring and got the engaged signal. So I didn't know if he was on his way in the car ready to drag me home, or if I was supposed to jog around keeping warm till he rang."

"So what did you do?" Lynn said.

"Well, I started to cry," Mandy said. Surprise, surprise. "And I started on at this complete stranger in the phone box. I was crying and shouting, 'How long you been on the phone?' I can't think what was going through his mind, with this mad woman in running gear, in floods of tears, banging on the glass, screaming at him."

"What did he do?" Lynn asked.

"Oh, he was lovely," Mandy said. "He came out and he was sweet to me. And he got me to tell him what was wrong. 'Course it all came pouring out—about the accident and the phones. He was ever so sympathetic. He really listened."

"And then?"

"Then Robin rang. He didn't know I was late to the second phone after all. So then, this feller took me in his van to the third phone. So we could keep on talking. And on to the fourth, and so on. All I had to do was run home from the last.

"Well, next time I went out running, there was the bloke in the van. He leaned out his window and waved a bunch of telephone receivers at me. What he'd done, see, was vandalize all the phones on my training route and collect all the receivers."

Lynn started to laugh.

"It wasn't that funny," Mandy said. "Not in the end. 'Cos when I got home that night, Robin wouldn't believe that every single phone on my route was out of order. So he took me in the car and inspected them. And then he gave me a right hiding, 'cos he thought I'd done it, and he suspected I had a boyfriend.

"And, it turned out, one of his mates actually saw me in this bloke's van in the cinema car park. Where we'd gone, see.

"And then he chucked me out of the house—bag and baggage."

"Just like that?" Lynn said.

"Just like that."

"And then?"

"And then he started going out with the girl on the cosmetics counter who didn't run. And he divorced me."

"What about the bloke in the van?" Lynn asked.

"Oh it was only the once," Mandy said. "I never saw him again after that one time in the back of his van. I sort of gave up interest in running after that."

Well, you could see her point, couldn't you? Anyway, running isn't much fun at the best of times.

"I had a bloke like that once," Bella said. "He thought I was having it off with every feller I talked to. So I avoided fellers like the plague. And then he turns round and accuses me of being a lesbian with all me girlfriends. You can't win. What tapes you brought, Mandy? I'm getting cold."

So Mandy put a tape on. It wasn't anything decent—like Megadeath or Guns'n'Roses—but you could do a simple eight-count to it. And I got to say, Mandy was right. They did look a lot better to music. You could almost forget what they were, and think they was a bunch of ordinary women at a keep fit class.

But I was thinking.

Bella thought she was so clever. She thought I made a mistake about Mandy. But I didn't. Well, all right, I was surprised that fat Mandy had ever been thin Mandy. But that was the only surprise.

Fat Mandy told a story about thin Mandy. The story wasn't about the London Marathon. No. It was about Mandy being totally under some bloke's thumb. Which is where I'd expect her to be. So I wasn't wrong, was I?

I grabbed Mandy once. In the alley where Dawn got clobbered. Remember? And she just stood there wobbling like a jelly-bag. She didn't do *nothing*. And that's what made me right and Bella wrong. Suck on that, Bella Big Mouth.

So I waited—'cos I'm a patient person. I waited till the girls had finished the stretch and warm-up stuff. And then I picked on fat Mandy again.

There she was, pink and breathless, fat little cheeks jubbling, right pleased with herself for taking charge.

So I picked on her. I didn't do nothing canny. I just caught her by the throat, two-handed, and shoved her back against the wall. She let out this squawk and went all boneless. Just like she did before.

"Oy!" Bella said. "Stop that. You're hurting her."

"No I ain't," I said. "I'm holding her. She's hurting herself."

And I let go. Mandy had gone all limp, so she fell on the floor.

"You got no call to do that," Bella said. She was standing in her favorite pose. Hands on hips. But she never moved an inch towards me. When fat Mandy fell all of a heap, though, she went to help her up.

"Too late," I said. "Pathetic."

"Bitch!" Stef said.

"That's better, coming from you," I said. "Last time I did that—in the alley—remember? Last time, you didn't even say gosh-o-golly. You stood there like a wet weekend and did nothing."

I waited till the girls got Mandy stood up again. And then I attacked her. Same thing. Two hands on her fat throat.

"Look!" I said. "She's got both hands and one foot free. And what's she doing? Nothing! That's what she's doing.

She's got her big mouth open. Is she shouting or screaming? No she isn't. And what are you lot doing?"

I let go of Mandy and turned to face them.

"You're doing nothing," I said. "She's your mate, ain't she? She's one of you. But you're all stood there with nothing better to say than 'Oy!' "

"Oh, I see," Bella said. "You're learning us. Well that's all right then."

"No it ain't all right," I said.

"Don't shout at us!" Stef said.

"Why not?" I said. "I can do anything to you I like. 'Cos you won't stop me. There's five of you and one of me. And you won't do nothing to stop me."

"I will," Bella said, and she took a kick at my leg. I could see by her hard painted face she meant it. I side-stepped.

"That's better," I said. "That's more like it. Legs hurt. Give someone a nice whack on the shin or the knee, and he'll know all about it."

"But you'll just get people angry," Mandy said, from her cringe by the wall.

"I didn't get *you* angry, did I?" I said. "Why the fuck not? I went for your throat. I was right in your face, pinning you up against the wall. You should be fucking angry. But you ain't. Why not?"

"Dunno," Mandy said. "I was scared. You took me by surprise."

"Surprise?" I said. "Surprise? Gimme strength! And you doing what you do for a living. Out alone at night with some bloke you never saw before in your life. *Nothing* should surprise you, girl, nothing. Now if he gave you a box of chocolates and a ticket to the ballet—*that* might be a surprise. But not if he does something nasty. Where you *been?*"

They really got up my nose, standing round gawping like they did. It was them who took the risks. Not me. It should be them telling me. Not me telling them.

"All right," I said. "Unroll them mattresses. Spread 'em out on the floor. We don't want anyone hurt too much."

They hopped to it. And I suddenly thought it was sort of okay being an expert—having people who did what I said.

"Right," I said, when they'd finished. "Mandy. I started with you so I'll go on with you. Come here. On the mat. Now, I'm putting my hands round your throat. Not surprised, are you?"

"No." Mandy giggled. "You're tickling me."

"Shut up. You got four weapons. What are they?"

"Um," Mandy said. "Two hands and two feet."

"Wrong. You got two hands and one foot. You got to keep one foot to stand on."

"That's only three," Mandy said. "You said I got four weapons."

"You got your fucking voice, dozy."

"Oh."

"Not 'Oh,' " I said. "AAAAGH!"

I opened my throat and blasted them all in the eardrums. Mandy nearly dropped dead of fright.

"Surprised?"

She nodded.

"So will he be. Okay, your turn. Shout at me."

"Aaah."

"Listen, stupid," I said. "You want to shock him. And you want to make enough noise to get help."

"If there's anyone around," Bella said.

"So when I say shout, you shout. Really shout."

Mandy tried again, and I thought a mouse would make more noise. Inside a python.

"All do it together," I said. Because, like I notice with the fight crowd, people will do things in a bunch they'd be ashamed of alone.

"On a count of three," I said, "one, two, three."

You wouldn't believe the racket those five pros made. I had

to cover me ears, and if the windows hadn't been boarded up the glass would've shattered. They was really enjoying themselves, stamping their little feet, screaming, laughing, and then screaming again.

"You can stop now," I said. Well, I didn't say it. I yelled it. But they never heard. Or maybe they heard but they took no notice. "SHUT UP!" I yelled. But they didn't.

Crystal came belting inside going, "Wha'? Wha'? Whassa matter?"

And Justin came down from upstairs, all pale and worried-looking.

But the girls went on screaming and rolling round on the mats.

"They was practising shouting," I told Crystal. "But now they won't stop. I dunno what got into them."

But Crystal was watching and smiling. And Justin had a big grin pasted on. So I went into the back and put the kettle on.

Everywhere I go I'm surrounded by fools. They all carry on like fruit-bats. Sometimes I think I'm the only one left with any marbles.

I made my tea and waited till the ruckus died down. Then I went back, and, stripe me pink and spot me blue, they were all lolling around on the mats chatting. I've never known a bunch like it for sitting on their padded parts and chat-chat-chatting.

"Right," I said, taking charge. "Where were we? Mandy? Come on."

"Do I have to?" Mandy said. "I'm knackered."

"You haven't done no self-defence yet," I said. "What you going to do about that?"

"Always use a condom," Bella said. And they all went off into fits again.

"It isn't funny," Justin said. "It's true. First line of defence."

"Don't teach your grandmother to suck eggs," Bella said. "What you think we are? Babies?"

"Shut up, all of you," I said. "Come *on*, Mandy."

So Mandy heaved herself up and stood there like a great blister. I went to her, hands out, to grab her throat. And, would you believe it—she kicked me!

Not an ordinary kick at my legs. Oh no. She went for the high kick. She knocked my hand, and if I hadn't swerved, she'd've landed one on my chin.

I went for her again, and she kicked me again. This time I caught her foot in my hand—just to show her how dangerous it was. For her. I could've wrenched her leg up higher and tipped her on her back. But I didn't. I just let her go. I waited till the leg was going down, and *then* I grabbed her throat. All the others were going, "Ooh, aah."

"Good stuff, Mandy," I said. "But don't try it more than once. High kicks put you off balance. And what about shouting?"

"Yaaargh!" she went. And she started hacking at my shins and ankles. She went at it like a frigging mule, and I had to dance this way and that to stop one landing.

In the end I let go. She stood puffing and sweating.

"Way to go, Mandy," I said. "But what you doing, just stood there? What next?"

And she came at me like a runaway train flailing her arms.

"No!" I yelled, sidestepping. "No, not that."

"Sorry," she said. "I just got pissed off, you always picking on me."

"Fuck it!" I yelled. "Don't say sorry. You *should* be pissed. S'pose I'm a bloke and I grab you by the throat. You fight me off. You don't stand there and say sorry. What *you* got to be sorry about? *He's* the one should be sorry."

"What, then?"

"Well," I said, "you don't go back and attack him either. He's faster than you and he's stronger than you. And sure as muffins he's nastier than you, or he wouldn't've grabbed your throat. No, when you've broken free, you run like the clappers and you make as much noise as you possibly can."

"Personal alarms," Crystal said. "I think I can get hold of some." No one asked her where.

"Can I sit down now?" Mandy said. "I'm sweating."

"Lynn," I said. I wasn't going to pick Bella because of those two-inch purple fingernails.

"Me?" Lynn said. "Do I have to?"

"Yeah. Come here." Lynn was from the country some-where. At least that's what she said when she told that dis-gusting thing about the frogs, but she looked pretty normal. Well, more normal than the others. Which was why I picked her. I couldn't pick Kath because I didn't know what to do about those bosoms. And Stef looked like one breath would blow her flat. Bella, as I said, would claw me eyes out, and suck 'em like gumballs, if I let her.

"This next bit's about hands," I said, when I had Lynn stood in front of me. "Mandy done good with her feet. She went for all the painful bits—shins, knees and ankles. But she forgot the groin, which was stupid. And she didn't use her hands."

"That's right, girls," Bella said. "It's stupid to forget the groin."

"Always use your hands," said Kath and then the whole bunch neighed and snickered like the dirty mares they were.

I said, "Why don't you two hang yourselves upside down and crap on your own heads?"

"I'll put the kettle on," Crystal said. "And before I forget, Stef, there's a message for you outside."

"Okay," Stef said. And she went.

Everything was falling apart.

"If that's the way you feel," I said, "I'm off home. You're none of you serious anyway."

"Don't be like that, Eva," Crystal said. "You made a start. Everyone learned lots. Didn't they Bella? Bella?"

"Okay," Bella said. "Don't mind us, Eva. We just ain't used to being organized."

"Well, all right then," I said. "But you better shape up next time."

"Tomorrow?" Crystal said.

"I got a fight tomorrow. I got to get sharp."

"Earlier then? A short session."

"Today could've been a short session, if they didn't spend all their time farting around and nattering."

"May I join in tomorrow?" Justin asked.

"You?".

"It sounded really interesting."

"You ain't a sl . . . a woman."

"Guys get picked on too, you know."

Which is true. I s'pose. Especially if they're young and pretty like Justin. Everyone pretty gets picked on. Actually, come to think of it, you only need to look out of the ordinary, one way or the other, and people think you're up for grabs. I used to get picked on myself when I was young. And it wasn't 'cos I was pretty.

"Money!" I said. I'd forgotten—which wasn't like me at all. "I'm not doing this for free, you know."

Chapter 12

The market was packing up. It was dark. I decided to go to Hanif's because I was running out of food at the Static. I'd only gone a couple of steps when someone in the shadows said, "Oy, Bucket Nut!"

I didn't stop. Why should I? Do you stop whenever any Tom, Dick or Harry says, "Oy?"

"Oy, you!" he said again.

"Oy you yourself," I said, and I went on.

"I'm talking to you," he said, coming out of the shadows.

"Talk to yourself," I said. "I'm busy."

"I *know* you're busy," he said. "I been watching you."

He had a sneery stoatish way of talking so I stopped to take a look at him. He was about my height—which is not short—but he wore his trousers at half-mast with a belly-roll oozing over the belt. His cap sagged over his little eyes and his nose had woodworm.

"Yeah," he said, "I been watching you. I seen your little set-up. And I reckon you could do with a partner."

"You what?" I said. "You seen nothing I want a partner for."

"I ain't offering," he said. "I'm telling. You need a partner. Fifty-fifty, and that's being fair—I could cut you right out. But I won't."

"No you won't," I said. "And shall I tell you for why? It's because if I see you stoating round my door just one more time I'll spread you flat and butter my bread with you. I don't like you."

And I walked off. I mean, what did a bloke with a belly-roll know about self-defence? What right did he have muscling in on my patch? I'd show him muscle he never even heard of.

"You better listen when I talk," he shouted after me. "I got mates."

"You need 'em," I shouted back. "But I don't believe you."

If he had mates, they'd have herpes. They'd be creepy-crawlies like him. They'd be miserable old blokes who never had a single idea in their lives except to make money off the backs of others.

I've said it before but I'll say it again—if you got something, stick to it like shit to a blanket. Because, no matter what it is, even if it's only a dirty old shop-front gym and a self-defence class, some miserable stoat will want to take half. Half he hasn't earned.

And let me tell you—Eva Wylie, the London Lassassin, did not come into this world just to make things easy for stoats.

It's not that I'm bloody-minded—I'm a helpful sort, really. I mean look what I'm doing to help Crystal and Bella and that crowd. It ain't for free, granted. But I work for my gelt. I put up with a lot. And, ask yourself, do *I* want anything for free? Do I complain? No I do not. There should be more around like me, and the world'd be a better place.

At Hanif's I bought bread and bananas. I bought tins of beef stew and a couple of pork pies. Then I went back to the Static to sort myself out and check my gear.

I let the dogs out. I changed their water. I dusted their bedding with flea powder. And that reminded me. I needed a bath.

Normally I shower at Sam's Gym. But these wasn't normal times. There is a little shower stall in the Static but it works off electricity. The Static is not connected to mains electricity. It could be. It once was. But not anymore. No electrics. No electric bills. Simple.

You think you need electricity, don't you? Well, you don't. That's what the electricity company wants you to think. They want you to think you can't do without. And when they've got you thinking that way they put their prices up. And up and up and up. And you suckers, who think you can't do without, pay. And pay and pay and pay.

Not me. I've got candles and torches for light. I got wood and paraffin for heat. I got gas cylinders for me stove.

What I ain't got is meters, or someone with his nosy little calculator totting up how much I use and how much I owe. I don't rent his equipment. I don't need him or his goods. I'm free. Hand on heart, can you say that?

I put a pan of water on the stove and ate a pork pie while it heated up. I like a nice hot shower—true—but I can get clean without.

After that, I checked my gear. I hung my black costume up to air, I made sure my boots were sound and the laces were strong, I inspected the straps on my kneepads. I don't want no broken straps or laces when I'm in the ring. I want to be perfect. Imagine a wrestler with her costume held together by safety pins! I don't want to spoil my image, do I? I'm a villain, and villains and safety pins don't mix. Mean hard villains got to have mean hard gear. I couldn't believe in myself if I was falling out of my gear.

I ran my black belt through my fingers, and tugged at the buckle. I like that belt. It looks like power and control. It's hard, and it's supple. Like me. I'm hard and supple. I can dish it out, and I can take it. I just wish there was more competition around so I could prove it to more people.

I just wish I could fight on TV like they do in America. Then everyone would know. I'd be mega-famous and filthy rich and no one, *no one,* would mess me around. There'd be no stinking stoats popping out of the shadows going, "Oy Bucket Nut." No—it'd be " 'Scuse me, Ms. Wylie, might I take a few seconds of your precious time?"

And I'd say, "Make it quick, my good man. The chauffeur's waiting."

I'd have all the erks and bims grovelling. Believe me, I would!

I'd have a proper trailer with a proper shower in it. The trailer would be made of reinforced stainless steel and polished up like a silver bullet. The trim would be black and it'd have "The London Lassassin" painted on the side so everyone'd know I was there.

I'd have a black and silver Rolls-Royce to pull the trailer.

I could go anywhere I liked and still be at home.

Ramses and Lineker could have a small trailer of their own. We'd be the Mobile London Lassassin and Her Hounds from Hell.

Crystal would have to make an appointment with my receptionist if she wanted to see me.

"Ms. Wylie'll see you now," the receptionist'd say. "Knock before you enter. Oh, and take this mug of tea and plate of doughnuts through when you go in. Ms. Wylie likes a little something this time of an afternoon."

And Crystal would knock and come in, and she'd see Mr. Deeds on his knees begging me to be top of his bill. He'd be arranging a fixture at the Albert Hall, and the only one who could fill the Hall would be the London Lassassin. *Me*.

He'd say, "Oh, Eva . . . sorry, I mean Ms. Wylie, I'll be ruined if you don't agree to make a guest appearance. There ain't no one more popular than you."

And I'd say, "I'll have to look in my diary. You don't want me to fight in a mask, do you?"

And he'd go, "I must've been bonkers to suggest that. It was all the fault of those two twats Gruff Gordon and Pete Carver. I fired them ages ago. They're sleeping at the Salvation Army Hostel these days. I'll go down there and pour battery acid on their beds if you like."

"Suit yourself," I'd go. "Pete who? Gruff who? I been too busy signing autographs to remember them."

And then, see, I'd notice Crystal. She would just pop up and grab my elbow like she does. She'd be standing there waiting to be noticed. So I'd notice her. In me own time. And I'd say, "What you want, monkey face?"

But I'd know what she wanted. Because I'd of just done this self-defence video. Y'know? Like Jane Fonda only serious. And Crystal wants to sell it on her stall. "Be Tough The Eva Wylie Way," that's what I'd call it. Or "The London Lassassin's Secrets of Personal Security."

"Oy monkey face," I'd say, "the deal's this—ninety-five percent to me, five percent to you. Take it or leave it."

And she'd go, "Oh thank you, Ms. Wylie, thank you. Five percent of what you make will keep me for a year."

And then Mr. Deeds'd say, "Please, please, please, Ms. Wylie, can I put your picture on my posters for the Albert Hall?"

"All right," I'd say, "but there's conditions."

"What?" he'd go. "Anything. You only got to say."

"I'm top of the bill. I get me own dressing room with a lavvy and a shower. I pick me own opponent. I pick the music. I don't want none of that sugar stuff like 'Three Steps to Heaven.' I want proper music. Maybe I'll get Axl Rose to do it live. I'm fed up coming out to 'Satisfaction.' Why should I come out to a song so old it was a hit before I was born? And I want gold chains for Ramses and Lineker."

"It's yours," Mr. Deeds says. "Everything."

So I go, "Don't you want to know who I pick to fight?"

"Who?"

And I wait and wait till his knees hurt—he's still kneeling—and then I say, "I think, seeing as it's the Albert Hall, and all the telly cameras will be there . . ."

"Yes?"

"And all those millions of fans will want something special . . ."

"Yes? Tell me."

"Maybe I'll do something different."

"What?"

"I think I'll fight . . ."

"Who?"

"I think I'll fight California Carl!"

He gasps. Crystal faints.

"But," he says, "you can't. You're a woman. It's never been done before."

"So much the better," says I.

"But California Carl is a maniac," he says. "We can't risk it. It's too dangerous."

"*I'll* risk it," I say. "We got a score to settle—California and me."

"But he's in chokey. He's banged up for seven years, for Grievous Bodily Harm, multiple murder and cruelty to animals."

"Get him out," I say. "Clean him up and bring him to me. Midnight at the Albert Hall. I'll show you how dangerous he is. Do it, or I won't be there."

So he does it.

Meanwhile, I've gone into strict training with Harsh as my personal trainer. We go to an island. Just the two of us. And while we're there he teaches me The Secret Eastern Method of Ultimate Strength which he is only allowed to tell someone as worthy and pure as what I am.

And that's how—at the Albert Hall, in front of millions of punters and viewers—I meet California Carl in a Titanic Struggle. Axl Rose is there in person, and the Royal family, and I see them standing up and hissing California. But they're cheering for me.

I've never actually been to the Albert Hall so I don't know

what it looks like, but I expect it's all gold and red. I'd be in black, so I'd really stand out under all them spotlights. And I'd have a black and silver satin cloak made specially for the occasion. And Harsh would hold it for me when I stripped down in the ring.

Oh, I was in a lovely mood when I went to bed that morning. A good mind-movie can keep you going for hours if you're lucky enough to get one.

The other bit of luck was that I didn't have any erk or bim spoiling it. I did my rounds, and went to The Enemy's places without seeing a single soul.

So I woke up feeling exactly as I ought on the day of a fight. Fight days are special days. I suppose they wouldn't be if I was on as many bills as the blokes are. But I'm not, so they are. A fight day is *my* day. Like a birthday. So I'm very particular about it. I'm particular about what I eat and how I train.

I had a few banana sandwiches and tea for my breakfast and then I went to the Premises to work out. All I need is a spot of light training. I don't want to tire myself out or cop an injury, but I want to be toned and sharp. And I want my brain to run on the right road. Harsh says if you can imagine moves right, you're halfway to doing them right.

The first thing I saw when I got to the Premises was Crystal with her stall parked outside the door like yesterday. The second thing I saw was Crystal had a face like a funeral.

Straight away she says, "Queenie died."

"Thought she would," I said. But it was a pity all the same.

"Justin doesn't know," she said. "I couldn't tell him."

"But you could tell me," I said. "Great."

"She ain't your dog. And then there's her babies."

Why can't she use the right word for things? Calling pups "babies"! She just makes things worse than they are.

"Pups," I said. "They're puppies. Not babies."

"They ain't doing too good neither. The vet says we may lose both of them. The littlest one's in a bad way."

"What you telling me for?"

"The vet says it's 'cos Queenie was old, and when she mated, she mated with a big dog with a big head. Like a boxer or a . . . a Rot-something."

"Rottweiler." Ramses has a lot of Rottweiler in him, so I know.

"So it killed her," Crystal said. "Who'd be female? Eh, Eva? If you don't get a hammering one way you get it another."

First she muddles up puppies and babies, now she was muddling up bitches and women. She probably still had Dawn on her mind. She was spoiling my special day.

"I got to go," I said. I hate it when Crystal gets soppy.

"So I was thinking," she said.

"No," I said.

"I was thinking, could you . . ."

"*No!*"

"Oh all right," she said. "But would you be *nice* to Justin?"

"I'm always nice."

"Yeah," she said. "But extra nice. 'Cos, like, he's got bad news coming. When I get round to telling him."

I went indoors and started warming up. The place smelled like hair spray from the women, but I took no notice and soon all I could smell was me working.

I don't know why soppy eejits like Monkey Wrench think hard news will be softer if you have a nice day first. What was she going to do—take him to the zoo? Cook him chicken and chips? Let him watch his favorite programme on telly? And then say, "Oops, sorry, Justin, your dog died"?

Life's hard. You got to be in training for it. If you're expecting life to be hard you won't go all to pieces when your dog dies. Having a nice day at the zoo won't make it any better.

I was skipping up a storm when Justin himself walked in. I didn't stop, so he lolled against the doorframe watching.

He said, "You've got really neat feet, Eva. It's deceptive. You look so big and heavy, but you're incredibly fast on your feet."

"Believe," I said, stone chuffed. Maybe the lad wasn't such a ninny after all. Or maybe he wanted something.

"What you want?" I said.

"Nothing," he said. "Just watching. If you don't mind."

I didn't say anything, but with training, someone watching helps. With someone watching, you don't skimp. You want to look good, so you do good. When you're on your own all the time you can get a bit blue about the hard work and wonder why you bother. As soon as you start wondering why you bother, you stop bothering.

So I worked and he watched, and after a while Crystal popped in and said, "You sure you're well enough to stand around in the cold, Justin?"

Justin said, "I'm feeling a lot better, thanks, Crystal."

She said, "You're looking better."

"I'll put the kettle on," he said. "It must be freezing out in the market."

Crystal sort of blinked at him in surprise.

He said, "Are you ready for a cup of something hot, Eva?"

And I sort of blinked at him too. What with all the girls fussing round him like they was, it never occurred to me he could do anything for himself. That and his ninny voice made him seem like everyone's baby.

He went out to the kitchen.

Crystal said, "Have you told him?"

"What?"

"About Queenie."

"Fuck off."

"Coffee or tea?" Justin called.

"Tea," Crystal said. And I started skipping again so Crystal couldn't talk to me.

After a bit, Justin came back with a tray. A freakin' tray! He'd got three mugs, milk, sugar in a bowl, teaspoons and biscuits. The biscuits were all arranged in a pretty pattern.

"Poop in the soup," I said. "This is better than the caff."

"I like things nice," Crystal said sadly.

"Have a chocolate biscuit," Justin said. "I know you like chocolate."

I put my sweat shirt on to stop me cooling down too fast, and we sat on the mats drinking tea and noshing chocolate biscuits. Or rather, Crystal ate the chocolate ones. I ate the plain ones 'cos chocolate makes me spotty, and no one wants to be spotty in a leotard.

How did Justin know Crystal liked chocolate? I didn't know that. I knew Dawn did, but Crystal just ate what she could get. Like me. It was the way he said, "I know you like chocolate," that made me think maybe she'd changed. Then I looked at her sitting cross-legged on the mat gripping her mug with her grubby little paws. Same old monkey face. She never cleaned her fingernails, and they were bitten down to the quick. Crystal would never waste her dosh on nail scissors.

After the tea, I didn't have the time to start work again because Mandy came in with her blaster. She gave me a leery look, and said, "It ain't going to be me you pick on all the time today, is it?"

Justin said, "She's got to pick on someone. That's the only way."

And Mandy said, "Oh hello Justin. You're looking better."

"I *am* better, thanks very much."

"You joining in today?" Mandy said. And she did a girly little giggle which almost made my breakfast hit the back of my throat.

Crystal said, "Maybe he could do the warm-up, but he doesn't want to tire hisself out."

"Is it okay if I just start and see how I feel?" Justin said to me.

"Suit yerself," I said, "but I ain't running no playgroup."

"Don't you go picking on him," said Mandy.

"I'll pick on who I like," I said, "till one of you stands up and stops me."

And then the others raggle-taggled in looking like rejects from the Fun-Runners Ball, and Mandy put on a Michael Jackson tape.

It was a bit like the day before. I watched them flopping around, giggling, and trying to balance on one leg, and I didn't know whether to laugh or cry. I mean, what *do* women think their bodies are for? You couldn't blame anyone for thinking this bunch had been built just to stuff food in one end and men in the other.

I suppose, years ago, they must have been little kids who could run and jump and hop and skip. So what happened? Why can't they do it anymore? Why did they let themselves get into the sort of state where they can't do it anymore? It's a mystery to me.

Didn't they ever run and run and run for the sheer buzz of it? Didn't one of them feel, if only she could get her little legs pumping fast enough she'd be able to take off, like a plane on a runway, and fly away from all the crap kids have to go through? Or was that only me?

"Me bra hurts," said Kath with the bosoms.

"I'm sweating. Yeugh!" said Stef.

And I thought, you can't help having bosoms but, if you've got them, what's to stop you buying a bra that fits? And I thought, what's wrong with sweating? You can't help that either. Whoever it was who started the rumor about sweating being wrong for women was a fuckin' genius. He must've made a fortune, and I hope he died in pain and went to hell.

"We're finished," Mandy said, all pink and proud. "How did we do?"

"Well," I said. "At least you know what you're trying to do even if you can't do it." I thought they needed some encouragement.

"Sod you too," said Bella.

"Right," I said. "Lynn."

"Not me," Lynn said. "I'm off." And she made for the door.

"You," I said. And I caught her by the arm just above the elbow.

"Get off!" she said, pulling away. I just stood firm and hung on.

"Don't you want to learn no self-defence?" I said. "You want to learn something. You can't even get out this door without I allow you to."

"Gerroff!"

But I jerked her in, and as she fell towards me I let go of her arm, wheeled round the back of her and got an arm round her throat. I wasn't squeezing or nothing, but she made the classic mistake of trying to pull away. Then she grabbed my arm and tried to haul it down. When that didn't work she tried to reach back over her head. And it was only when she found she couldn't reach me that she tried her elbows.

"Yeah," I said. "Twist a little and then slam back."

She twisted a bit and then drove with her right elbow. I let her hit me a glancing blow. I could tell she enjoyed it because she started to yell.

"Yaaagh!" she went. And because she'd remembered to yell, I let go and stood back.

"I did it!" she said. "I did it."

"Yeah," I said. And I rubbed my ribs like I was hurt.

"It's your own fault," she said. "You shouldn't be so rough."

"But *you* can be as rough as you like," I said. "Now, Bella . . ."

"What?"

"Get behind Lynn and put an arm lock round her throat like I did."

"Why me?"

" 'Cos I say so. I want to show her something."

"Can I stand on a chair?" Bella said. "She's taller than me."

"Who isn't?" I said. "Use your imagination. Grab her by the waist or something."

So Bella went behind Lynn and put her arms round Lynn's waist.

"Ooh lovely," Lynn said. And all the others started laughing.

"Shut up," I said, because I had a plan and I didn't want them all gooey and giggling.

"You got four weapons," I said. "What are they?"

"Two arms," Lynn said, in a kiddy sort of voice, like she was at school and I was the teacher. "I got two arms, one leg and me voice."

"Right. Now, don't pull away. 'Specially if someone's got you by the throat. If you pull, you'll only throttle yourself and make his job easier. Step back into him so you know where he is. Go on, Lynn, step back."

So Lynn stepped back into Bella's arms.

"Right," I said. "Now. You know where his feet are, don't you? And you know where his legs are. Right?"

"Right," said Lynn.

"So you can stamp on his foot or hack him in the shins. Right?"

"Right," said Lynn.

"Do it," I said. "Slowly."

And Lynn trod back onto Bella's foot. As soon as she made contact she got off again.

"Now," I said. "Kick back like a horse. Gently."

And Lynn kicked back and found Bella's kneecap.

"Good," I said. "Let go, Bella."

Bella let go.

"Now," I said. "Let's make it more real. Stand with your back to the rest of us, Lynn, and shut your eyes. You're out on your own in that alley. Right?"

"Right," said Lynn.

"Someone's going to come up from behind and attack you. You don't know who. You don't know when. Right?"

"Right," said Lynn. And she stood with her back to me and the rest of the bunch.

I pointed at Bella and then held my hand up to make her wait while I counted slowly up to fifteen. I wanted to give Lynn time to get nervous. Then I gave Bella the nod.

Bella tiptoed up behind Lynn. She was so stupid I had to stop myself grinning. Bella crept up to Lynn and grabbed her round the waist.

Lynn gave a little squeak of surprise. Then she stomped back onto Bella's foot. And then she kicked back with her other foot and really whacked Bella's kneecap. I hadn't told her to do both things together, but I was ever so chuffed when she did. It worked a treat.

"Ow-ow-ow!" screamed Bella. "You bitch! You hurt me." And she let go of Lynn's waist and hopped around screeching. And the best thing was, I hadn't laid a finger on her. Lynn done it. I could hardly stop myself laughing out loud.

"Sorry, Bella," Lynn said. "Sorry, sorry. I didn't know it was you. I didn't mean to hurt. You startled me."

"Bitch!" hissed Bella.

I had to talk fast or she might cotton on. I said, "Brilliant, Lynn. Now listen all of you. When you go out at night, what do you wear on your feet?"

"Proper shoes," Stef said.

"With heels?"

"Yeah."

"You could really hurt someone if you did what Lynn just done only you did it with high heels. Think about it."

They thought about it. I could see them thinking. But I

could also see Bella beginning to give me the eye. Her foot and her knee still hurt and she wanted someone to blame

"You forgot to yell," I said to Lynn, real quick.

"Bella yelled louder than Lynn," said Kath with the bosoms. Which was true, but I didn't want to remind Bella.

I said. "Yelling should come second nature. So pair off, all of you. Bella, you'd better go with Stef—she's more your weight."

"I want to go with Justin," Stef said.

"*I* want to go with Justin," Mandy said.

"I said first," Stef said.

"Shut up!" I yelled. "Stef, go with Bella. Mandy, go with Lynn. Kath, go with Justin." Justin seemed like a gentlemanly lad so he might know what to do about the bosoms.

I waited while they grumbled and got into pairs. They couldn't do *nothing* without making a big salad out of it.

"Okay," I said. "This is what you do—Stef attacks Bella, Lynn attacks Mandy, Justin attacks Kath."

Justin said, "I'd find it really difficult to attack a lady."

"You won't mind attacking Kath then," Mandy said.

Kath said, "Do you mind?" And everyone started laughing again.

"Shut up!" I said. "All right, Kath, you attack Justin. It doesn't matter, see, 'cos all I want is for the attackers to grab, and the defenders to yell and push. No hitting or kicking, mind. Just yell and push."

So that's what they did for a while. And then the attackers switched and played defender. I got pretty fed up with them, but at least they were learning to make a lot of noise and fuss. Which was peculiar, really, 'cos they made a lot of noise and fuss about silly little things, but when it came to being jumped on they did sweet FA and got their teeth kicked out.

The next thing I wanted to do was to get them to help each other if one of them got attacked, but Crystal came in from the cold and said it was tea time.

She said, "You've got your accountant coming, Bella. Remember?"

"Okay," Bella said. "I'll have a bath."

"You got the bathroom working?" I said.

"Kath's Billy fixed it yesterday," Crystal said.

"Great," I said. "Me first." And I ran upstairs as fast as I could because Bella was the sort of rat who'd take all the hot water.

And it was great. It was a proper bath with scented soap and towels and shampoo and all the stuff. I didn't know where it all came from but it seemed everyone was falling over backwards to make Justin comfortable, and I didn't see why he and Bella should be the only ones to benefit. Specially since it was Bella's mob got me drummed out of my gym and I couldn't take a shower there no more.

When I came downstairs again I found everyone drinking tea and gassing on the mats. The room reeked of smoko. So I left without saying goodbye. I was sick of them anyway, and I had a fight coming. A proper fight, not a cat fight—which is what I'd get if I stuck around. Bella was shooting bullets through her eyeballs.

Chapter 13

I quite like Lewinsham Sports Centre. It's modern and fairly clean. But it isn't very dramatic. It ain't got the atmosphere of some of the older places. It's too well lit. And when you come out to fight you don't get that feeling of exploding out of the dark into the light. Which is what I like. I like to come walloping out with a great crash. The crowd is usually booing already—they start as soon as they hear "Satisfaction"—and I give 'em a moment or two to rev themselves up before I come out howling and revving 'em up even further. I like a nice angry crowd. I like 'em to hate the villain. Give me a good angry crowd and I'll work it up into a lovely rage.

They build the ring in the middle of the basketball court and they fill the rest of the space with seating. What with that and the observation decks, there's room for hundreds of people. But it ain't like them old theatres. Theatres are built for drama. Sports halls are built for sport. Wrestling's a sport, but it's a drama too, and all in all I like a dramatic setting. It's easier to make a crowd go nuclear in a dramatic setting.

But the nice thing about modern sports halls is you got proper changing rooms with pegs for your clothes, and showers and benches. You aren't poked away in a draughty broom cupboard with no lavvy and no mirror.

But it don't matter to me. If I'm going to be somebody I'm going to be somebody in places like Lewinsham. Anywhere. Everywhere. I don't care if it's got a lavvy or not, 'cos this is where the action is. This is where I can make my name.

Oh yeah, I was well up on my toes when I walked into the sports centre that night. I walked in and I saw Mr. Deeds, all official, with his clipboard in the foyer.

"Oy, Eva," he said, when he saw me. "I thought you wasn't coming."

"Whatcher mean?" I said. "I always come. When haven't I?"

"You weren't training," he said. "I didn't see you at the gym. I thought you dropped out."

"Me?" I said.

"Don't fucking yell," he said. "Harsh said you was injured. You said you had tooth trouble. I thought you dropped out. So I stood Gypsy Jo down."

"You *what?*"

"Don't fucking *shout*," he said. "I stood her down."

"You stood Gypsy Jo down?" I said. "You don't tell me. You don't ask me. It's my freakin' life. It's what I live for. And you stand Gypsy Jo down?"

"Shut up and listen . . ."

"*You* listen," I said. But I didn't know what to say. A big hole cracked open under my feet and I was falling down it. He was stood there with his clipboard, a bulgy blowfly sucking on a sick cow's turd, telling me he was chopping me off at the knees. I could squash him flat, I could grind him into . . .

"Eva!" he shouted.

"What?"

"Put me *down!*"

He straightened the lapels of his smelly black jacket. And took a couple of paces backwards. Drops of pure lard squeezed past the blackheads on his nose.

"You got a problem, Eva," he said. "You're a maniac. Know what? You're a maniac."

"Don't you tell me what I am," I said. "You've got no right. You stood Gypsy Jo down, and you've got no right. You've no right to fuck with my life like that. Don't you tell me what I am. I'll tell you what you are. And in case you don't understand I'll write it down for you. I'll write it with the toe of my boot on your bum."

"All right!" he yelled. "Get your hands off me! I'll sort it out. But don't you ever lay hands on me again. I'm an entrepreneur. Show some respect."

"Respect?"

"I said I'd sort it out," he said. "I'll get someone else."

"Who?"

"Never you mind who. What do you expect at short notice? Klondyke Kate?"

"When?" I said. "When you going to sort it out?"

"When I get a minute."

"When's that?" I said. He wasn't going to fob me off. He wasn't going to leave me dangling.

"Get out of here," he shouted. "You're nothing but trouble. You're a nutter and a hooligan. You're a bad influence. You upset the boys."

"When you going to sort it out?"

"*Now!*" he said. "Gerroff me. I'm going to sort it out now."

So I let go of his stinky old suit. And he waddled off to the office as fast as his fat legs would take him.

You got to be firm with dops like him.

I sat down. I was cold. My heart felt like it wanted to kick its way out of my chest. I was still falling down a hole. Mr. Deeds actually stood Gypsy Jo down. He scratched my fight. The bastard took it away from me. He stole it. It was mine. And he stole it.

Wrestling's my life. If I'm not the London Lassassin, who can I be? Who?

It's the key to my life—being the London Lassassin. I'm the villain. That's me. No one has the right to thieve it off me.

Kids ask me for my autograph. I write my name on their programmes. I write, "Eva Wylie," big and bold, right next to where it says "The London Lassassin" in the programme. Because that's me. Me.

Mr. Deeds has got the key to my whole life in his dirty fat hand. He scratched my fight, and when he scratched my fight it was like he said, "Eva Wylie, you can't be the London Lassassin no more."

He took the key and chucked it down the sewer and said, "It ain't yours. It's mine to do what I want." And he left me in a small dark place where I can't breathe. And if I scream and shout no one hears. And if I'm big and strong no one sees. What's the point in doing all that work to be big and strong if no one sees? What's the point shouting if no one hears? I might as well lay down and die.

Like I nearly died and my sister Simone nearly died when Ma locked us in a cupboard under the stairs. And we screamed and cried and wet ourselves. But she never heard us because she nearly died too, dead drunk on the sofa she set fire to.

No one heard us—we were too little to make ourselves heard. And we were too weak to break the door down. If the bloke next door hadn't been out of work, and if he hadn't been home to smell the smoke, and if he hadn't called the fire brigade Simone and me would have been dead. We'd have laid down and died because we had no other choice.

Well, I'm big and strong now and I can kick any bloody door down. And I ain't going to lay around whimpering when Mr. Deeds fucks with my life.

"Eva!" Harsh said.

"What?"

"Do not hit the door. You will break the glass and damage your knuckles."

"What?" I said, because he was talking nonsense. The sports

hall doors were made of safety glass with wire laminated inside. You can't break safety glass.

"Harsh?"

"Yes, Eva?" he said. "What is it?"

"Mr. Deeds scratched my fight. He can't do that, can he?"

"He can," Harsh said. "Mr. Deeds can do as he pleases. He's the promoter."

"But if he says turn up for a fight. And I turn up. He can't just turn round and tell me there's no fight."

"He *should* not do such a thing, Eva," Harsh said. "But he *can* do it. Unless you have a contract."

"Contract? I got nothing like that."

"Then, you see, Mr. Deeds is contracted to nothing where you are concerned."

"Oh."

"If you are not fighting, Eva," Harsh said, "why are you standing in the foyer hitting the door?"

"I wasn't," I said. "I got a fight. Mr. Deeds is bringing someone in. I made him."

"You made him?"

"Yeah, I sodding made him. He can't fuck with the London Lassassin like that."

"Eva," Harsh said, "this might not have been the cleverest thing you have ever done. This is a bad time to impose your will on others."

"Why?" I said. "I thought it was pretty clever. He thinks he can get away with anything."

"He is correct," Harsh said. "You have no contract. This is why you should think carefully before imposing your will on him. Force should only be employed with wisdom. I have told you this before." And he went away to the men's changing room.

"Bollocks," I said. Because this time, Harsh was wrong. Mr. Deeds wouldn't do nothing about my fight without I forced him to. No one does nothing unless you force them.

Take Ramses—he wasn't always the obedient dog he is today. When I first got him he was on his way to the knacker's yard because the dwerb that owned him couldn't control him. He weighed about eight stone and if he stood on his hindlegs he could bite your nose. Even so, he wasn't full-grown. He was barely more than a puppy and his owner couldn't control him. Can you believe it?

So I saved his life and trained him up. But it wasn't easy. You see, Ramses thought he was top dog. He thought he could do anything. He thought he only had to show his teeth and I'd turn to jelly like that dwerb had. He thought he could control me.

We had a couple of knock-down-drag-out fights, Ramses and me. I got five stitches in my hand to prove it. See, he'd never even come when I called. He just wouldn't. He ignored me. He reckoned I had no business calling him 'cos *he* was leader of the pack. Not me.

So I put him on a chain and when I called him I pulled on the chain so he had to come. He came all right when I pulled his chain—he came straight for my face. And let me tell you, even half-grown he had a full set of gnashers. I just got my hand up in time to fend him off or I'd of lost me chin and he'd've had my adam's apple for afters.

When I got back from the hospital I found an empty squeezy bottle and I filled it with salt water. Then I called Ramses again. And he ignored me. So I pulled his chain. And he came straight for my face. Again. Only this time I was ready for him. He came for my face with his teeth bared and his mouth open, so I squeezed jets of salt water in his mouth and down his throat and up his nose and in his eyes. 'Specially in his eyes. And his eyes really stung. He dropped like a rock and tried to rub the salt out of his eyes. And when he was down I knocked him off his feet and stood on him.

Yeah, I really stood on him. Want to know for why? I'll tell you why—I stood on him because that's what dogs do to other dogs. And that's what Ramses would've done to me. He'd've knocked me down and stood on me because that's what the leader of the pack does to any other dog who fucks him around. If you don't believe me, you go down the park one day and watch dogs. Really watch them. Pick a top dog— and remember, the top dog ain't always the biggest one—and watch him.

You think I'm cruel, don't you? Go on, admit it. You think dogs are pets and you got to be kind to them. Well you're wrong. Dogs are pack animals, and most dogs accept humans as the leader of the pack. But if you meet one who doesn't, and if that dog's a big fierce dog, like Ramses, you've only got a couple of choices. If you don't force him to accept you as leader of the pack you can only beat him or kill him. And where's the kindness in that?

Beating didn't work on Ramses. I know, because when I met him that dwerb had already beaten him rotten. He had welts as big as my finger all over him. Beating didn't make him submit, so the dwerb was going to kill him.

I ain't cruel. I didn't beat him or kill him. He's alive and well, and he's still waiting for me to show weakness. Because when I do he'll take over. He's itching to take over. Meanwhile, he's a good dog who does a good job. And that's a lot better than being a dead dog.

But he only does a good job because I forced him to.

And that's what makes Harsh wrong. If you don't force people to do the right thing they fuck you around and treat you like the lowest dog in the pack.

Chapter 14

I waited in the foyer. I waited and waited.

All the blokes turned up, one after another. They all stared and sneered, but none of them said a dicky-bird to me. They all knew, and they were all sneering. That barrow-load of dick-wits—they'd just love to see me wiped. They'd love if it I laid down and died. No more London Lassassin sharing the bill with them. No more Eva Wylie.

Well I'm not going to do what they want. I'm not going to give them the satisfaction.

It was dark outside. The audience was beginning to turn up at the front entrance—everyone pudgy in anoraks and scarves, rubbing their hands against the cold—waiting to get in—waiting for warmth and light. They were waiting for their burgers, crisps and hot dogs. They was ready to be entertained.

And I was waiting for Mr. Deeds. I was ready and waiting to entertain all those people. I'd warm their blood for them. I'd make them howl and yell and jump up and down in their seats. I was ready to do what I'm good at. But I had to wait for Mr. Deeds.

All those people were waiting to see me. My name was on the programme. They were expecting to see me. We'd all been promised by that wet snot-wipe, Mr. Deeds.

I went to look for him. But he wasn't around. No one had seen him. They said.

I went back to the foyer and waited some more. I could hear the loudspeakers from the main hall. They were beginning to make birthday announcements and play "Three Steps to Heaven." They were beginning without me.

I raced up the stairs to the office floor. All the doors were locked. Mr. Deeds wasn't there. I ran to one of the observation decks and looked over the balcony. The audience was thickening up—people taking their coats off and finding their seats. The MC was down by the ringside making announcements. But there was no Mr. Deeds.

My teeth ached. They pounded like a pulse in my mouth. I knew where Mr. Deeds was. He was hiding from me in the men's changing room. He thought I wouldn't go in there looking for him. He thought wrong.

I went downstairs again. I'd find him. I'd nail his balls to the wall. He had let me down. Things happen to people who let me down. Bad things.

I charged through the foyer and into the corridor which led to the men's changing room. The door slapped back against the wall and flattened the person behind it.

"Oy!" said this voice.

"Out me way," I said.

"Oh my God!" she said. "You're the London Lassassin, aren't you?"

"Who's asking?" I said. "Move! I got to find someone."

"Incredible," she said, "amazing! Eva Wylie."

So I stopped to take a look at her. She wasn't much to look at, but she was very solid. And I suppose spots do clear up some time.

She said, "I saw you fight in Warminster last year."

"Yeah? So?"

"You were mega."

"Yeah?"

"Mega mega."

Which was all very nice, but it didn't help me find Mr. Deeds.

"If you want an autograph," I said, "see me later."

"I can't believe it." She said 'oy caarn't' in that dozy haystack way.

"Gotter go," I said.

"I never would of thought it," she said, still blocking me out.

"What?"

"You," she said, "and me. Against each other. Here. In Lunn'n."

"What?"

"In Lunn'n. I only just came up last week. From Brissle. Mr. Deeds said it'd be ages before I were ready. Now look at me."

I looked at her. If she was saying what I thought she was saying it wasn't a conversation I wanted to have in a passage outside the gents' changing room. I wanted to have it somewhere I could throw a punch.

"Who are you?"

"Olga," she said. "Volga Olga. Olga from the Volga, Mr. Deeds says. D'you like it?"

"Love it," I said. "Follow me." And I went further down the passage to the women's changing room.

"It's Mary, actually," she said, trotting along behind. "Mary Spragg. But Mary doesn't sound very . . . you know."

I pushed the door open and turned on the light. The strip lighting flickered on the benches and tiled floor.

"Ooh, lovely," said Olga from the Volga. "They don't half give you lovely places to change in Lunn'n."

I dumped my kit on a bench. She stood there gawking at the white tiles like it was Buckingham Palace.

"Now see here," I said.

"Where I was before," said Volga Olga, "where Mr. Deeds

came to see me, we only had a screen to dress behind. And I swear the audience could see bits of us poking out. It was a village hall, see. And Mr. Deeds, he came to speak to me after. He said I had potential. He's a lovely man, Mr. Deeds. Don't you think he's a lovely man? He was ever so sweet to me. Like a father, really."

Like a syphilitic ape's father, I thought. I said, "Shut up a minute. He called you in to fight me?"

"He gave me a ticket from Brissle to Lunn'n. I never went to Lunn'n before. It's a bit big, like. And my mum never went neither. So I had to come on my own. But he's been lovely to me, Mr. Deeds. He found me lodging. And he's been teaching me, private. Polishing me up, like. He says I'm not ready yet, but then he calls me up tonight. There's a phone on the wall outside my room . . ."

"Shut up!" I said.

"You don't have to shout," said Olga from the Volga. "I know I do go on a bit."

"A bit?"

"But it's only 'cos I'm nervous. Meeting you for the first time an' all. You a star, and everything . . ."

There was a rap on the door, and Mr. Deeds poked his head in.

"You decent?" he said. "Ah. You met. Okay, Mary?"

"It's lovely, Mr. Deeds," Olga said. "Eva's been ever so sweet to me."

Mr. Deeds looked gob-whacked.

I said, "Now, see here . . ."

"Later, Eva," he said. "I'm putting you on after the interval."

"Crap in a trap, Mr. Deeds . . ."

"Gotter go," he said. "Look after her, Eva." And he went.

Look after her? I'd look after her all right. After I'd looked after him.

I flung the door open but the passage was empty. Mr. Deeds could sprint when he wanted to.

He'd left me with a baby wrestler, a great chunk of raw meat with a mouth like Mary Poppins on speed. It was stone out of order. I didn't know what she could do. I didn't know what she knew. She wasn't a professional like me. If she just blundered about in the ring like she did when she talked someone was going to get hurt. And it wasn't going to be me.

"It's going to be lovely," she said, "My first Lunn'n fight. With you. Ooh, I'm *that* excited." She had a big soppy grin on her big soppy mush, and all her spots were glowing pink on her chubby cheeks. If she was a dog I'd think she was going to lick my face. I hated her, but I ignored her and started to organize my kit.

"Do I change now?" she said.

"Suit yerself," I said.

"Don't look," she said.

Don't look? What the fuck was that supposed to mean? Look at what? Don't tell me the great goof was shy! You can't be shy *and* be a wrestler. If you're a wrestler you've got to go out and strut. You got to strut in front of an audience. Not wearing much. Whatever you look like. You can't be *shy*.

"Ooh look," she said, after a few minutes. "We're both wearing black."

I turned around. Shit-double-shit. She was wearing a black costume just like mine.

"What's your game?" I said. "You taking the piss, or what? I wear the black. *Me*."

"Nice," said Olga from the Volga. "We're both the same. Like twins."

"Take it off," I said. I could hardly speak I was so choked.

"Mr. Deeds gave it to me," she said. "Lovely, isn't it? Sophisticated. I think it makes me look slimmer, don't you?"

She looked like a pyramid. She had legs like brick posts, huge hips and no chest at all—a very low center of gravity. It wasn't a bad build for a wrestler. It'd take a tank to knock her down. But tank or no tank I was going to try.

"Are you deaf or only stupid?" I said. "You can't wear black. I wear black. I'm the villain. See?"

"Wait," she said. "You haven't seen the best bit."

She rummaged in her bag. When she stood upright and turned to face me again she was wearing a black mask.

"I don't bleeding believe it," I said.

"Good, isn't it?" said Volga Olga.

I couldn't think of anything bad enough to say. I tried, but I couldn't.

"Mr. Deeds says I got to wear it to look sinister and mysterious," Olga said. "I think it's great. It does make me look sinister and mysterious, doesn't it? And slim."

"Where are you going?" said Olga from the Volga.

Chapter 15

I threw my robe over my shoulders and slammed out the door. I marched over to the men's changing room. I didn't knock. I kicked the door open.

I said, "Where's Mr. Deeds?"

"Get out," shouted Mr. Julio, Flying Phil's dad. He had his jockstrap at knee height.

"Aha, oho," said Gruff Gordon. "Bandits."

Pete Carver said, "Let me guess—she's met Mary Mouse."

"Mary Super Mare," said Gruff, "the Russian ram-raider."

Gruff and Pete hadn't changed yet. They were smoking cigarettes and playing poker with the Mavericks.

"Where's Mr. Deeds?"

California Carl got up from a bench. He was wearing his gold lamé trunks. His body looked like oiled gold metal too.

He said, "Get out, cunt-face."

He came the full length of the room, saying, "This place is for men only. Not you. You don't belong. Get out."

He stood in front of me. "Fuck off," he said, and slammed the door in my face.

I'm not sure what happened next, but my toes and knuckles were hot and bruised when Harsh opened the door.

He said, "Come with me."

"Harsh . . ."

"Quiet," he said.

I followed him further down the passage to a games room at the end. A door from there led to the main hall and I could hear the music and the crowd through it.

"I'm going on in a minute," Harsh said, "so there isn't much time."

"Harsh, she's wearing my costume," I said. "She's wearing the black. Black's mine. I'm going to kill her. I swear to God, Harsh, I'm going to tear her into little pieces and ram them down Mr. Deeds' throat."

"Be quiet, Eva," Harsh said. "Stand still. What are you afraid of?"

"Afraid? I ain't afraid of nothing. It's her should be afraid—that Olga. She's taken what's mine."

"Her name is Mary," Harsh said.

"What the fuck's it matter what her poxy name is?"

"Stand still," Harsh said, "and use her proper name. She will not seem so threatening."

"She ain't threatening me. I'm threatening her. I'm going to . . ."

"Eva."

"What?" I said. "You don't understand. She's even got a mask. She don't look human in a mask, Harsh. Mr. Deeds said he wanted *me* to wear a mask."

"And do you wish to wear a mask?"

"No I fucking don't."

"Why?"

"You can't see proper. You can't breathe."

"Then why are you so angry with Mary for wearing one? Why are you not sorry for her?"

"Sorry?" I said. "Sorry for *her?* Harsh, she's dressed like a villain. There's only one sodding villain on the women's circuit. *Me!*"

"There are no villains," Harsh said. "There are only professional wrestlers. I repeat, what are you afraid of?"

"I *ain't* afraid!"

Harsh said, "Are you afraid that Mr. Deeds has brought Mary all the way from the country to replace you? Do you know how old she is?"

"Old?"

"Ask her," Harsh said. "Your fear and anger are misplaced. And ask yourself why she has been forced to cover her face."

"She's got spots."

Harsh sighed. "Then ask yourself why you refused to wear a mask. And why she consented. And then see if she is some-one to fear."

He was stirring my brains into pudding. He wasn't talking about what I was talking about.

I said, "I *ain't* afraid of her. I could beat her ten times round any ring in the world, blindfold, with both hands tied behind me back, without breaking wind."

Harsh sighed again. "Yes. Well. Excellent. So if there is no need for fear, there is no need for anger either. A rich man should not heed where fall his crumbs."

"Eh?"

"Oh, Eva," Harsh said. "You are exhausting yourself. Don't waste your energy on what does not matter."

He was making sense now. Because I *was* feeling tired. I couldn't think why—I hadn't done anything but a little light training earlier—but I was feeling whacked. And suddenly, I was right chuffed because Harsh had noticed. Not many people notice if another person's feeling tired. But Harsh noticed me.

I said, "Yeah, all right." And I cleared my throat which was feeling a bit tight. Maybe I was coming down with flu or something—feeling tired and tight throat are the first signs. I'd been spending a lot of time with Bella and the other slags so who knows what I'd caught off them. Harsh is always right even when he's talking garbage and doesn't understand splotch.

I went back to the ladies' changing room. Olga-Volga-Mary was sitting on a bench with a raincoat round her shoulders. She had a Snoopy-dog on her lap, but when she saw me she stuffed it in her bag and blushed.

"It's for luck," she said. "My mum gave it me when I left. She came to the station with me and she had it all wrapped up for me to open on the train. A surprise, like. She always knows what to do to make me feel better, my mum."

Gawd gimme strength to keep me hands to meself! A baby wrestler who played with toys!

Harsh told me to, so I had to ask. I said, "How old are you?"

If she'd blushed any more her spots would've burst.

"Eighteen," she said.

"Oh yeah?"

"Well, nearly eighteen."

"Eighteen months or eighteen weeks?"

"Mr. Deeds said to say eighteen," said Olga from the Volga. "I'm big enough to be eighteen. Aren't I?"

She was big enough, all right. She was big as a medium-sized horse. But she wasn't as tall as me, and she didn't have any muscle definition. She was just an unformed slab.

"You don't believe me, do you?" said Olga. "Can't hide anything from you. I'm fifteen, well, almost sixteen. But I can trust you, can't I? You wouldn't tell anyone, would you?"

Harsh is a genius. He knew I'd feel better once I knew she really was a baby. He knew I'd be okay if I had something on her. Because, now, if she gave me any trouble, I could give her trouble back. Real trouble, from social workers and dead-heads like that—for working underage and not going to school. That's what people kept trying to do to me when I was fifteen. It didn't work, but it made my life a misery. And that's what I'd do to Olga if she got in my way. Don't think I wouldn't. It's a dog-eat-dog world—the wrestling world—

and I ain't going to lie down and let some overgrown puppy walk all over me.

But if Olga gave me no grief I'd show her a thing or two. Call me a soft-hearted fool if you like. I could help her a bit. I could help her enough to make me look good. Because it doesn't make me look good if I mash an opponent too easily. If she wants to look good on her own account she'll have to help herself. Like I had to. I'm soft-hearted, but I ain't daft.

"Right," I said. "Let's find out what you know, and what we got to do to make a fight of it tonight."

Olga said, "Mum told me to watch out for myself in Lunn'n. She said everyone was out for themselves. But it isn't like that at all. You're being like a sister to me."

I nearly told her—I'm a sister to my sister, wherever she is, but I ain't no sister to a pumpkin I only just met. She had a lot to learn, that Olga, but, like Harsh said, I wasn't going to waste my energy on stuff that wasn't wrestling.

I took her along to the games room where we could spread ourselves out a bit.

Harsh was gone. He was in the ring. Mr. Deeds often puts him out early, before the crowd gets too hysterical to appreciate him. The crowd likes to think it can appreciate skill. But that's not what it's there for. It's there for blood and thunder, thud and blunder. You don't get thud and blunder from Harsh. You get skill. 'Cos Harsh is a shooter. He wouldn't stoop to dramatics.

I opened the door a crack and peeped out at him. Just watching him work makes me peaceful. He's quick, supple and strong—everything I wish myself. And he flows. He flows from throw to fall to escape to hold to pin like water flowing over rocks.

"See that, my girl," I said to Olga, "that's poetry in motion, that is. Look and learn."

But I didn't let her look too long 'cos I didn't want her to learn too much. A pumpkin like her can't take it all in, see. She'd just get confused.

She was big, but she was soft. Kids are. Their muscles haven't hardened. I'm not saying she wasn't strong—she was. Or she would be if she did the work. But when I grappled with her it was like grappling with a sponge. I suppose I must've felt like that a couple of years ago when I was raw. And it made me think. I spent all my fighting life up against women older than me. This was the first time I copped someone younger.

Of course she was soft in the head as well as soft in the body. But at least she wanted to learn. She was keen. Keen but clumsy. And that made me think too. About Bella, Stef and the others. And how they didn't want to learn to use themselves except for rumpty-tumpty.

If I said to them, "Do so-and-so," they'd moan. And when I said, "No, that's wrong, do it again," they'd go, "Do I have to? I'm sweating."

Olga didn't mind doing stuff over and over again. Which was just as well, seeing how wrong she got it first off. She liked the work. She thought it was fun. I know, 'cos she kept saying so. She said it so often I had a good mind to wire her mouth shut.

Even so, it was better to be with a woman who wanted to be an athlete than to be with the frilly kind. The frilly kind try to make you feel like a freak for having muscles, and they bad-mouth you for being sweaty—as if being sweaty's the same as being dirty. Which it isn't.

I was just thinking maybe I'd dump the self-defence lessons and start a wrestling school instead when it was time for me and Olga to go on.

Chapter 16

Going on first after the interval is a bad slot.

You've lost half the audience. They're still trickling back from the bar. They're more interested in their bags of sweets, their beer and their burgers than they are in you. They're wondering if their bladders will hold out for the whole of the second half. They're making last minute trips to the bog. They're buying the kids a last packet of crisps. They don't have their minds on the job.

Mr. Deeds knows it's a bad slot. That's why he gave it to me. He knew Olga wasn't ready and he thinks I don't matter. But I do matter. And if I've got an aim in life, it's to show Mr. Deeds and all the piss-piddle-poohs like him how much I matter.

I sent Olga out first. She toddled down the aisle and climbed into the ring. And nobody hardly noticed. There she was in her black mask, looking like a lady executioner, and no one noticed.

She stood in her corner like a good little girl and waited. And waited.

Then, out of the speakers, came "Satisfaction." I didn't move a muscle.

I was peeking through the door, so I could see people beginning to turn in their seats to see where I was. I stayed shtum. I was going to show Mr. Deeds. If he thought he could mail-order some little pumpkin-bumpkin in from the country to replace me he had another think coming. He'd never get a better villain than me. Never.

My music died away, and still Olga waited. I couldn't see her face because of that stupid mask, but I bet she was getting nervous.

The MC was standing in the middle of the ring with the ref. They were waiting too. Let them fucking wait. Nobody takes the London Lassassin for granted.

The MC held the microphone to his lips and said, "We're expecting the London Lassassin any moment now." And he waited. Everyone waited.

Then the MC said, "We've got a new attraction here for you tonight. I want to introduce her to you. Since the Iron Curtain came down, you may have wondered what happened to all those bad people from the KGB. All those bad men and women who walked in the shadows. The Soviet Union's secret army. Well one of them's come thousands of miles to be here tonight . . ."

"Where's Bucket Nut?" some bim in the audience yelled.

"Maybe she's afraid to meet her new opponent," said the MC quickly. He's a fast thinker, the MC. That's what he's paid for. "Maybe she's heard about Olga from the Volga. Ladies and gentlemen—she's still a paid-up member of the Russian Secret Service . . ."

"Where's Bucket Nut?"

"So secret, in fact, that her identity still has to be protected . . ."

"Bucket Nut."

"Ladies and gentlemen, let me introduce you to *Olga* from the *Volga.*"

There was some half-hearted clapping, some half-arsed booing.

"Where's Bucket Nut?" someone yelled.

"Play her music again," someone else suggested.

"Play 'Roll Out the Barrel,'" a boozy bum shouted. "*That'll* make her come out."

"Well," the MC said, "I never thought the London Lassassin was a coward."

The boos were growing louder.

And louder.

The hair on my arms was up. My spine was tingling.

I started to count, "One, two, three . . ."

Olga stirred nervously.

More people joined in the booing.

I counted to twenty-three, and then I couldn't wait no longer.

I hauled the door open and came walloping out.

"Boooo!" went the crowd.

"What's your trouble?" I yelled at the first howling face I saw. "Got the gut ache?"

I marched down the aisle.

"Boooo!"

"Sheep!" I yelled. "Yer all sheep and cows."

"Boooo!"

"Ba-a-a," I screamed back. I stuck my face right up to a woman in a blue cardy. "Mooo!" I yelled, right into her ear. She took a whack at me with her handbag. Another lady lashed out with her umbrella. I snatched it off her, and poked at a feller on the other side of the aisle.

"Boooo!" went the crowd.

"Shut yer silly face," I went. "Moooo," I shouted at the fella I'd poked. "A goat could bleat louder'n you."

He got up. I dropped the umbrella. I danced backwards away from him going, "Ba-a-a," taunting him till he chased me to the ring.

One of the bouncers picked him off and led him back to his seat.

"Mummy's boy!" I shouted at him. "Yeller!" And he tried to come back at me.

The front rows were standing up, screeching and throwing programmes and bits of burger.

I had them. They was mine.

I pulled myself up on the platform and vaulted the ropes.

"*Boooo!*" went the crowd.

"I thought you wasn't coming," said the ref. "Jesus! Talk about cutting it fine!"

Olga came over. "What happened?" she said.

I gave her a shove. "Back off," I said. "We ain't pissing about up here."

I gave the ref a good shove too, and he staggered back. I marched round the ring giving the crowd the finger. The ref trotted after me.

"You behave yourself," he said, loud enough for the front rows to hear. "I want a fair fight . . ."

The MC started the ritual—"In the red corner . . . in the blue corner . . ."

But I didn't go to my corner. The ring was mine and I used it for a parade ground. I strutted. I flexed my muscles. I backed Olga on the ropes. And the fight hadn't even started.

"BOOOOO!" went the crowd. It was music to my ears. They were yowling fit to burst. I was giving them what they came for. That'd teach Mr. Deeds to fart around with my life. He'd have to think twice before dropping me.

The bell went, and while it was still clanging, I whipped into Olga's corner, grabbed her by the arm, swung her round and ran her, head first, into the ropes on the other side of the ring. As she hit the ropes, I kicked her in the bum.

She grabbed the ropes for balance. I snatched one of her hands, twisted it behind her back and started biting her fingers.

I don't know what it is about biting—but if you want the crowd to go totally ape-shit, take a nibble on your opponent.

It works every time. Oh yeah! Young pumpkin-bumpkin would have to get up very early in the morning to beat me in the villainy race.

The ref came over, outraged. He tried to pull me off. I gnashed my gnashers at him too. The crowd went critical. The MC got on the microphone and gave me a public warning. He was almost drowned out by the boos.

Things were going very well indeed.

The ref hauled me back. I hipped him out of the way and went on a parade of the ring. I punched the air and went, "Easy, easy, eee-zee!"

"Dirty, dirty, dir-tee!" went the crowd back.

I leaned over the ropes and went, "Shut yer mucky mouths!"

A little old lady leapt out of her seat and tried to clobber my feet with a beer bottle. I jumped back, pretending to be scared, and the front rows collapsed in laughter.

All this gave Olga time to catch her breath. She came off the ropes and aimed a forearm smash. I ducked under it, and she grabbed my head and hair. She was too nervous to do it right so she gave my hair a rotten yank. She was new to the game so I let it go. This time.

She scissored my head and neck between the crook of her elbow and her hip. She was over-excited and squeezed too hard. My ear got bent the wrong way. Otherwise it was a passable side-headlock.

"Get her!" yelled the crowd. "Hurt her!"

I grabbed Olga's arm to loosen her grip.

"Twist her ugly mug off!" screamed a bloke in the front.

"Ow-ow-ow!" I went at the top of my voice. The front rows just love to hear a villain beg for mercy.

Olga hung on like grim death. I dragged on her arm. We swayed, twisted, tottered. I pulled. She squeezed. Slowly I pulled her down to the canvas. We both knelt. She held the headlock tight. I got both hands down on the floor, bunched my legs under me and kicked up in the air.

I shot up in a handstand. I straightened my arms and, thank Christ, Olga remembered to release my head.

The handstand escape is a right classy move and, if I say so meself, I done it perfect. But it silenced the crowd.

Then, from somewhere, I heard a lone voice shouting, "Come on, Bucket Nut, come *on!*"

I was all amazed. Something was wrong. No one cheered *me* on. I squinted into the lights, trying to see. I thought it sounded like . . .

And that's when Olga decided to take a dive at me knees. She launched herself and hit me on the backs of my legs. 'Course I tipped over backwards and came down on my arse. The only trouble was, Olga was still there. She hadn't rolled on through or dodged. So there was a real clash of arses—mine on top.

I rolled off backwards and left her flat on her face.

Now, take a tip from the expert—if you find yourself up on your toes while your opponent's flat on her face, don't wait for no second invitation. Jump her.

"'Orrible skaggy cow!" some bloke shrieked.

I flung myself across Olga's back and snatched her arm.

"Mmf!" went Olga from the Volga. "M-m-mmf."

"What?" I said.

"Mmf-mmf-umf!"

"Eh?" I was twisting her arm up her back and taking a nip at her elbow.

"Boooo!" went the crowd.

"Oy," said the ref, "that stupid fucking mask's slipped. She's choking on it."

"What?"

"Gerroff, Eva! She's suffocating!"

I leapt up and started to put the boot in. That's another thing that makes the crowd go berserkers—kicking when your oppo's down. Try it sometime and see if I'm not right.

The ref jumped in to give me a ticking off, so Olga took the chance to sit up and straighten her mask. She didn't hurry.

I danced round the ref to get at her again but he kept stepping in between. He wanted to give her more time. But she was so slow the crowd went quiet again.

The only action for them to see was me and the ref so I turned on him instead. I gave him three quick shoves back to the ropes.

"Okay?" I said.

"Careful," he said.

And I chucked him out of the ring.

He's an old fighter himself, so he landed well. But he made a lovely stew of it, hobbling, staggering onto the front row.

Quick as a flash, the MC was on his mike again giving me my second public warning.

And in the hush which followed that, I heard the voice again. "Way to *go*, Eva," it went, "*sock* 'im one for me."

I knew who it was now. It was Kath with the bosoms. What the freakin' hell was she doing at Lewinsham? I glared out through the lights, and, stone me, but the whole sodding bunch of them was there.

Loads of people had stood up to see what happened to the ref, and there, in the middle, standing on their seats, waving their arms in the air were Crystal, Bella, Mandy, Stef, Kath and Lynn.

I could have *died*.

The only people supporting me in the whole sodding sports hall was a gaggle of prossies.

"Don't just stand there," the ref said. "Get on with it." He climbed back into the ring.

I turned. Olga, with her mask straight, came galloping across the canvas. I gave her my arm and she swung me over the ring into the ropes. I twanged off and back to her. She hit me with a body-check. I bounced off her and fell back on the canvas. She should've caught me with a head throw, but she forgot, so I had to fall down on me own.

She remembered the next bit though. She came down with a knee-drop to my throat.

"Aaaagh!" I screamed.

And she flung herself on me in a cross-press.

"Yeah, yeah, yeah," yelled the crowd. "Kill her, *do* it to her! Smash her skull!"

It was like having a mattress drop on you. I could've dealt with a mattress, but this mattress had elbows, and she wasn't clever enough to get them out of the way before she landed. And she landed on my chest.

"Fucking ow-ow-ow-ow!" I yelled, for real. Well, really! I don't know what you'd say with ten tons of teenage meat on top of you with its elbows grinding into your tits.

So instead of doing the usual bridge and escape I hauled my arm off the canvas and whacked her in the side of the head.

"Nnnf!" she went. But she didn't get off me tits. Grind, grind, grind.

"Bury her!" shrieked the crowd. "Break her legs!"

I hit her again. I got her in a bear hug. I pushed, pulled, squirmed and then rolled her over. When I was on top I banged her head on the canvas, jumped up and did a knee-drop on *her* tits.

Usually when you do this you pull out just when you're landing. It's the other knee on the canvas which comes down—thud. Ladies' parts are sacred. You protect your own and you try not to damage your oppo's. If you didn't, it'd be out and out warfare. It's the same with the blokes. If they really landed any of those kicks to the goolies there'd be real murder and real blood on the canvas.

But accidents do happen. 'Specially when you're fighting a clumsy great pumpkin. It was her own fault—grinding on my painful parts like that. She got me so narked that when I knee-dropped on her I didn't quite pull out in time.

I'm not a sadist. I didn't do the full business on her. But I didn't let her off either. I gave her a bit of a clip where it hurt—where she'd hurt me. She needed a lesson. She needed learning not to be so clumsy.

She doubled up, rolled in a ball, howling, and the ref dragged me off.

And that's when I got me third public warning and disqualification. Which was a pity really. It was supposed to end with a pile-driver. I like pile-drivers. They're nice. Spectacular.

But we couldn't carry on with her rolled in a ball going, "Wmf-wmf-woomf," and rubbing her tits the way she was. I could've been rubbing mine, but I had more pride.

A woman in the audience started shrieking, "Lesbian! You should be ashamed to call yourself a woman!"

And a bloke yelled, "If your face looked as good as my wife's bum-hole I wouldn't feel so sick."

I yelled, "A bin-bag's got more brains than you!"

"Mouth like a cat flap!" someone else shouted.

"Mouth like a garbage truck!" I said.

"Barn door!"

"Grand Canyon!"

Ooh, they was really wetting themselves out there.

"Good show," said the ref. "Now get your arse out of here. You're holding up the programme."

So I climbed out the ring and dodged handbags, walking sticks and flying food all the way back to the games room door.

Pumpkin came tottering along behind, sweating and whimpering. I wasn't feeling at all tired now, but I had mustard in my hair where a hot dog hit me.

There were two blokes in the games room waiting to come on. One was Bob "Hacker" Smith who I don't know well because he doesn't train at Sam's Gym. The other was California Carl.

Bob said, "Some wind-up! What were you doing out there—swinging from the ceiling?"

Bob's a bit of a villain himself so he wasn't being rude.

But California said, "Sure, that's what big ugly apes do. They swing from the ceiling, pick their arses and screw each other in public."

"And you'd shag sheep—if they'd let you," I said, trying to push past. I didn't want to talk to him. I was feeling good, and his eyes were on the boil again.

Volga Olga came in behind me and stood there looking like lost luggage.

California said, "Who's that with her head in a bag? You should take a tip from her, Eva—it's the only way you'd ever get a man."

"What dick-drip says I want one?"

"All you slits want one," he said. He had acid oozing out of every pore, and his eyes were on fire.

"Nniff?" said Volga Olga.

Bob said, "Ease down, Carl."

I said, "You got a mouth like an open drain, you got as much talent as a coat hanger and I see better manners than yours scrawled on the lavvy wall." And I bulled him out of the way and went to the changing room with Olga tagging along behind.

I like getting the last word. I like winning an argument. I bounced on my toes, feeling good.

Olga tore the black mask off. Underneath, her face was sopping, and if she'd been any redder she'd've stopped traffic. More fool her for wearing the sodding thing.

She'd forgotten about the bumps on her lumps or the lumps on her bumps. She said, "Who was that man in the gold lamé?"

"California Carl," I said.

"What's the matter with him?"

"Hormones."

"Eh?"

"Steroids," I told her. "It's enough to make any whore moan."

"Eh?"

I couldn't be bothered to explain. I wanted a shower. But she said, "He's serious. Isn't he? The way he looked at you like, y'know, like he could've killed you. Like he's really truly dangerous."

I didn't want to talk about him. I kept remembering the Eva mouse.

"You keep clear of him, girl," I said.

"But he's gorgeous," said Pumpkin, and sighed. The girl was a giant eejit. She was much too young to be taken out of her vegetable patch. She needed advice from someone older and wiser.

So I said, "Take a cold shower, fool. California's a psycho—don't even think about him."

I stripped down and went to the shower. My own lumps and bumps needed hot water. The elbow was swelling up again but I was quite chuffed with tonight's show. It'd been very short, but I'd shown what I could do against the odds. That pillock, Mr. Deeds, handed me a know-nothing baby whale to fight against, but even so, I gave the crowd something to shout about. It could've been boring, but it wasn't. Okay, so I had to get myself disqualified so that it didn't look like a one-sided mess. But I'm prepared to make sacrifices for my art.

Olga must've got into the next stall because I heard water. And after a bit, through the splashing, this pitiful little voice went, "I was awful, wasn't I, Eva?"

Which was a good sign. At least she didn't think she was all right.

"Hey, Eva?"

"What?"

"I said I was awful."

"I heard you."

"You mean you thought I was awful too?"

I was feeling generous, so I said, "Everyone got to start somewhere."

When I got out of the shower Olga was already nearly dressed. She said, "I don't know if I could take it."

"What?"

"All that, y'know, what those people say to you. They're so, like, angry. And rude. I don't know if I could bear it."

She didn't know *nothing*.

I said, "It's being a villain. It's how you know you done good."

She couldn't even think about being a villain if she didn't understand that.

"But, out there, the people *hate* you."

"What are they supposed to do?" I said. "Pat me on the head? It's what a villain's *for*. To be hated."

"But I don't think I want to be hated," said Olga from the Volga, KGB agent. "I don't like people not liking me. It really upsets me."

Maybe God actually exists! Maybe He, She, or It was rewarding me for doing a good show.

I said, "Then don't wear black, don't wear a mask. That's what villains wear. If you want to be a blue-eyes, wear pretty colours and lipstick."

"But Mr. Deeds . . ."

"You tell Mr. Deeds a good villain's born, not made. You can't be a villain 'cos someone tells you. You got to want it."

That fight with Olga had been better than cash in my pocket. That fight showed Olga she couldn't have what's on my plate. She couldn't have what I wanted. She didn't want what I wanted.

I could've *told* her, but she wouldn't've believed me. So I had to show her. I express meself best out there in the ring.

And out there in the ring I showed her she couldn't have what was mine. She wasn't up to it.

I won by being disqualified.

Maybe, when Mr. Deeds saw Olga in her veggie patch he said to himself, "She's big. She ain't pretty. I'll train her up and she'll do as a villain."

Maybe he thought, "I'll use her as a stick to beat Eva with."

Wrong! Wrong, wrong, wrong. I showed him how wrong he was. And I showed Olga how wrong he was.

I won.

I was going to tell her the difference between villains and blue-eyes but just then we heard a great kerfuffle in the corridor. It sounded really interesting, so I opened the door.

The corridor was full of St. John Ambulance men faffing around, telling each other what to do. They were carrying a stretcher but I couldn't see who was on it. I didn't know if someone was really hurt, or if someone had pulled a gag. I thought what a perfect night it would be if California Carl slipped on an ice cream cone and broke his neck.

But it wasn't California on the stretcher. It was Bob "Hacker" Smith.

When the corridor cleared Flying Phil came over. He said, "Shit, Eva, poor old Bob. He'll be on the dole for a few months."

"What happened?"

"California Carl," Phil said. "He went crazy. I don't know what actually happened—maybe Bob said something—but Carl lost his rag. Bob's got a torn groin and a broken leg. He'll be out for ages."

Chapter 17

When everything was all over I went out into the night. There was a bunch of fans waiting by the door, and some of them had come to see *me*. Crystal and the gang were there too—but I didn't mind anymore. I was glad they were there, 'cos they had to wait, see. They had to wait and watch me sign programmes and pictures.

Nobody bothered to ask Olga for her autograph. But they asked for mine. And bloody Bella saw them asking. That way she knew how important I was. So next time she thinks of some sarky thing to say, maybe she'll think twice. Because now she knows I'm someone who signs autographs, and I'm not to be pissed around with.

A little kid tugged my sleeve. She didn't say nothing—she just gave me her pen and programme. She was a wiry little thing with wanty blue eyes. I almost took her for a boy, but the bloke with her said, "Get a move on, Peggy."

I signed her programme with a flourish—making sure Crystal and Bella could see. The little kid didn't go away. She stood there wanting more. But she never said nothing.

"Come *on*," the bloke said. But she never, and I got on with a couple of other fans.

"Do what you're *told!*" the bloke said and made a grab for her. But she dodged round the other side of me, and there she stayed till I was ready to go. She didn't say nothing, she didn't ask for nothing but she definitely wanted more. I know that look. "More," it says, "there isn't *enough!*"

Well, there isn't, is there? 'Specially when you're a kid. You got to get big and strong and shout very loud if you're going to get more. No one just gives it to you.

I snatched her programme back and I scribbled, "Stay bad," under where I'd wrote my name. Then the bloke grabbed her and dragged her away. I could see him giving her a right verbal. And I could see her not listening.

"What did you write?" Olga said. She'd been hanging around breathing down my neck although she was in my way and ought to be gone home.

"That's private," I said. Then I said, "I told her to be good." And that was my secret laugh.

Then Crystal said, "Kath's Billy brought everyone in his van. Want a ride back?"

So we all piled in his old Ford Transit and left Olga waiting for Mr. Deeds outside the sports centre. Gruff Gordon and Pete Carver watched us go. They were still poncing around for the fans. They're a terrible pair of diddleoes but the fans don't know that, and they're a lot more popular than they deserve.

"You were monster," Kath with the bosoms said to me. "When you came in a little kid near me wet hisself. I mean really wet."

"Yeah," I said. Maybe Kath wasn't as daft as she looked.

"I'd forgotten what it was like," Stef said. "I ain't been to the wrestling for years."

"It's a good night out," said Kath, nodding. "Takes you out of yourself."

"That California Carl's a gorgeous animal," Mandy said. "A real animal. The way he threw that Hacker Smith out of the ring! It made my hair stand on end."

"What happened?" I said.

"Didn't you see?" Mandy said. "Well, there was a lot of

needle. You could tell they hated each other. Old Hacker was really winding Carl up."

Which is what Hacker's paid for.

Mandy said, "And then the time came when Carl couldn't take no more. He'd been a real gent up till then—y'know, taking the abuse and the cheating. So he picks Hacker up and held him way above his head."

"We was all cheering and shouting," Stef said.

"And then he threw him right over the ropes," Mandy said. "And he sort of caught one of Hacker's ankles as he was flying out the ring."

"So he flew out like a starfish," Stef said. "It was ever so dramatic. It looked like his leg was getting tore off. I swear I could hear something tearing—even where we was sat."

"Bollocks," said Bella. "It's all a fix. They learn all that in wrestling school. Don't they Eva?"

"No they bloody don't," I said.

"You can't kid me," Bella said. "That Hacker's at the pub right now sinking pints and swapping dirty jokes with California Carl."

"No he ain't," I said. "They took him down the hospital in a frigging ambulance."

"There!" said Mandy to Bella. "I *told* you."

"You're so naive," Bella said to Mandy. "He's no more hurt than I am."

"He *was*," Mandy said. "Wasn't he, Eva? I saw with my own two eyes."

"He's got a broken leg and a torn groin," I said. "He'll be out of the game for months if not forever."

"*Told* you," Mandy said.

"You're plain daft."

"Not!"

"Shut up," said Crystal.

I said nothing. The trouble with outsiders is they can't tell fact from fancy. I wasn't going to put them straight, 'cos it's an unwritten rule with insiders that you're not to. Let them believe what they like, so long as they believe. There's lots of fact, and there's lots of fancy in wrestling, and I'm not saying more than that. If you want to know which is which, go and see for yourself. Don't expect me to do your seeing for you.

"Anyway," Mandy said, "that Hacker got what was coming to him. California Carl's a real hunk."

And then she and Stef started talking about what a hunk he was, about all the things he probably never showed off even at his Boy Beautiful contests. Which surprised me—I'd of thought they'd be clagged up with men's bodies, seeing as it's men's bodies they do for a living.

Kath's Billy stopped at the Full Moon at the top of Mandala Street and everyone got out. I could've done with a beer but I was choked off with them all by then—there's only so much you can take about California Carl's mustard bum. Besides, I was more hungry than thirsty, so I trekked off to the nearest burger bar.

But Crystal caught me up. She said, "I didn't want to say in front of the others, but Justin's got some food in for you."

"For me?" I said, and I stopped in surprise. "What for?"

"Well, see, he wanted to," Crystal said. She blinked her little monkey eyes like it was the most normal thing in the world. "Y'know, for letting him join in the self-defence. He's strapped for cash—what with being sick and the vet's bill an' all. He thought you could do with something hot after your fight."

"He did?"

"'Course, he wanted to come to your fight but he still ain't got all his strength back."

"Oh," I said. I was stone mystified and I couldn't think what else to say. No one ever cooked my dinner for me. Ma sometimes brought in takeaways, but she never cooked. I was never at her place much anyway, and you don't count the food you get in homes and secure units. They may be homes, but you don't get home cooking there.

We walked down Mandala Street to the Premises. Crystal didn't say much, and I kept looking at her out the corner of my eye 'cos I thought she must be up to something. But when she let us in I could smell onions frying, and my mouth started watering so I couldn't be bothered to find out.

Justin popped out of the kitchen and said, "Go on up and make yourselves comfortable. I won't be a tick. There's beer upstairs."

So we went up to his room. I had to stop in the doorway. I couldn't believe my eyes. The last time I was up there, when I went to look at Queenie, there was a mattress on the floor and that was all. Now it was all pretty colours and lamps with lampshades on, and little rugs, and chairs with material thrown over them. And there were dark red curtains and pictures hiding the stains on the walls. He'd made a proper nest of it.

Crystal wasn't surprised so I guessed she'd kitted him out with all her spare bric-a-brac. But it didn't look like her room. Her room looks like a stockroom for her stall. This looked like home, like Justin lived there permanent.

Crystal poured beer into mugs. We didn't drink it out of the cans. And there was a plate of little cheesy things. You needed about five of them to make a mouthful, but they tasted nice.

And another thing—the place smelled sweet. The rest of the Premises ponged of mouldy damp. Justin's room smelled lavendery and cedary.

"Don't just stand there," Crystal said. "Park your arse."

So I sat in one of the chairs. What I couldn't get out of my brain-box was the picture of when me and The Enemy bust in on Justin the first time we saw him. Him squatting on a pile of rubbish downstairs, with his little gas camping stove and his sleeping bag. And Queenie panting in the corner. He didn't have a pot to piss in then. That was hardly a week ago. *Now* look at him!

He came up then, with a big tray. He said, "Crys said you'd like steak." And he gave me a plate, and a knife and fork wrapped in a red paper napkin.

There was steak, and onion rings, and little mushrooms, and fried potatoes, and peas.

"Dig in," said Justin. "You must be starving."

And I was, so I got stuck in, and it was the most dynamite dinner I had in my life. If someone asked me, "How do you like your meat done, how do you like your spuds cooked?" I'd say, "Just like this." But Justin hadn't asked. He'd done it like he already knew.

Every so often I'd sneak a look at Crystal, and she was noshing away too, like there was no tomorrow. And every so often I caught Justin sneaking a look at Crystal and me noshing, and he had a little curly smile on, like he was our mum or something.

"All right?" said Justin. But I couldn't answer because I'd just wiped my plate with the last chunk of potato and stuck it in my gob.

"Magic," said Crystal.

"Mmm," said I.

"Pudding?" said Justin.

He brought up a huge dish of sweet dark chocolate pudding, and he spooned dollops of it into bowls for Crystal and me. I still couldn't say a word 'cos my mouth was always full of pudding.

He made tea and put a tape in his tape deck. And then he said, "What was the wrestling like?" And Crystal started to tell him.

It was like seeing it again at the movies. Crystal told him all about it—all the people, like Gruff and Pete and Harsh, and Phil and Hacker and California, sounded like characters in a movie. Me too. I sounded like The Terminator. And I wanted to say, "Tell it again, Crystal. I want to hear that part again." But my mouth was full of sweetness and I started nodding off.

Because there's nothing like it, is there? Sitting in a comfy chair, too full to move, hearing someone talk about you like you're the heroine in a movie. I could bottle that and take it in little sips every night of my life.

When I opened my eyes a little later on Crystal was curled up in her armchair and Justin was stretched out on the bed. It couldn't of been much later, 'cos the light was still on and the room was still full of music and the smell of chocolate.

I sort of thought I shouldn't be there. There was something I ought to be doing. But my eyelids dropped like fat cushions over my eyes and I nodded off again.

And then I was dreaming about something horrible. I was looking in a mirror only the face looking back at me wasn't mine. There was a thing in a black mask looking at me, so I couldn't see what it was except the eyes were blood red. I struggled to tear the mask off because I couldn't breathe. But I wasn't wearing a mask. The thing in the mirror was wearing the mask. It pulled its mask off, and underneath was this deformed face with blood red eyes. One side of its cheek was ripped open and there were hundreds of maggots crawling between sharp dog's teeth. The thing reached out and tried to drag me through to the wrong side of the mirror. I kept trying to make the sign of the cross because that always works in Dracula movies. But the monster didn't take a blind bit of notice, and it kept dragging me. It was much stronger than me.

I woke up with a yell. At least, I thought it was me yelling. Crystal was sitting bolt upright in her chair. Justin was halfway off the bed—his eyes out on stalks.

"AAARGH!"

It wasn't me yelling.

"Wha?" said Crystal. It wasn't her either.

Justin had his mouth open but he never made a sound.

"AAAARGH!"

I shot out of my chair. I was still half asleep but I flung the door open and staggered out into the hall. There was light leaking from under the next door along.

I threw it open. And saw Bella. Well, I saw her face and legs. What really caught my eye was a hairy arse bumping up and down between her legs.

"Oy!" I said.

"Downstairs!" Bella shouted. Her black-red lipstick seemed to be moving of its own accord. "Downstairs," she said. "They're downstairs." And the hairy arse never missed a beat.

"Gerroff!" she screamed at the hairy arse. But she might've been nailed to the mattress for all the notice it took.

I couldn't get out fast enough and I fell over Crystal on my way.

"AAARGH!"

"Downstairs!" Crystal shrieked. And we stumbled to the top of the stairs.

Down there seemed to be full of people.

I raced down, Crystal behind me, through the hall and into the gym. My gym.

Except it didn't look like my gym no more.

The hanging light bulb was shaded with a dark red scarf so everything looked dusky pink.

And the mats were all stacked up so they seemed like beds.

It was Mandy yelling.

There were three blokes.

Mandy and three blokes.

They were doing something. I couldn't see. It wasn't nice. It was making Mandy scream.

In my gym.

"Yaaaa!" I roared. And I went in with fists and boots.

I punched. I kicked.

"Oof!" I heard. And, "Ow-ow!"

I grabbed a handful of hair and smashed a head into a wall. And then Crystal came flying in with a big frying pan, and I heard, "Boing-boing-boing," so I guessed she was walloping away too.

I wished I had something to boing with. But I didn't, so I laid about me with feet and elbows. I hit everything that moved.

A stack of mats toppled, and suddenly we was all on the floor except Crystal who was beating seven bells out of the back of someone's skull.

I leaped to my feet. There was a bloke lying on his back on the floor. He was struggling up. He made a grab for my ankles.

So I jumped on him.

I jumped on his knob.

Both feet. Full weight.

If you think Mandy screamed loud, you should of heard this bloke! He bellowed like a bull dying.

I didn't care. He was one less to worry about.

And then Crystal came sailing past and landed on her back in the corner. The frying pan only just missed me.

I ducked, and the bloke who threw Crystal staggered into me.

I came up and caught his chin with the back of my head. The blow shook my teeth loose, but he went over backwards like a falling tree.

I had to get them out.

Out.

I went after the one who fell over backwards. I caught him by the foot, and his shoe came off in my hand. So I got his arm and heaved him up. I twisted his arm up his back till I heard the elbow crack and ran him out the door.

That left one.

And that was when Justin came in with a socking great kitchen knife.

"Gimme!" I yelled, and I snatched the knife off him.

I found the last one squashed under a mat with Mandy pinned under him.

I jabbed him in the thigh to tell him I had the weapon. I took him by the hair and yanked his head up. I stuck the knife under his nose.

"Get up," I said. And I shaved his nostril.

He got up. I stuck the knife into the pouch under his eye. "Don't!" he said.

I recognised him then. In spite of the dim red light I recognised the stoat-faced pillock who'd gone, "Oy, Bucket Nut," at me from the shadows two nights ago.

I pricked him under the eye.

"Back off," I said.

"My eyes!" he said. His breath was gob-turd.

"Out," I said. "Back out."

His nose was dribbling blood where I shaved it. The blood looked black in the red light.

Back he went. Slowly. Ever so careful. He didn't want to jog the knife.

It would've been all right.

I know it would've been all right. Except for fuckin' Mandy.

She came from behind me. She'd got to her feet. She'd found her handbag somewhere.

"AAAARGH!" she went. And she clattered him on the side of his head with her handbag.

His head hit the knife. It wasn't me. Honest.

I wasn't going to cut him 'less he made me. For *true*.

His head hit the knife. The knife sliced clean through his cheek.

First there was this thin black line from his eye to his jaw. Then the slit opened up and I could see his teeth. Just like in my dream. And then the blood began to pour.

His hand went up. His eyes went glassy. And then he fainted dead away.

He crumpled down.

And that left us with three bodies on the floor.

There was Stoat. There was the one with the squelched knob. And there was little Monkey Wrench, all of a heap. Three.

But I counted wrong. There was four.

There was Stef. I hadn't even seen Stef, but I'd probably trod on her.

Me and Mandy and Justin stood there with our gobs hanging open, looking at the pile of human parts on the floor. What a total, mega wreck.

And I'd forgotten Bella and hairy-arse upstairs.

Do you know who hairy-arse was? Can you guess? Well, *can* you?

Hairy-arse was Pete Carver. *Pete fucking Carver!*

I couldn't believe it. I really couldn't. No.

What a mind-blowing, bloody, shit-hole of a shambles!

Pete Carver walked in, still buckling his belt and hitching up his trousers.

"Farkin'ell, Eva," he said. "What you been teaching in your self-defence school? Farkin' butchery?"

'Cos Stoat was flat out on the floor with his face in tatters and blood everywhere.

And Stef was a goner too, now I could see her—blood was oozing out of every opening in her body. And believe me, you could see all of them. She wasn't wearing hardly nothing.

If you ever wanted to know how really wrecked a human body can be, you should've seen Stef. It's so easy to hurt a body. 'Specially one that's expecting love. I didn't want to look.

"I gotta go," I said. "I got my dogs to see to."

Because I remembered what it was I ought to be doing. What I forgot when I nodded off. I got my own life. I got my dogs. I got duties. I'm Armour Protection. I'm in charge.

Chapter 18

I lost my lovely dinner outside. That lovely steak, the onion, mushrooms, those peas—all sicked up in the gutter.

My guts were sore. Someone had punched me there.

I didn't remember anyone landing a punch on me. But they must've. I was sore all over.

"Eva?" Justin said. "Are you okay?" He started to rub my back. I was still bent over the gutter. The smell of old vegetables from the market was heaving.

"Leave off," I said. "I'm all right."

"Don't go," he said.

"Got work to do," I said. Who was looking after the yard? Who was checking on The Enemy's properties?

"Please don't go," Justin said. "I think Crystal's concussed. And we've got to get Stef to hospital."

"Why bother? She's dead, ain't she?"

"No she isn't," Justin said. "But she's badly hurt. Please, Eva. It's an awful mess in there. And someone has to get rid of those men."

So I went back in. I didn't want Pete Carver to think I'd thrown up.

The bloke with the cracked elbow had gone. I don't know where. I didn't see him go. Bella was crouched over Stef. Mandy was looking after Crystal.

Pete Carver said, "Don't suppose you've got a phone. I'll call an ambulance on my way home if you like." He was looking at Stoat who was still in a dead faint on the floor.

"No ambulance!" Justin said.

"Who's the nancy-boy?" Pete asked.

"No ambulance," Bella said, standing up.

And Crystal mumbled, "No," too.

"No?" said Pete. "Well, you got a point. The cops'd come too, and you don't want them knowing this address."

The bloke with the squashed danglies was sitting up moaning and retching. "Jesus!" he squeaked. "Not the cops! Jesus!"

Mandy went to him. She said, "What happened to you? You okay?" Silly mare!

"No I'm not fucking okay," he said. "Some bastard beaned me. And then a bus fell on my wedding tackle."

Something was wrong.

I said, "Ain't you with Stoat?"

"Who's Stoat?" he said.

Mandy said, "He's all right. He's my . . . What did you say your name was, dearie?"

But Dearie didn't answer. He groped his way to his feet and lurched out bent double.

"Well, well," said Pete. "They don't call her Handy Mandy for nothing. You ain't losing your, ho-hum, *grip,* are you, darlin'?"

"Shut up," screamed Bella. "Just *shut up!* All you're good for is a dirty joke. If you'd got up when I told you, none of this would've happened."

"Get up?" said Pete. "You don't interrupt the vinegar strokes. I got what I paid for. And now I'm going home."

"No you fucking ain't," said Bella. "You're taking this sod with you." And she kicked Stoat with her pointy little shoe.

"We can take care of our own," she said. "But you get this bastard out of here or I'll find your fucking wife."

Which amazed me. I didn't even know Pete was married.

"And you!" She turned on me. "You're so fucking clever—you get us some wheels. Now!"

I was stone chuffed to go, I can tell you. It was a stinking, dirty mess. It made me feel little and weak and sick. Like I felt when Ma locked us in the cupboard under the stairs. And we heard her. And Simone said, "What's she doing? What's *he* doing. He's *hurting* her!" But when Ma let us out again she seemed glad of it, even when it hurt. And Simone and I didn't understand. Except after the fire. Ma wasn't glad then. They took her away to hospital then. And the social workers took Simone and me into care.

I let the dogs out. They were ever so pleased to see me. They charged around, stretching themselves. They were hard and glossy and clean. All full of muscle and hard clean bone. And their eyes were shiny and they didn't have no dirty thoughts. Except Ramses who's always waiting for me to crumple.

"Wait on," I said to Ramses. "I'm not like the rest of 'em. I'm the London Lassassin, me. I'm still top dog, and don't you forget it."

But I didn't sound like the London Lassassin. My voice sounded little and weak. I expected Ramses to notice, but he had his ears pricked. He'd heard something more important.

"Ro-ro-ro," went Ramses, and he galloped off to the gate.

"Rap-rap-rap," went Lineker and charged off after him.

"*Eva!*" shouted Justin, from the gate. "Where are you? Have you found a car?"

"Piss off and leave me be," I said. "I done my bit. You're on at me and on at me—you and monkey face. Fuck off—you're doing my head in."

He climbed up on the gate, and he would've come over if Ramses and Lineker wasn't circling around, like sharks in the water, waiting to take his legs off.

"Please, Eva," he said. "I know you're upset . . ."

"I ain't upset," I said, 'cos I wasn't. I was just choked they kept taking me for granted. I came when Mandy screamed, didn't I? I stopped the bastards hurting her. What more did they want? Did they say, "Thanks, Eva, nice job?" No they did not. They just wanted me to stick around and get my head done in some more.

"We can't manage without transport," Justin said. "You said you'd get us some. We've got to get Stef to hospital. She's hurt."

"She ain't hurt," I said. "It's only smoke."

"Smoke?"

"From the fire," I said. I couldn't breathe either. That's what fire does.

"I don't understand," Justin said. "Help us take Stef to hospital, Eva. We need you. We need a car."

"Oh," I said.

Then I said, "What d'you think this is? A rose garden?"

"What?"

"It's a breaker's yard," I said. He was so dim. "And what do they break? *Motors*." He was so thick, he didn't see transport all around him.

But it wasn't reliable transport. I know that. I'm not brain-damaged.

I did what I've never done before. I took wheels from the second-hand lot. I took a minibus the manager rebuilt to sell. I never do that. It's too risky. But I did it that night because I wanted Justin, Bella and Monkey Wrench off my back. I never wanted nothing to do with them ever again.

Crystal wasn't hurt. She was only shook up and lazy-eyed. When the time came she refused to go into the hospital.

"No way," she said. "They kill you in there if you're not dying already." Which went to show she wasn't concussed.

So Bella and Mandy went in with Stef. Justin, Crystal and me waited round the corner in the minibus.

"What fire?" Justin said, at last.

"What about a fire?" Crystal said.

"There weren't no fire," I said. "What you on about?"

"You were talking about smoke and a fire."

"Was *not*," I said. "Clean yer ears out. There weren't no fire."

"Oh," said Justin. And we sat silent till Bella and Mandy came back. And that gave me time to think.

But the more I thought, the more narked I got. And when Bella and Mandy came back I was seeing scarlet.

I said, "You think I'm stupid. You think I'm thicker than a bricky's lunchbox."

"Don't shout," said Crystal. "My head's splitting."

"Let it split," I said. "You're using my gym for a knocking shop."

Nobody said nothing, so I knew I was right. I remembered the bathroom. I ought to have known when I saw all that perfumed bubbly stuff. Who did they think they were fooling?

"Who do you think you're fooling?" I said.

"Don't shout," Crystal said, in a wobbly monkey voice.

"Please, Eva," Justin said. "Let's go home and talk about it later."

"There you go again," I said. "Expecting favours. You turn my gym into a slut's rogering parlour and you expect me to fucking drive you home. Dream on!"

I was waiting, just waiting, for Bella to stick her spiky oar in. But she didn't. She just sat there looking about fifty years old with her make-up smeared and her hair all rat tails.

"Y'know, Eva," Mandy said, "you was so right. About the shouting and kicking. I'd of been mince meat, like poor Stef, if I hadn't remembered shouting and kicking. And then you came. It was like on telly, when the cavalry rides over the hill. You was Joan Ranger or Dirty Harriet."

"The cavalry?" I couldn't help laughing even if I was narked bad.

"You were brilliant, Eva," Justin said.

"Brilliant," mumbled Crystal.

So that was all right, and I drove them back to Mandala Street. It was only Bella said nothing. But she always was a right prickly little witch, and three out of four of them grateful was a pretty good number where I come from.

I took the minibus back to the yard and parked it in the exact same spot I borrowed it from. It'd be a fine thing, really typical, if the owner caught me borrowing without permission. He'd give me the old heave-ho, and that way I'd lose my home as well as my job. And it'd all be Crystal's fault. Just like it was her fault I was in the sewer with Mr. Deeds and the gym.

If she hadn't got her monkey wrench clamped on me about self-defence classes for the girls, if she hadn't gone conkers about Dawn dying, none of the strife would've happened. And I'd be living and fighting peaceful, as per normal.

It wasn't, none of it, my fault. Yet if any sucker got the blame it'd be me. That's what comes of standing out in a crowd. Anyone who looks different gets shot.

So I was extra careful when I parked the minibus and did my rounds. I didn't want anyone picking holes in my work. Pick-pick-pick—that's all some people do.

It was morning—almost too late to matter—when I went round with the dogs. They were grizzling and griping because they'd had their routine screwed. I couldn't fault them. I didn't like it either, and I grizzled and griped back at the dogs. All three of us was in a foul mood.

I kept thinking—what's Pete Carver going to say back at the gym? He seen me in a knocking shop. He'd tell Gruff Gordon, and Gruff Gordon can't keep his mouth shut without three rolls of sticking plaster and half a pint of super glue. He'd tell everyone—"Eva's knocking around in a knocking shop." So Harsh'd know. Everybody'd know.

And who would they all laugh at? I ask you.

They wouldn't laugh at Pete for bonking witchy bitchy Bella, would they? No. That'd be just another blokish trophy for the stud, wouldn't it? All the sniggers and pointed fingers would be aimed at yours truly. Me.

And what had Pete done with Stoat? Stoat needed stitches. What was he going to tell the hospital and the polizei? He wouldn't say Mandy swiped him with her handbag, would he? He'd say I knifed him.

I copped time in solitary once, for knifing. It wasn't me that time either. I was in one of them units where all the bad girls get sent. And there was a sort of fashion for razor blades—small pieces of razor blade. A razor blade can be broken in small pieces. The trick is to wedge a little bit of razor blade under your thumbnail with soap. The sharp edge hardly pokes out at all—you can barely see it—but it can slice rotten. And because it's such a tiny weapon you can hide it or dump it really quickly.

Anyone who's been in a secure unit knows there's all sorts of gang stuff going on. You've always got to be on one side or another, even if you don't care bloomers for any of them. And you got to protect yourself from all of them. So if there's blades about, you better find yourself a blade double quick. And you better *tell* everyone you got a blade. If you don't, you'll be grated cheese before long. Usually, you find if everyone's got one, no one uses them much. Except if someone goes bonkers.

I don't know how it all started. I can't even remember which side I was supposed to be on—but five of them trapped four of us in the lavvies, and all hell let loose. I've got two long white scars on my left forearm and one on the back of me neck as a keepsake. But, y'know what? I never cut no one myself. Not a single girl got sliced with my bit of blade. And y'know for why? I'll tell you. It was when I took a swipe at the first girl to come my way. She dodged me, and I hit the wash basin. And the blow forced my bit of blade right up under my thumbnail. It bled like a stabbed hog. And it hurt. Oh boy, did it hurt!

So when the screws turned up to stop the fight everyone dumped their blades in the lavvies or washed them down the drain. All except me. Mine was driven up into my thumb and I couldn't get it out.

Mine was the only blade the screws found. Everyone was cut, including me. But mine was the only blade. So them geniuses decided it was me who done the cutting. No one bothered to ask who cut *me*. I suppose they thought that was me too—me having a fine old time slicing meself.

See what I mean? If there was a prize for always copping the blame, I'd cop that as well.

I was feeling pretty moody, and the dogs was feeling pretty moody. And I didn't do a check on The Enemy's property because I didn't want to leave the yard or the dogs. But I should of, 'cos all we did was sit around and snarl at each other. And that way, Friday night turned into Saturday morning.

Usually, on the night after a fight, I make the night last. I go over all my triumphs in my mind—over and over—so I can hear the oohs and ahs when I pulled off something really stunning. That handstand escape I brought off in spite of Olga from the Volga being such a vegetable—usually I would've done a slow-mo replay of that, again and again. But I couldn't.

When the blokes came to work, and I penned the dogs and went to bed, I tried to replay my handstand escape. But every time I shut my eyes I saw Pete Carver's hairy arse. I saw Stef on the floor. And I saw Stoat's cheek flopping open. My eyelids would fly open and my heart felt like a rubber ball bouncing in my chest—bounce, bounce, bounce.

But time passed, and I must've slept because Crystal woke me up. She banged on my door and when I staggered out to open it I saw a piece of paper on the floor. I picked it up and opened the door.

Crystal's eyeballs looked like raw eggs. In fact, Crystal looked like I felt. I wasn't pleased to see her. If you must know I'd rather've seen giant spiders.

I said, "What you doing here?"

"Came to see you."

"Came once too often," I said. I would've slammed the door in her face but she squirmed in.

"I'll put the kettle on," she said, as if that made everything all right.

"You'll put nothing on," I said. "What you'll do is fuck off out of here. You've screwed my life, and I ain't had any kip yet."

"Yes you have," she said. "I came round two hours ago and knocked. You never answered but I could hear the snores from outside. I'll make us both a cuppa. We got to talk."

"We don't gotta do nothing," I said. But she lit the gas and filled the kettle. And I did fancy a cup of tea. My mouth felt like something crawled in it and died.

I should of slung monkey face out on her little monkey ear, but I read my bit of paper instead. It was from The Enemy. It said, "Dear Eva, Thanks for the good work you did this week. I have now made permanent arrangements for the two properties in question so you won't have to bother with them this weekend. But don't worry, I think there will be something else next week.

"I need to speak to you urgently on another matter. So, when you come to the office for your money, please make sure I know about it. If I'm out, *wait*. Anna Lee."

Typical. Typical polizei. Typical Enemy. She came round to see me. She could've brought my money. She could've slipped it under the door and saved me the bother of going to her office to get it. But did she? Oh no. She never does nothing to suit me. All I get is another one of her stupid notes giving orders. If I want my money—what I worked for, what's due me—I have to suit *her*. Typical.

"What's up?" Crystal said. "Bad news?"

"Business," I said. "I got business and it's nothing you can stick your hooter in."

"Oh," she said, and gave me my tea. She gave me this woeful look over the rim of her mug.

"What?" I said.

"It's Dawn," she said.

"No," I said. "I've had it up to here with slags. I don't want to know."

"You promised," she said.

"I never," I said. "What did I promise?"

"You said if I ever found out who did for Dawnie, you'd help me to kill him."

Chapter 19

"I fucking did *not!*"

"Don't shout," Crystal said. "You was standing right where you're standing now."

"Was not!"

"Was. Don't shout."

"*Not* shouting!"

"You said, 'You find 'em, I'll kill 'em.'"

"Fuckin' did not!"

"Did," Crystal said. "It was right after Dawnie died. The night after. You was stood right there. I told you about her and me when we was little. About the bloke with the red car and the fancy suit. And you said, 'You find 'em, I'll kill 'em'. You *did.*"

"Not!" But it was coming back to me. I remembered Dawn's story. Some of it. And Crystal moaning on about the blokes who tap-danced on Dawn's teeth. And I s'pose I said something. Well, I must've, mustn't I? You don't just stand there like a parking meter when someone's lost a sister, do you? Even if the sister's only Dirty Dawn. So I must've said something, y'know, out of sympathy, but I wouldn't never've said I'd kill someone. Not over Dawn. I'm just not like that.

So I stood there with my mug of tea. And Crystal stood there with hers, looking woeful.

Then she said, "It's 'cos of Dawn, isn't it?"

"'Cos of Dawn what?"

"You never liked Dawn. What you got against prostitutes?"

"I don't like anyone," I said. Which is true. Except for Harsh. "I've got nothing against . . . them other girls."

"You have," Crystal said. "You're always rude to them."

"That's 'cos they're fuckin' stupid."

"No," she said. "It's more than that."

"What do you know about it?" I said.

"Don't *shout*," Crystal said. "Why're you shouting?"

"Who's going to look after Stef's kid while she's in hospital?" I asked. Because Stef was one of the ones who had kids.

"What do you care about Stef's kid?" Crystal said.

"I don't fucking care about Stef's kid. No more than she does."

That shut her up. She stood there drinking her tea, looking at me. Then she put her mug down.

"Buy you breakfast," she said.

"No," I said. "I know your game."

"What game?"

"You're always trying to play pinball with my head."

"Am not," she said, and without any warning at all, she burst into tears. Which really took me by surprise. Crystal is not a crier. Crystal's like me. She'd rather die than cry.

I could only gape at her, and she ran out of the Static slobbering all over her sleeve.

I suppose you think I should've run out after her. I suppose you're the type who goes all weak and woolly when someone breaks down and blubs in front of you. Well, more fool you! You don't know Monkey Wrench the way I know her. She'd try anything to make me do what she wanted—including pretending to cry. She's a lying little madam.

Once I knew she was only pretending, I forgot about Crystal and decided to go and get my money off The Enemy.

Don't get me wrong—I wasn't broke. I had money in my pocket from the self-defence classes, I had wages coming from looking after the yard and Mr. Deeds owed me for the Lewinsham fight. But the self-defence dosh wouldn't go far, and being owed isn't the same as having a big wad in the hand. I like to keep my wad where I can see it. Owed money is no money at all until you get your fist round it. Take my advice—if you're owed any ackers, you go out and grab it fast before the bim who owes you spends it on himself.

But by the time I got to her office The Enemy was out and the old secretary-bird was packing up to leave.

She said, "Anna told me to ask you to wait."

"Where's my money?" I said.

"It's all ready," she said.

"So am I," I said, and I held my hand out.

"Anna locked it in her desk," the secretary-bird said. "She won't be gone long."

"Not long's too long," I said. "It's owed me and I want it *now.*"

"Please," she said, "don't thump the fax. You'll break it."

"*Now,*" I said. See what I mean? That old secretary-bird would rather part with her knickers than part with dosh that was already mine.

She said, "Please, Eva, calm down. Why don't you make yourself comfortable? Anna's coming shortly. You could read a magazine while you wait."

And then The Enemy herself walked in. She said, "Bleeding hell, Eva, why're you throwing magazines round the room?" And the secretary-bird scuttled out like she had a fuse lit under her heels.

"I don't want to talk to you," I said. "I don't want to talk to her. I don't want to wait and read a poxy fucking magazine. I want my money."

"Keep your hair on," she said, and unlocked her private door. "Come in."

"I don't want to come in," I said. "You're all jerking me

around. You all want me to do things. And you're holding my money ransom so I'll do what you want."

"Take your money," The Enemy said. But she took her time unlocking her desk, and while she was at it she said, "I just wanted to pass on a warning, that's all." She handed me my money.

While I was counting it she said, "I had a visit from the police this morning."

"I don't want to know," I said, and I stuffed my dosh in a back pocket.

"I know," she said, "but I think you should."

"Who're you to tell me what I should know?"

"Why are you so upset today?"

"Not upset."

"Okay," The Enemy said. "Okay, okay. But all the same you should know that the police say that a brothel has been opened on Mandala Street at that property you and I would have taken charge of if we hadn't found the squatter."

"What?"

"For God's sake, Eva, don't shout at me. You're splitting my eardrums. Don't rush off. Talk to me."

"You don't want to talk to me," I said. "You just want to tell me what to do."

"Have it your own way," she said. "But you'll look pretty silly if the police charge you with keeping a disorderly house or living off immoral earnings."

"*What?*"

"And I'll look bleeding silly for employing you."

I couldn't believe my ears. I said, "All I done was teach those slags a bit of self-defence. What fart-arse you been listening to?"

"Just the local beat copper," she said.

"What did he say?" I said. "What does he know about me? What you been telling him?"

"Nothing," she said.

"Nothing?" I said. "You dobbed me in."

"No," she said. "Sit down. Calm down and shut up."

I sat down. What else could I do? My life was turning rotten. I could smell it. I could smell the stench of a life turned mouldy, and believe me, it's a sick, rancid stench.

"It's that turdy gnome," I said.

"Who?"

"Crystal," I said. "Monkey face. She done it."

"Crystal?" The Enemy said. And she got that puckered look around the mouth she gets when she wants you to think she's thinking.

"It's Dawn, getting herself stiffed," I said. "It tossed Dwarf's brain down the bog-hole."

I expected The Enemy to say "nonsense" or "rubbish" like she usually does. But this time she just sat there all puckered.

Then she said, "I'd better have a word with young Crystal. Meanwhile, don't you take any more money from those women. And if you're wise, you'll give Mandala Street a wide berth for a few days."

"Can't do that," I said. "It's where I train."

"But I thought . . ."

"You thought wrong," I said. "You always *think* you know, but you don't know shit from shaving cream. Them premises on Mandala Street—that's my gym."

The Enemy looked like she wanted to spit tin-tacks. She said, "It's the law, you see."

"What law?"

"If more than one prostitute shares a place, that place is deemed a brothel."

"It's my gym," I said.

"In fact," The Enemy said, "almost anything sensible a prostitute might do to protect herself—like hiring a minder or setting up in a collective—is illegal for someone."

"I told you—it ain't a knocking shop. It's my gym."

"Aren't you listening?"

"It's you that's got bum-fluff in your lug-holes. It's my gym. I saw it first."

"Don't bleeding shout!" The Enemy yelled.

It was turning out to be a stone septic day—a day when you're dragged backwards into evil-smelling flob. A day when everything you ever done up till now counts minus. It didn't happen, you didn't try, you're back wallowing in the cesspit where you started.

And I hadn't even had my breakfast yet. My feet were gummed to the pavement by everyone else's snot and phlegm, and, since getting up, I hadn't had time to get my gnashers round a bacon sarnie.

So I went to the caff on Mandala Street, but would you believe it—the first person I saw when the door banged behind me was Justin. Justin hunched over a table by the steamy window. Justin with his eyes all red and swollen.

"Eva!" he said.

"Fuck off," I said, and I turned round and walked. "Out me way," I said to the bolly who whacked into me as I left. "Need the whole bleeding road?" I said to the woman who nearly ran me over in her car. Weepers, bims and bollies everywhere you looked.

I stopped looking.

When I was a kid with nowhere to go I would sometimes fetch up at Waterloo Station. It was somewhere to get out of the rain. I wasn't the only one. Lots of kids went to Waterloo. Sometimes there'd be quite a crowd and you could get quite matey—shouting at the railway police and passing round a bit of blow or a jar of cider. I never stayed long because there was always the chance of polizei, parents and social workers lolloping around looking for runners and IRA bombs.

Come to think of it, Waterloo was probably where I first ran into Crystal. Because a station can be an ace place to cadge a bob or two or a free cup of tea.

See, what happens is that your average train traveller mongs around waiting, gets bored, buys tea and munchies. Train gets called, passenger dumps tea and munchies. And someone like Crystal, after a quick dip into the passenger's pocket or purse, gets to scoff his tea too. Easy-per-deazy.

You may wonder, if Waterloo was where I first met Crystal—which maybe it was, maybe it wasn't—why I fetched up there after leaving the caff on Mandala Street. Well, keep wondering. I ain't telling you 'cos I don't know myself. It was one of those times when time eats its own tail. I went to Waterloo, and that's all I'm telling you. You don't have to know why I do every little thing, do you? Well, *do* you? You're not polizei, are you? No. So you'll hear what *I* want to tell you. No more, no less.

Anyway, that's where I was—Waterloo. And I started looking round for something to eat, because I'd walked a long way and I was feeling quite light-headed.

But the station wasn't a friendly place no more. There was nowhere to sit to take the weight off your feet. There was no bins for dumped food. There was no one I recognised.

And why should there be? All the people I knew was gone ages ago. And me. I was gone too. I wasn't a kid no more. I don't hang round stations. I'm a professional with a career and relaxed mental attitude. I don't got to look in bins for bits of burger no more.

"What're you looking for?" Justin asked.

He made me jump out of my boots. "What?" I said.

"You're looking for something," he said.

"What you doing here?"

"I followed you," Justin said. "You stormed off. But you looked really, sort of, weird. So I followed you."

"Who said you could?" I said. "I never said you could follow me."

"I was afraid you might, sort of, *do* something. But you just walked. And then, I saw you were coming here, and I thought I'd like to come here too."

"Why?"

"Oh, I don't know," Justin said. "This is the station I came to when I first came to London."

"So?"

"I'd just got off the train," Justin said. "And I was standing over there with my suitcase in my hand, wondering which way to go, what to do next. And then this well-dressed guy— all silk suit and handmade shoes—came up and started to chat. Was anyone meeting me? Did I have anywhere to stay? That sort of thing." Justin stood with his hands in his pockets, and he looked at the station concourse like it was a picture someone painted. He said, "This guy took me in a taxi to Shepherds Market. I'd never been in a taxi before. I'd never been in London before. As a matter of fact, I'd never been anywhere alone before."

He stopped looking dreamy and smiled. "Oh well," he said, "it could've been a lot worse. At least he was clean and fairly normal. You wouldn't believe some of the things I've heard since."

"Yes, I would," I said.

"He's dead now," Justin said. "Let's go, shall we? I'm getting the shakes, thinking about it."

So we went. I wanted to go anyway. I was afraid Justin was going to tell me how his young life got knocked pear-shaped. And I didn't want to know. Somewhere between the ages of nought and eighteen *everyone's* life goes pear-shaped. I don't need the details.

Chapter 20

Justin said, "I'm surprised you're so upset. I didn't think a thing like last night would upset you."

"Whadya mean, upset?" I said. "I ain't upset."

"The violence," he said. "I thought that was your stock in trade."

"Takes more than a little bam-a-lam to upset me," I told him.

"That's what Crystal said. But maybe she's wrong for once."

I just kept walking. If he thought Crystal was only wrong once he was a bigger melon than even I thought. As far as I was concerned Crystal was wrong every time she came out of the water to breathe.

"Don't look like that," he said.

"Like what?"

"Like you kill kittens for fun. Crystal's been good to me. She looks after me. I owe her."

"Buy a brain!" I said. "That's what she wants you to think. You're just another mark. She wants you for something—only you don't know what it is yet."

"Yes I do," he said. "She's lonely, she's sad and she's frightened. We need each other."

"Wait while I get me violin out," I said, and I started running.

"Don't go," he said. So I stopped. I don't like running, and I sodding loathe running on an empty stomach.

"All right," I said, "only don't talk to me about Crystal. My whole life got gangrene since she showed up."

So we walked down to the Embankment. I found a van selling hot dogs, and I bought a few which made me feel better. And Justin kept his trap shut till I'd eaten which was a good thing too. He didn't want a hot dog and he spent the time kicking a stone around like it was a football, and that made me remember he was only a kid. Which was weird—he didn't talk like a kid and he didn't cook like a kid.

He waited till I'd stuffed the last crumb in my gob and then he said, "Queenie died, you know."

"Who?"

"My dog."

"Oh, right," I said. And that explained why his eyes were all pink around the edges. I was afraid it'd been something to do with Crystal, but anyone can understand a bloke being cut up about his dog. That's the way it should be.

He said, "I wanted to ask you about her puppies."

"What?"

"The vet won't keep them any longer, and I've got to collect them."

"So?"

"Well, they're newborn," he said. "I don't know what to do."

"Oh," I said. "You got to feed 'em and keep 'em warm just like Queenie would've."

"Oh," he said, like he never thought of it. "But what do I feed them on?"

"Milk," I said. "There's stuff you can get like bitch milk. But you'll have to bottle feed 'em. They'll be too small to gnaw a bone."

"This bitch milk," he said, "is it expensive?"

"How should I know?" I said. "I always got my dogs full grown." I knew, I just fuckin' *knew,* he was going to ask me to help, so I said, "Has anyone been to see Stef?" Which was really stupid. I didn't want to know about Stef. I didn't want to know about anyone.

"You could go and see her yourself," Justin said. "She's right here."

"Where?"

"St. Thomas's," he said.

And I looked. Sometimes, see, I don't bother about what's around. I know where *I* am. But Justin was right. We were on the Embankment, a stone's throw from Waterloo, with St. Thomas's right behind. If I'd've known that I'd've walked in the opposite direction.

"The funny thing is," Justin said, "the man who hurt her, the one who got his face cut, is here too."

"Stoat?" I said. "Wasn't my fault. It was you gave me the knife, and Mandy clattered him with her handbag."

"You knew him?"

"Do me a favour!" I said. "Would I know a deformed pile of parts like that? He tried to talk to me in the street once."

"What did he want?" Justin asked. And I looked at him. He still had his hands in his pockets, and the wind from the river was blowing his curls around like an angel's halo. But his face had gone white and tight.

"What did he want?" Justin asked again.

"Dunno," I said. "Something about taking over half the gym."

"The gym?"

"But I soon told him where to stuff his partnership."

"Oh Christ," Justin said. "Why didn't you tell us?"

"Tell who?" I said. "Tell who what?"

"About him wanting a partnership."

"Why should I? He wasn't horning in on my gym."

"Oh Eva," Justin said. "It wasn't the gym he wanted. It was the women. He thought they were paying you for protection and he wanted half."

"He what?" I said. "The dirty stinking bastard—he thought I was a whores' minder?"

"I suppose he must have."

"How do you know?"

"Because Bella talked to Stef and Mandy. Stef couldn't say much—she could hardly talk. But Mandy was there, remember, with her friend. And Mandy said."

"What did Mandy say?"

"She said that he and the other man did what they did to Stef to prove that the women needed their protection. Mandy said they kept shouting, 'You work for us or you don't work at all.'"

I looked up at St. Thomas's—all the glass, all the concrete. Stoat was in there somewhere. And Stef.

Justin said, "You should've cut his throat."

I said nothing. What could I say? I didn't even know what to think. If the polizei found out they'd blame me for slicing his face. And here was Justin blaming me for not slicing his throat. Buggered every which way. And me not knowing which end was up.

There was only one thing to do. A rhyme came into my head—if you're in doubt, get the fuck out. I was quite pleased with it because it saved me from thinking other thoughts. If you're in doubt, get the fuck out. If you're in doubt . . .

I started off up the Embankment. I was going back home to the Static, back to Ramses and Lineker who didn't lie to me and didn't try to get me to do things I didn't want to do. I was going back to Sam's Gym and I was going to heave those weights till the sweat poured off me. I was going to sweat. Till all the poison poured out of me like a filthy river.

St. Thomas's, Stoat and Stef. Bella, Mandy, Justin, and Crystal—most specially Crystal—could all crumble into the

Thames and float out to sea with the rest of the sewage. I didn't want to know.

So I started off, and I was stepping out nicely when Justin hopped round in front of me saying, "No . . . wait, Eva, you don't understand."

"No," I said, striding on, "*you* don't understand." And I walked right through him.

But up he popped again right under my nose.

"Wait, Eva," he said. "It's Dawn. You haven't got it yet. The men who hurt Stef killed Dawn."

I kept going. Buzz-buzz-buzz, he went. He was a fly on sugar, buzz-buzz.

Justin went, "Eva, please. Think about it. Two men took Dawn out of the Full Moon. Two men hurt Stef. Crystal says it's the same two. She says they want all the women in Mandala Street working for them or giving them a cut. Crystal says . . ."

Crystal says. Fucking Crystal says. Says, says, says. Buzz-buzz-buzz. In my face. In my ears. Up my nose.

I swatted the fly.

Well, no. Not swatted exactly.

I nutted him.

It was his own fault—buzzing in my face like that.

It was only a little nut. But it hurt my forehead and it made him sit down a bit swiftish.

You can't blame me. A woman can only take so much.

But I was sorry. Soon as I done it, I was sorry. After all, he did cook a lovely steak and mushrooms for my dinner. It wasn't his fault I sicked it up after.

My eyes were watering but I squatted down to pick him up. It looked as if his eyes were watering too, and he had a bloody nose.

"Oh Eva," he said.

"Get up," I said. "You ain't hurt."

But he sat there looking sick. I pulled the tail of my shirt out of my jeans to help mop the blood. But he pushed me away.

"Don't get it on you," he said. "I've got a handkerchief."

"Be like that," I said. "I'm only trying to help."

"Thanks," he said. "It's all right." And he sat on the pavement mopping his nose till it stopped bleeding.

The funny thing was, although he didn't want my help, he didn't seem too pissed off with me. I'd've thrown him in the Thames if he'd put the nut on me. But he didn't seem that put out. Maybe he was used to people bopping him.

Well, that's the way of the world, ain't it? You got to get used to people bopping you when you're young and weak. Till you're all grown up and it's your turn to do the bopping.

What really hit me was how bad I felt about it. I don't often say this, because it doesn't happen much, but I felt I'd done something wrong.

'Cos Justin was such a harmless little git. He was pretty and he spoke nice. Well, more than spoke nice—he *was* nice. He never had a hard word to say about me. Everyone else does. But he didn't, and I wondered why I hadn't noticed before.

I s'pose he had been buzz-buzz-buzzing at me but that was Crystal's fault. He wasn't out to get me. He wasn't trying to make my life a misery like she was. So, really, when you think about it, I shouldn't have head-butted him.

I should have head-butted Crystal instead. But she's so little I'd have had to kneel down to do it.

I felt blue, and I wanted to borrow a car to take him home to Mandala Street. But he wouldn't let me. He said it was a risk in broad daylight. And he didn't want trouble with the polizei any more than me.

Nutting Justin made me feel sort of peaceful—peaceful but very blue and I couldn't understand it.

So I said, "You shouldn't of buzzed in my face."

"Yes," he said, "I can see that."

He was so understanding, I said, "I ain't killing no one for her."

"Who?"

"What?"

"Who aren't you killing?" he asked, but he knew what I meant.

"Stoat," I said. "Crystal says I promised. But I never."

We were walking slowly because he was still wobbly.

"It's all balled up," I said. "Everything. I ain't got me own routine no more."

And I told him about training, and fighting, and the yard, and the dogs.

"It's my life the way I *made* it," I said. "But everybody, 'specially Crystal, screwed it up. Taking advantage of my sunny nature, see. I want to be heavyweight champion. I got a life. I got ambitions. I ain't topping no Stoat for Crystal."

I couldn't explain and I was beginning to feel all prickles and aches again.

"I can't top no one," I said. "It'd put me right back where I started. I've come a long way from where I started. You don't understand."

"It's okay," Justin said. "I do understand."

And maybe he was talking for true.

He said, "Perhaps Crystal didn't realize you had so much to lose."

"Not much to lose!" I said. "I got everything to lose."

"I know that," he said.

"Everyone's got something to lose."

"Well," he said, "nearly everyone. I'll talk to her, shall I?"

"Yeah," I said. "You talk to her."

Maybe he was the only one who could. But there's not many people can talk to a monkey wrench when it's got its jaws clamped round your throat.

But it was a weight off my mind. Crystal wanted straightening out, and Justin was going to do it. Bingo! I was free. No worries.

I could jump back into my own life same way I could jump into a warm bath. I could wash the dirt off and ease the aches. Screw Mandala Street. Screw the Premises. I was going back to Sam's Gym where they had proper equipment, proper mats, proper showers and lavvies. Where they had proper professionals training. People like me—in my business. *My* business. Not a bagful of tarts who don't know an armlock from a padlock, or a forearm smash from bangers and mash, or a body press from a trouser press.

'Cos those slags, well, they ain't my kind. You can't buy me for the price of a drink. I came a long way to hide from all that.

"I can't keep up," Justin said. Puff, puff, puff.

See what I mean? He ain't my kind neither. He didn't have a proper hard body. He didn't have no control. Maybe he couldn't keep up—but believe me, I wasn't going to let him hold me back.

"Bye," I said. "I'm off."

And I went.

Chapter 21

Things don't never happen the way you plan. There's days when I ask myself why I bother planning. It's not like I don't think, 'cos I do. I think and *think* about what ought to happen. I think till steam shoots out me ears. And then—splat—it's like I built a house in my head and the bricks start dropping off one by one, till there's nothing left—all that thinking in a heap of rubble.

I hardly got to Sam's Gym when the first thing went wrong. I was going up the steps when I saw Bella going up too.

I said, "What the fuck you doing here?" Because she oughtn't to be there. It wasn't in my plan. In my plan I'd never see bitch Bella ever again. I wouldn't see her on the stairs up to *my* gym all painted and powdered and pouting, all ready for work in a tiny little skirt which practically showed her knickers—if she was wearing any.

She said, "The trouble with you, Eva, is you're just too warm and cuddly for your own good."

"Screw you!" I said. "What you want here? You looking for me?"

"Yeah," Bella said. "I need the name of the charm school you graduated from so I can take lessons."

"Shit worms," I said. "What you want?"

"Nothing from you," she said. "But your mate Pete owes me money. He thinks I've forgotten but I ain't."

I would've laughed if I hadn't been so peed-off seeing her where she didn't ought to be. I thought Bella would've grabbed the dosh up front. It didn't seem like her to make a mistake like that.

I said, "I didn't know you worked cash on delivery."

"I don't," she said, "but the bastard nicked it back when Stef started screaming."

"Can't trust anyone these days," I said. "You should pick your punters more careful."

"Like your mother did?" she said. And she showed her sharp little fox teeth.

"What you know about my ma?"

"Hah!" she crowed, and grinned even wider. "I *thought* so!"

I started to see spots. I shouted, "What you saying about my ma?"

"Nothing," she said. "I never met your ma. I only know her daughter."

"Then shut yer dirty little mouth!"

"All right," she said, and she went on up the stairs. I stood where I was, breathing hard.

My ma is not like Bella. She isn't! Bella's a dirty, filthy, shitty liar. My ma has a hard life and she gets by as best she can, but she is *not* like Bella. I won't stand for it! And if you believe she is, you believe *lies.*

I went up the stairs slowly. I felt like I was choking. I felt like someone put a blanket on my head and I couldn't breathe proper. I had to stand outside the swing doors waiting for my lungs to work regular.

The doors swung open and Flying Phil and old Mr. Julio came out like they'd finished work and were going home. It was later than I thought. The Julios looked at me but they didn't say nothing.

"What you looking at?" I said. But they went on downstairs without saying bugger all.

A bit later Harsh came out. He said, "Go home, Eva."

"What?"

"Take a week's holiday," Harsh said. "When the time is unfavourable, every action brings misfortune."

"Eh?"

"The dog who crosses a flooded stream gets its tail wet," Harsh said. "Now is not the time, Eva. Go home."

And he was gone before I could draw enough breath to ask him what he meant.

I went into the gym.

I was hardly through the doors when Mr. Deeds came running. He was all strawberry coloured. He said, "I'm surprised you've got the nerve to show your face round here. But now you're here you can collect your evil-minded little friend and take a long walk off a short pier."

I looked, but I couldn't see Bella. I said, "She ain't no friend of mine, Mr. Deeds."

"You've brought this business into disrepute," he said. "You're finished."

"Don't give me that," I said. "I ain't done nothing. I've come to train, same as always. I done a good show for you last night, Mr. Deeds, and I want my money."

"Get knotted!" he said. "You got the *neck* to talk to me about last night after the way you behaved to me. I don't allow anyone to shove me around like you did last night. And never a woman!"

"You was going to stand me down," I said. "But you didn't, and I done a stone brill show. You should thank me."

"*Thank* you!" he said. "You're through. You're barred. You're out!"

"You can't do that," I said. "You owe me my purse for last night."

"You're fined too," he said. "Now fucking hop it. And don't come back—not now, not next week, not next year. *Not ever.*"

I was boggled—strapped for words. The only thing I could think of to do was jump up and down on his throat.

But I didn't, because that's when Bella started screaming.

"What the fuck?" said Mr. Deeds, and he made for the men's changing room.

"I want my money," I said, and I went after him.

"Gruff!" yelled Mr. Deeds. "*Gruff!* What the fuck's going on in there."

Gruff Gordon came out of the men's changing room and stood with his back to the door. He looked like someone pulled him through a briar patch backwards and he had a silly limp grin on his pan. Bella was shrieking behind the door.

"What're you boys up to in there?" Mr. Deeds said. "Keep it down, for Christ's sake. I can't hear myself think."

"Just a bit of fun," Gruff said.

"*Give me my money!*" I said.

"The girl can't take a joke," Gruff said.

Bella screamed.

"She shouldn't be in there anyway," Mr. Deeds said. "Get her out."

"Eva!" screamed Bella. "Eva!"

It made my teeth ache hearing her scream my name. I said, "You give me my money, Mr. Deeds. You *owe* me."

"Shut up!" he yelled. "Where's Pete? Where's Carl?"

Gruff said, "Don't go in."

But I kneed his knob and hit the door with my shoulder.

My whole face hurt with Bella's shrieking and I had to shut her up.

"Watch out!" Gruff said. "Carl's let the snake out!"

The poxy python. Carl hadn't just let it out. He had it in his hand.

Pete had Bella spread on a bench.

Carl was trying to ram Bella with the python's head. She was kicking, twisting, screaming. And who could blame her?

I never seen anything so disgusting in all my life.

Carl trying to stuff Bella with a six-foot python.

Even Mr. Deeds was floored.

"Oy!" he said. "Oy, Pete! What in hell d'you think you're playing at?"

Pete let Bella go.

He said, "Oh. Sorry Mr. Deeds. Just having a bit of a giggle."

Mr. Deeds said, "Just . . .?"

But I wasn't looking at Pete. I was looking at Carl. Because the man was badly off his head. He was serious. He was foaming. He'd boiled over.

He went, "You want it. You want it. You-want-it-you-want-it. Split-your-slit-split-your-slit . . ." On and on. Over and over. And he looked at me the way he looked at Bella.

I grabbed Bella. Bella grabbed her knickers and her bag. We ran.

I ain't afraid of much. You know I ain't.

But running out of Sam's Gym then I was almost wetting myself. I couldn't run fast enough. And neither could Bella. She was gripping my hand like she wanted to break my fingers off. I was dragging her. And she was dragging me.

Because Carl was barking mad. He was a total freak.

And that is frightening.

Never mind the python. I'm not scared of snakes.

But I was scared of Carl.

I stiff-armed the swing doors and we sprinted through. We ran and tumbled down the stairs. Bella broke the heel off her shoe but we kept on running till we were out on the pavement, and then we huffed and puffed all the way to the tube station.

"Stop," I yelled. "I'm not going down there."

"Well I am!" Bella said. "You go where you like. I'm getting out of here." She was shaking and hopping around on her one good shoe.

"Typical," I said. "Fucking typical. You only think of your cowing self. You've done me up like sliced sausage. You've got me booted. And now it's 'fuck you, bye-bye.' No wonder the blokes rough you up."

"Shut up," Bella screamed. She was stood there on the kerb with her knickers in one hand and her handbag in the other.

"Shut your stupid fucking mouth," she screamed. "You just don't get it, do you? You think you're so wonderful. You think, 'cos you got a couple of muscles, you're above it all. You think you're one of the boys."

"You're raving," I said. "You're disgusting."

"Oh yeah?"

"Yeah!"

"Well, let me tell you Mr. High and Mighty Eva Fucking Wylie. You ain't one of the boys. You piss sitting down like I do." She was spitting in my face. She was shouting so loud I could see her tonsils waggle.

"I don't do *nothing* like you," I told her. "I wouldn't even step on you—you're dirtier than cat crap."

And she swung her handbag at me. I caught her wrist, and her wrist was angry red from when Pete held her down.

We were nose to nose, only I had to bend double to get in her face.

I swear I would've clumped her but just then a scarlet Honda Prelude pulled up alongside. Maybe the driver was stoned. Maybe he thought Bella was waving to him with her knickers. How should I know what a bog-brush like him thinks?

He leaned across the passenger seat and said, "You girls looking for business?" And he grinned an evil dirty grin.

A funny humming started in my ears. My teeth felt like iron spikes. I spun on my toes and lashed out with my boot. I landed a thudding kick on the passenger door and saw it dimple like a belly-button.

"Oy!" the bog-brush yelled. "What the fuck are you playing at?" He opened his door and climbed out.

Suddenly everything was clear and simple. Just me and the metal. The metal and me. There was an empty space in my head. It was peaceful.

I vaulted onto the red bonnet. Just me and metal. And I was stronger. The red nose buckled as I jumped up and down on it. Thud-crimp-crump.

I leaped on the roof and danced on its red head. I made its scarlet skull bend under my weight. Thud-crimp-crump.

I jumped down. I got my hands under the doorsills. I rocked. I heaved. I wanted to turn the fucking motor over and send it rolling like a dead red dice across the road.

I could have. I'm strong enough.

The bog-brush swung and hit me on my back.

Bella hit the bog-brush with her handbag.

I straightened. The bog-brush took one look at my face and he started running.

"Yeah!" Bella screamed, "and I hope your cock drops off!" She was all pink and hopping, like she'd been savaging a motor too.

Then she said, "Shit, Eva, the law!"

I looked and saw polizei coming my way, trotting along with its pointy blue hat under its arm.

Bella vanished, whoosh, down the tube station steps.

I took off running after bog-brush.

Bog-brush turned and saw me coming. He thought I was coming for him so he put a sprint on.

I turned and saw polizei galloping after me, so I put a sprint on.

I caught up with bog-brush. Polizei caught up with me.

Bog-brush was jibbering. He went, "No—don't—you're mad . . ."

I grabbed him—like I do in the ring. I swung him round so fast his feet left the ground. I let go. I threw him at polizei.

If we'd been in the ring he'd of twanged off the ropes. We weren't in the ring. He crashed into polizei. Polizei stumbled and almost swallowed his walkie-talkie. They went down, ker-rash, all arms and legs. Polizei's helmet rolled into the gutter. Bog-brush landed on his chin.

It was ace. I felt a laugh rising like a burb in my throat. It exploded.

"Ha-ha-ha-ha," I went. Then I got up on my toes and pounded away.

I ran up the main road, dodging in and out of the crowds.

"Ha-ha-ha," I went. And people stopped to look. But I just ran on, turning into side roads, zig-zagging up alleys.

And then it started to rain, and no one was looking no more. I stopped laughing. I looked round. It was dark. It got dark on me when I was running and laughing.

Polizei was gone. There was no reason to run anymore.

Carl and the snake came rushing back into my head, and there was no reason to laugh anymore neither.

And in my head, Mr. Deeds said, "You're through. You're barred. You're out!"

So I stood there, not knowing where I was. I'd run so far I was lost.

The rain dribbled down the back of my neck—cold, tickling fingers of rain, making me shiver.

"Oh yeah, you too!" I shouted up at the sky. "Come on! Piss on me! Everyone else does."

An old woman said, "I know what you mean." She was selling evening papers on the street corner. She'd put one of her papers over her head like a roof.

"Here, dearie," she said, "have this on the house." And she handed me a paper roof. I stuck it on my head. The rain tit-tatted onto it and ran off over my shoulders.

"Keep yer head dry, dearie," the old woman said. "That's the important thing."

And I stood there wishing the python had turned on Carl, wound round him like a knot and choked the living shit out of him.

"Cheer up, dearie," the old lady said. "You're young. You got plenty of time. When you get to my age and you're still out in the rain selling papers—that's the time to worry."

"Where am I?" I said.

"You're in dead trouble, if you got to ask," the woman said.

And she croaked and coughed with laughter. But she told me where I was, and I set off home.

Chapter 22

My life was over.

Everything I ever wanted. Everything I ever worked for. Over. Finished. Kaput. Gone. Lost. Dead.

In my chest, under my ribs, was a great empty hole. My heart was all alone in there. It went dum-dum-dum, and I wondered why it bothered.

I let the dogs out. Ramses sneered at the rain. He sneered at me, and then he set off round the perimeter fence. Lineker looked at the rain and tried to get back into his shed. I barred his way.

"Oh no you don't," I told him. "If I've got to get wet, and Ramses got to get wet, you got to get wet too."

I followed the dogs round the fence. My beam of torchlight joggled along the ground. But I wasn't seeing things. I was seeing that glare of light. I was seeing the arc-lights bounce off the canvas and hit the red, white and blue ropes. The cage of light. I was hearing "Satisfaction," and a whole hall full of people going, "Bucket Nut! Bucket Nut!" I was seeing all those faces turn towards me. All those craning necks. All those eyes. Watching. Watching for *me*.

Only now they could watch till the North Pole melted away. I wasn't coming no more. None of it was mine no more.

It was all gone. There was nothing. Nothing except for my heart going dum-dum-dum in a big empty hole.

And the rain came down. And my paper roof sagged heavy on my head and fell apart. Like everything else.

But I kept on walking. And I kept the dogs going too. Every time Lineker tried to skive off under a wreck or a hoist I hauled him out.

"Feel sorry for yerself?" I shouted at him. "I'll give you something to be sorry for." And he gave me a pitiful look like I was the one who fixed the rain.

Ramses shook himself, and a great rainbow of water flew off of his thick coat and whacked me in the face.

"You did that on purpose!" I yelled at him. And he bounded off a couple of yards where I couldn't get at him. He grinned at me. His big yellow teeth gleamed in my torchlight.

"You'll pay for that, my lad," I told him. "Just wait and see."

But there was no one waiting to see. The crowd shut up. Their faces turned away. The arc lights went out. But my heart dum-dum-dummed, all by itself, in an empty hole.

And I didn't have no one to talk to. Not that it mattered. No one would of understood.

Dum-dum-dum. Dumb. Dumb. Dumb. All alone.

In solitary confinement. Doing time. Behind a socking great wire fence. Again.

It rained cold sheets of slimy water till about two in the morning. Then it stopped.

I went into the Static where it smelled of mould and old stale seaside. I lit the gas cylinder. I made a cup of tea. I towelled my hair till my scalp burned. I put on dry trackies. I opened a can of beans and ate them. I opened a can of corned beef and ate it. I opened a packet of custard creams and ate them too.

I still felt empty.

I opened a can of leek and ham soup and drank it cold from the can.

Nothing filled me up.

"I want," I said. But I couldn't say what I wanted. I wanted . . . everything.

"Ro-ro-ro," went Ramses from the gate. And I was glad because it took my mind off my stomach.

I picked up the torch and the tyre iron.

"Yak-yak-yak," went Lineker, getting there late as usual.

I lugged on my trainers and sloshed out through the muddy puddles to the gate.

"Ro-ro-ro," went Ramses. And he gave me a look which said, "Trust you to go indoors and get comfortable when there's work to be done." He pointed at the gate with his big muzzle.

"Eva. Eva?" called fat Mandy. "Eva, are you there?"

"Where would I be?" I said. "Who do you think looks after this place—the sugar plum fairy?"

"I can't see in the dark," she complained.

"You got any chocolate?" I said. Fat Mandy was the right person to ask.

"Chocolate?" she said. "Why?"

"Just fancied some," I said. "Got any?"

"I 'spect so," she said. "Somewhere. But, Eva, why I came is 'cos some of us decided to do the old fish trick, and we thought you'd like to be in on it."

"In? On it?"

"Yeah," she said. "Bella told us."

"What?"

"About the snake," Mandy said. "About those filthy pervs at your gym. About how they stole her money."

"And mine," I said. "Don't forget mine. *And* I got tossed. Don't forget that either."

"You got fired?" Mandy said. "Bella never told us that."

"Don't suppose she cared. She was too busy getting snake-raped."

"Isn't that the lowest?" she said. "None of us heard of anything like that before. I had a friend once who made a dirty movie with a donkey. But snakes! That's revolting." Fat Mandy shuddered, and her chins shook.

She said, "We had to do something. But we couldn't think of anything nasty enough, so we decided to do the old fish thing because it'll drive them crazy."

"Who?"

"The blokes at your gym, of course. Aren't you listening?"

"The fish thing?" The penny dropped. "At Sam's Gym?"

"That's what I'm telling you," fat Mandy said. "Lynn went to the wet fish stall at closing time and she's got cod, coley heads, mackerel. She's got shrimps, prawns, cockles, whelks and even a couple of duff oysters. Pounds of the stuff. And none of it cost us a penny. It was being chucked. Are you in, Eva? Because Kath's Billy brought his van and we're all waiting."

"I'm in," I said. I didn't bother with the padlocks and chains. I climbed over the gate and dropped down beside Mandy.

Kath was in the front of the van with Billy. I got in the back with Lynn and Mandy.

"Where's Bella?" I asked. Not that I wanted to see her.

"She stopped in," Kath said. "We took her some rum and coke to settle her nerves. She was feeling poorly."

"She didn't want to come out," Mandy said. "We told her about the fish."

"She said it was pathetic," Lynn said.

"Well, it *is* pathetic," Mandy said, "considering the provocation."

"You agreed," Lynn said.

"Never said I didn't," Mandy said. "You're in, I'm in. It's just a pity we couldn't think of something nastier."

"In the time," Kath said. "We didn't have long to think."

"Bella said she wouldn't take a step out of doors unless we were planning to torch the place," Lynn told me.

"No fires," I said.

"There's people living nearby," Lynn said. "Bella wasn't serious."

But I thought Bella was serious. She was just the type to set fires and not care who got hurt. She was also the type to stop indoors with her rum and coke and let everyone else do her dirty work. It's a good job I was doing dirty work for my own reasons, or I wouldn't of set foot outside the yard.

Kath's Billy brought his tool box and I brought my tyre iron and torch. But I did not have to break the doors down. Kath's Billy's tool box was full of interesting stuff. Maybe I should've asked myself why he didn't have a day job when he was so handy. But you don't get anywhere asking handy blokes why they don't have day jobs.

Anyway Kath's Billy got us in without leaving a mark on the doors. Then he sat in the van with headphones on and left the dirty work to us.

Let me give you some advice—if handling old fish turns your guts over, the old fish trick is not for you. The trick, you see, is to hide it where it won't be found. You have to stuff it into small places, into hollow tubes where it will ripen and melt and rot.

Once, when I was a little kid, a bunch of us put a kipper under the bonnet of the social worker's motor, right up close to where the fan blew air into the interior cooling system. The social worker was a dab hand at tinkering with people's lives, but she was hopeless at tinkering with cars. I don't think she looked under the bonnet from one month to the next. And when, each time she visited, her clothes smelled more and more of fish, and her anxious little mush got more and more anxious, we knew we'd won.

When you think about it, a gym is an ace place to pull a stunt like that.

"All these tubes is hollow," whispered Lynn.

Well of course they are, silly moo! A lot of gym equipment is made up of hollow steel tubes—like bicycle handle bars. You can stuff pounds of old fish into miles of hollow tubes in a gym. Specially if you thought ahead like Mandy and brought a handful of knitting needles to push it in.

"People have been known to move house when they can't get rid of a bad smell," Mandy said. And for a while I had fun thinking about Mr. Deeds, Gruff, Pete and Carl having to leave Sam's Gym because of the smell. They'd shoved me out. Now it was their turn.

None of the girls would go in the men's changing room because of the snake. There was a lot of argy-bargy about the snake. Mandy wanted me to let it out. Kath wanted me to kill it.

"It's only a snake," Lynn said. "It wasn't the snake's fault." But she hated snakes too.

I wanted to take it home but the girls wouldn't have it in the van. I quite fancied the idea, but feeding it would be a problem. I mean, think of keeping a pet you had to feed with other pets! Besides, I don't think Ramses and Lineker would stand for it.

I went in the men's changing room and I didn't touch the snake. It lay sleeping in its heated tank, all muscle, and thick as a big man's arm. I looked for the mice. I wanted to let the mice go. I found the boxes with Bella, Crystal, Mandy, Kath, Lynn and Stef written on them. But the boxes were empty. The mice were gone, and the snake was asleep. I decided not to tell the girls.

Instead, I took down the rails the shower curtains hung from, and I stuffed them full with prawns and shrimps. The heat and damp from the showers would make them stink to high heaven in no time at all.

The shrimps were wet and messy. They were whiffy already and some of their legs were dropping off. So I started thinking about Carl. Well I didn't actually think about him— I sort of saw him. I saw him and his boiling eyes and the look he had on his face when he had his hand clamped round the snake's neck and Bella spread out in front of him. And how he'd given me that very same look when he stared at me.

And I thought, if he could do that to Bella in front of Gruff and Pete, with Mr. Deeds right next door, what would he have done to her if he'd caught her somewhere where no one could see him? In an alley for example?

And I thought—Crystal's wrong. She's so wrong. She thought it was Stoat who clobbered Dawn. But she was wrong. It wasn't Stoat, it was Carl.

And then I was in a hurry. I wiped the shower rails clean and put them back up where they came from. I ran back to the gym.

The others were just finishing. They were tidying up the mess and leaving everything spick and span. Because the only way the old fish trick works is if no one knows you've done it. They mustn't know or else they won't clean the drains or take up the floor boards or bring in the sanitation expert. They've got to be ignorant, and go slowly crazy with a horrible smell they can't find and stop.

The old fish trick is a very sneaky sort of revenge. If it works you can drive people raving mad. Slowly.

But Bella was right—it wasn't enough. It wasn't strong enough and it wasn't bad enough.

I'd been enjoying meself because I wanted to do something—anything. But as soon as I thought about Carl and his 'roid-rage eyes I started to feel empty all over again. There just wasn't enough you could do to make him suffer.

I wanted him to suffer. I wanted Mr. Deeds and Gruff Gordon and Pete Carver to suffer too. They still had their lives but they'd taken mine away.

Old fish wasn't enough.

"Don't just stand there," Mandy said. "We got to go."

So we went. We piled back in the van and waited while Kath's Billy locked up the same way he'd unlocked. And then we drove off down the empty wet streets. And I'm surprised all the cats in the neighborhood didn't follow us.

I felt dirty. I sat there listening to Kath, Mandy and Lynn giggling and chat-chat-chatting. But I felt dirty and I dreamed about tearing Mr. Deeds' legs out of their roots and feeding them to Ramses and Lineker. One each. I dreamed about sticking Gruff's motor, with Gruff and Pete still in it, into the metal crusher at the yard. But I couldn't dream anything bad enough for Carl except perhaps sucking his boiling eyeballs out of his head—plop, plop, and frying them in deep fat and feeding them to him on a fork.

"There!" I'd say to him. "You've gone and eaten your own eyeballs. That'll teach you to look at me and Bella like you did. You won't do that again in a hurry." And I'd laugh. I would! I'd laugh.

"What's the matter?" Mandy said. "You sound like you're choking."

"Me?" I said. "It's the smell."

"You can wash," she said. "But just think what it'll be like at the gym next week!"

They all hooted. They were easily pleased.

Chapter 23

I had this idea. And I couldn't let go.

When Ramses catches a rat he spikes it with his yellow teeth. He grips it and crushes it till he breaks its back. He shakes it. He rattles its bones. He won't let go till it's dead three times over.

I had this idea about Carl and I could feel it between my teeth.

Carl beat Dawn to death.

I saw it in his eyes when he looked at me.

Carl killed Dawn. Crystal wanted me to do it to the man who did for Dawn

Well, maybe I would. Only I wasn't going to do it for Crystal. I wasn't going to do it for Dawn. Or Bella. Not them. No way.

But I'd do it to Carl for me. Not for them. Not 'cos he killed Dawn. But for what he did to me. He took my life. See? All the shit—with the women and the gym—all the shit with Mr. Deeds, all that started because Carl killed monkey face's sister, and monkey face wouldn't let go.

He took my life.

A life for a life. That's justice. Everyone says so. An eye for an eye. A tooth for a tooth. A life for a life. It's only right and proper.

Well, I'd let Carl keep his eyes. I'd let him keep his teeth—which is more than he let Dawn keep. But his life was mine because he'd taken mine.

No more body beautiful for Carl.

I was going to smash it. I'd wait for him. In a car. A Volvo would do the trick. It's well made. I'd wait for him in a Volvo. I'd rev the motor till he noticed. Then, when he was looking at me, I'd run him down. I'd crush him up against a brick wall. And I'd look him bang in the eyes while I did it. The last thing he'd see would be my eyes looking at his eyes. And he'd know. He'd know it was me. And he'd know for why.

Then I'd get out the Volvo. And I'd walk away.

That was my idea. It filled me up, and I wasn't hungry no more.

But first I had to find a Volvo to borrow. And before that I had to find Crystal.

Because, what if I couldn't walk away? Who would feed Ramses and Lineker? If something went wrong, someone had to look after my dogs. And that someone had to be Crystal. She owed me.

It was Sunday. On a Sunday I don't put the dogs in their pen. On a Sunday they roam free because no one comes to the yard to work.

I called them. "Ramses," I yelled. "Lineker! Come here yer bastards." And they came, all eager, tongues lolling out, because it was morning and time to be fed.

I fed them. I mixed up their meat and their biscuit, and I threw in a bit extra—just in case. And I gave them each a big Bonio biscuit to gnaw on. For a treat. Just in case.

"Listen, you wossoks," I said, "don't think I'm going soft. Don't think you can take advantage. Right? But if Crystal comes instead of me, you watch out for her, see?"

They wouldn't. Of course they wouldn't. They'd make sausage meat of her unless she had the brains to feed them with a very long spoon.

"You behave," I said. And Ramses snarled at me with his bass rumbling snarl because I was standing too close to him while he was eating.

"All right," I said. "Have it your own way. This once. But you'll miss me when I'm gone. See if you don't."

Then I left them.

Crystal would make Justin help. Justin knew a bit about dogs. He was too soft—I mean, hadn't he made tea for Queenie in his own bowl? But he knew a bit. Together, him and Crystal would see my two were all right. Crystal owed me.

I was doing her dirty work for her. As usual. So she fucking owed me.

I went to her gaff. I knocked on the door. I waited. I knocked again. She didn't come.

Don't worry, I said to meself. She's at the Premises. With Justin.

So I went down Mandala Street where I didn't want to go because I hadn't been there since the ruck when Stoat got sliced.

I went down Mandala Street and walked into the Premises.

Someone had tidied the gym. All the mats were in a neat pile in the corner. The kitchen was clean too. All in apple pie order.

I went to the bottom of the stairs and I yelled up.

"Crystal," I yelled. "Justin!"

But there was no one there. The place felt dead and empty.

"Crystal! Justin!" I yelled. I knew there was no one in but I wanted to hear a living voice even if it was only me own.

"Don't shout," said The Enemy from behind me. More fool me—I wanted to hear a living voice, but I didn't want to hear hers. Because, what do I hear when I hear her poxy voice? I hear, "Don't do this, don't do that, don't hit, don't shout, don't, don't, don't." I hear the voice of screws, of social workers, of polizei. "Don't," they say to everything worth doing.

Every time I want something, every time I want to get there first, make something of meself, every time I got me hand out to grab . . . "Don't," they say.

"Don't you tell me 'don't'!" I said.

"Okay," said The Enemy. "Okay, okay. What's the matter, Eva?"

"What's it to you?" I said. "I'm looking for Crystal. I got business with Crystal. And it's none of your business."

"I know," she said. "It's all right."

"It ain't all right," I said. "Where's Crystal? I can't do what I got to without she promises me to look after my dogs."

"I'm looking for Crystal too," The Enemy said.

"Who cares?"

"Wait!" she said. "It's important."

"To *you*," I said.

"To her," she said. "And it may be important to you too."

"Nothing's important to me," I said. "It's over. I got nothing to lose no more."

"That's silly," she said. Her with her nice coat, nice shoes, nice car. Her with her own business premises, with her own name written on the door. Her with her own bank account, her partner, her secretary-bird. Her with her polizei ways.

We stood toe to toe in the little kitchen and I told her how much she knew. She didn't listen.

"I'll make us a cup of tea," she said. "I don't suppose Justin will mind. He's a nice lad." She wasn't listening to me. She never does.

"You never fucking listen to me," I said.

"Yes I do." She filled the kettle at the tap and put it on the stove. "Why do I bother with you, Eva?" she said. "You're rude and rough—you're always stroppy. You shout at me. You blunder around like a rogue elephant with a burr up its backside. So why do I bother? What's in it for me?"

"Fucked if I know," I said. "You need muscle. I got muscle."

"True," she said. "You're useful when you're not in a terminal strop. But it's more than that."

"What?"

"Fucked if I know," she said. "Maybe, just once in a blue

moon, it's refreshing to see a woman who doesn't pretend when she's angry."

"I ain't angry."

"Liar," said The Enemy, giving her evil polizei grin. "But whatever it is, Eva, don't push it too far or too hard. Even I can lose patience."

"You can't threaten me," I said.

"I'm not trying to," she said. "I'm looking for Crystal. The police have arrested someone they think might be responsible for her sister's death."

"What?" I said. "WHAT? They nicked Carl?" I didn't know whether to howl or holler.

"Who?" The Enemy asked. "Carl?"

"Yeah," I said. "California Carl. You'd know him if you ever went to the wrestling. He's the one with the gold knickers and the body beautiful. The one all the girls wee themselves for. He clattered Dawn."

"A wrestler?" The Enemy said. And she stitched that pucker on her face. "Surely not. This is a little bloke—an out of work plasterer from Norwood."

"Gimme strength!" I said. "Typical fuckin' polizei! They nabbed the wrong bloke."

"Wait a minute," The Enemy said. And, knock me sideways, she made the tea. Everything in order. She warmed the pot. She stuck teabags in—one, two, three—everything just so.

Then she hopped up so she was sitting on the draining board. She said, "Tell me about Carl."

But I didn't. I'd said too much already. I'd told her Carl bumped Dawn. So now, if I bumped Carl she'd know it was down to me. I'd broken me own golden rule—don't say nothing. I've said it before, but I'll say it again—even a fish wouldn't get itself caught if it kept its big trap shut.

I said, "You ain't saying it was Stoat after all? Don't tell me Crystal got it right?" Because it'd give me a big laugh if Crystal *and* the polizei cocked up, and it was only me who knew about Carl.

"Stoat?" The Enemy said. She looked as if she was going to fall backwards into the kitchen sink.

Don't you just love it when someone who thinks she knows the lot finds out how pigging stone ignorant she is? I do. I just *love* it.

"Where's this tea?" I said. "I'm gasping."

The Enemy said, "What the *hell* have you lot been up to?"

And I said, "Always the stupid questions." I said, "You always ask. You never tell. So why should anyone tell *you* anything? What's it to you, anyway? What's Crystal got to do with you?"

"I thought you knew," she said. She poured some tea into two mugs and gave me one.

"Crystal's your mate," she said. "You're the one who told her I was in security."

"I never."

"Yes you did. The night we came here and found Justin squatting. She came to see me the next night. It was at that other property. Remember? I was installing security locks and you came in shouting about junkies."

"Oh yeah," I said. And I did—vaguely.

"She told me about her sister, and she said she was afraid the police wouldn't do anything about it because her sister was on the game. She asked me if I knew anyone on the local force. She said no one was telling her anything."

"That figures," I said.

"It does, actually," The Enemy said. "So I told Crystal I'd keep my ear to the ground for her. She said she was doing the same. She said she knew most of the other women and, if anyone was having any particular trouble with one of the customers, she'd hear about it."

It made me feel very bitter. Because that was why Crystal got me doing self-defence classes. That was why she turned my gym into a knocking shop, and stuck her stall right outside. She wanted to keep her little monkey eye on everyone. She was using me as her patsy.

"She had no right," I said, "getting me into it up to me neck."

"Self-defence lessons were a very good idea," The Enemy said.

"Yeah?" I said. "I thought so meself when I came up with it." I mean, why should monkey face get all the credit? It wasn't as if she had any of the talent.

The Enemy drank her tea and looked at me over the rim of her mug.

"But it went a bit too far, didn't it?" she said. "When you were actually staying here, protecting the women."

"I never!" I said. "I never done that. Justin cooked me dinner, that's all. And I nodded off in his armchair. I never knew the dirty slags was humping away in the same house."

"Didn't you? Didn't you really? I'd have thought something like that would be hard to miss."

I could of stuffed her down the plughole and turned on the cold water to wash her away. Her and her dirty mind.

"I was sleeping!" I said. "I didn't know nothing till Stef and Mandy started screaming. It wasn't my fault. And Stoat'd never've got cut if Mandy hadn't walloped him with her handbag."

"Ah," said The Enemy.

"Ah, what?" I said. "You don't know crap from a carpet."

"How right you are."

"Yeah."

"Well," The Enemy said, "whatever you think, and whatever Crystal thinks, the police picked up a bloke early this morning. He and a friend had beaten up a prostitute and taken her money. She was pretty badly hurt, but she managed to identify him. He wasn't cut or scarred in any way."

"So it ain't Stoat. Half Stoat's face fell off. Anyway he's in that hospital."

"The bloke I'm talking about made a statement," she went on. "But later, he retracted it. The police don't believe the retraction. They think he and his mate could be responsible for several attacks on prostitutes. Including the one on Dawn."

"Hah!" I said. "Shows how much the polizei know."

"Okay, Eva," The Enemy said. "Fair exchange. I told you what I know. Now it's your turn. You say Crystal thinks the man who killed her sister is this Stoat character? The one who got cut? Why?"

"You're simple," I said. "She's a monkey wrench. That's why. She gets an idea and it's the wrong idea. But will she let go? No she fucking won't. She'll hang on and hang on till her little jaw gets cramp and still she won't let go."

"Sounds like someone else I know," The Enemy said. "So who is Stoat?"

"No one. Just another tart-raker wanting a percentage."

"And he got hurt?" The Enemy said with that polizei gleam in her all-seeing peepers.

"Dunno," I said. "Fell on a steak knife, I heard."

"Last night?"

"Yeah."

"So that's him out of the frame," The Enemy said. "We'd better tell Crystal before she does something silly."

"You tell her," I said. "I've had a belly-full of her."

"Okay," The Enemy said. "Now, what about Carl?"

I put my mug down. "I don't know nothing," I said. "Except I got things to do." And I walked out the door.

"Hey, Eva!" The Enemy shouted. But I kept walking. And while I walked I laughed. Just for once in my life I got more out of The Enemy than she got out of me. So who's got the brains now, I ask you. Me. That's who.

The polizei was wrong as per usual.

Crystal was wrong.

The Enemy, Anna-know-it-all-Lee, actually knew as much as a fly on a tiger turd knows about a tiger.

The only one who *really* knew was me.

Chapter 24

I knew it was Carl, see. But I'd gone and said his name to The Enemy. And she wouldn't forget. Which meant I couldn't just go out and squash Carl without her putting two and two together. I had to wait. Which was a pity. When I get an idea I want to act straight away. But that Enemy's a door slammed in my face. Always in the way. Always saying, "don't."

So I went to Hanif's instead. I hadn't had any shuteye. And I'd eaten all the food in the Static. Whatever happened, I had to get my rest and keep me strength up.

But when I was in Hanif's, schlepping up and down the shelves, looking at the price of stuff, I remembered I didn't have nothing to keep me strength up for. I remembered I was finished in the ring. I remembered I'd been fined my fight money, and there was no more where that came from.

I was back on scag rations. But it's sod's law—as soon as you know you're back in Hunger-town, you want an enormous blow out. I wanted steak and fries. I wanted chicken pie and mash. I wanted six gallons of ice cream and tinned peaches. I didn't want to watch the pennies.

I was going to have to scratch around for more scratch if I wanted to live like I had been doing. I almost went back to talk to The Enemy. I almost went back to tell her all about

Stoat and Carl. Maybe she'd take me in as a partner and give me an office of me own with my name on the door—Eva Wylie, Security Expert. And I'd have my own secretary-bird to bring me tea at teatime. And regular wages. But I never went back. I don't care how hard it is—I don't gob to the polizei.

I bought a loaf of bread and a bit of bacon. That's all. And a tin of spaghetti hoops to wash it down. And some chocolate to keep my blood sugar from dropping off the scale. The bare necessities. Then I went back home. Scratch-city, here I come.

But did I get there? Did I—cobblers! Did anything—even walking home with a bit of bacon—turn out how it ought?

I just about made it to my gate when a motor pulled up alongside—a silly little green Renault with woolly dice, skeletons and furry rabbits dangling from the windscreen. And I was just asking meself who'd have a prat motor like that, when Bella leaned out and yelled, "Hop in, Eva."

"Hop in and hop off yerself," I said. I never did like Bella.

"Please yerself," Bella said. "I might've known you'd turn your back."

And then a little kid leaned over the back seat and said, "Please, please, please. Mum's doing her nut."

"Who's this?" I said.

"My Elton," Bella said. "He's a fan of yours, but he's normal otherwise."

"Are you really the London Lassassin?" Elton said.

I nearly said I wasn't, no more. But you don't like to disappoint the kiddies, do you? So I got in and sat with my knees under my chin. Trust Bella to pick a car that didn't fit me.

"We're going to the hospital." She jammed the car in gear and lurched away from the kerb. It didn't surprise me she was a crappy driver. I got whiplash, and little Elton got thrown in a heap on the back seat.

Bella said, "We got to hurry. The hospital's letting that bastard out today."

"Who? Stoat?"

"The one who, you know, with Stef." Bella glanced in her mirror to see if Elton was listening, which of course he was.

"So what?"

"Shut up and listen. Me and Elton went round to Justin's, didn't we, Elton? We was going to have a look at the puppies. Isn't that right, Elton?"

"Bang, bang," said Elton. He was playing with a Terminator toy, pretending he wasn't all ears.

"Justin's out," I said. "I was looking for Crystal earlier."

"They are now," Bella said. "We caught them both on their way out." She was grinding along at forty miles an hour in second gear.

"Listen, Eva," she said. "I know you don't give a toss, but this is serious. Crys and Justin's gone to meet Stoat. Crys thinks Stoat killed Dawnie."

"She's a pillock," I said. "Carl killed Dawn. You and me both know that."

Bella stalled the car. She turned to look at me and she took her foot off the pedal to do it. Bad drivers are like that.

"You're insane, Eva," she said. Cars piled up behind us hooting.

"Shit!" said Bella, and started off again, lurching and grinding.

"I thought Crystal was bonkers," she said. "But you're ten times worse. How could it be Carl? If Carl had come in the pub and gone out with Dawnie don't you think someone would've noticed? Carl's outstanding. All the girls would've seen him. If Dawnie'd scored a hunk like Carl it would've been big news."

"It was him," I said. "I saw it in his eyes. He could've killed you. He could've killed *me!*"

"Who could've killed you, Mum?" little Elton said.

"Shut up, Elton," Bella said. "Could've! Could've! 'Course he could've."

"There, then!"

"But he didn't, did he? And he didn't cut Stef. And he didn't kill Dawn. So don't be stupid!"

"Who you calling stupid?"

"You!" Bella said. "Okay, so Carl's a total freak and he hates us. So what? So do thousands. Millions. I said the same to Crys. I said, 'The bastard knifed Stef. He wants our business. So what? Does that make him different? He's not worth ruining your life over,' I said. But she won't have it. No. The bastard who knifed Stef killed Dawn, she says. 'Why?' I said. 'There's bastards all over the streets who want to hurt us or take our money. Why pick him?'"

"The polizei nicked another one last night," I said. "They say *he* killed Dawn."

"There you are, then," Bella said. "I'm surprised they haven't nicked twenty. But try telling Crys that! *She* says that Stoat bastard killed her Dawnie, and he's going to pay. Pay! She's the one who'll pay. Her and Justin. They'll pay and pay and pay. They could spend the rest of their lives paying."

There was this big black hole under my ribs and my heart went dum-dum-dum, all by itself in there. I said, "What's she going to do, Bella? What's that stupid little monkey wrench going to do?" Because I knew Crystal wouldn't give up. She's like that—take it from one who knows—if she gets her teeth into someone, she never lets go. Never. Not till she's had satisfaction.

"Something," Bella said. "I don't fucking know. They had two boxes. Crys had one, Justin had the other."

"What was in the boxes?"

"Puppies," said little Elton. "There was puppies in the boxes. But they wouldn't let me see."

"Shut up, Elton," said Bella.

"Why did you bring him along?" I asked.

"No one to leave him with," she said. "Granpa went to church."

And we bumped and ground all the way to St. Thomas's hospital with Bella swearing at the traffic, and everyone else swearing at Bella.

She swung in where it said, "No Entry," without using her indicator, and whizzed round the side of the hospital in second gear—always in second—and then she stalled.

"Where are we?" she said.

"Just get the fuck on with it," I said. What with her driving and all I was feeling an up-chuck coming on.

"Over there!" shouted Elton. "They're over there with the puppies." He was kneeling on the back seat pointing with his Terminator toy.

"Shut up, Elton," said Bella. She was twisting the car key and squinting over her shoulder at the same time.

But Elton was right. On the other side of a little wall, where the sane people had parked their cars properly, was Justin and Crystal.

I flung my door open. Bella twisted the key. But she hadn't put the motor in neutral so the car bucked forward and stalled again. The open door crashed against the wall. I tangled my foot in my plastic shopping bag and I fell out the car on my arse.

"Hurry," Bella squealed. "Stop them."

"Stop what?" I said. I jumped to my feet. I climbed on the little wall. I looked.

And from up on the wall I saw Crystal and Justin with two cardboard boxes resting on the bonnet of a car.

I saw Crystal pointing and Justin turning to look.

I saw Stoat walking slowly down the entry ramp, half his face hidden in white bandage.

I saw Crystal reach in one of the boxes. She pulled out a bottle. An ordinary glass milk bottle. It was full of liquid. The neck was stuffed with rag.

I jumped off the wall.

"Stop!" I yelled. But the wind from the river whipped the word out of my mouth and blew it the wrong way.

I started to run. I dodged between parked cars. I whacked into wing mirrors.

I saw Crystal hand the bottle to Justin. She took a cigarette lighter from her pocket. She cupped her hand round it. She struck the flint.

"Don't!" I bellowed, and the wind blew it back down my throat.

I couldn't run fast enough. The cars were parked too close together.

Justin shielded the flame with one hand. He turned and started to trot towards Stoat. All unawares, Stoat walked slowly towards him.

I was close. But I wasn't close enough.

"Justin!" I howled. "Don't!"

Crystal turned to me. Her little face was all bare and waxy. "Eva," she said. "You came."

Stoat saw Justin. He saw the flaming bottle. He threw up his hands to protect his face.

Justin chucked the bottle.

I stopped. There was nothing I could do anymore.

The bottle flew in an arc. The flaming rag fluttered. Over and over, it spun. It landed at Stoat's feet. Stoat watched it coming. He watched it somersaulting over and over till it fell at his feet.

The glass splintered. Crack.

Two ladies with flowers in their hands started to scream.

The bottle shattered. For a split second nothing happened. And then whoosh! Justin ducked. Crystal ducked. I ducked. The ladies with the flowers flung themselves down on the ground.

The flames went ker-flump whoosh. They shot up Stoat's legs. They bloomed on his clothes like red and orange roses.

Justin picked himself up and legged it to Crystal. He grabbed her hand. She tried to grab the second box, but it fell.

They ran. They raced away to the Embankment. They looked like two kids playing. They ran hand-in-hand as fast as their legs would take them.

I could smell burnt meat.

Everyone was screaming. People poured out of the hospital entrance.

I closed my eyes. I couldn't stand to look. I sank down on my haunches between the parked cars.

"You wasn't quick enough," Bella said from behind. "You just wasn't quick enough."

"Oh yeah?" I snarled. "And where was you?"

"Oh look," said little Elton. "Puppies!"

"Fucking shut *up*," Bella screeched. "Shut up and get back in the car. Who said you could follow me?"

"No, *look*," said Elton. He ran away from us to the car where Crystal had waited for Stoat. He was right. The box which fell had fallen on its side. And tipped out, near it, was two small grey balls of fluff.

"He's fucking right—the little tyke's right," I said. I scrambled to my feet. I turned my back on Stoat and the screams and the smell. Bella didn't want to watch either.

She said, "Let's get out of here, Eva, before someone starts taking names and asking questions."

"We never saw nothing," I said.

"'Course not," she said. "But let's go before anyone asks."

"We better take the pups," I said.

"Fuck the pups," she said. But she went to where Elton was bending over the two balls of fluff.

"What's wrong with this one?" Elton asked. He picked up one pup, and its head lolled out of his hand like it was hanging on a thread.

"Oh shit!" Bella said. "Put it down, Elton. It's sleeping, isn't it, Eva?"

Stupid cow. She brought little Elton to a cremation, but she couldn't admit to him that one of Queenie's pups had died.

The burnt meat smell on the air was Stoat, but Bella wouldn't tell her kid a pup was dead.

"Come away!" she shouted at Elton. "Do as you're told." She snatched his hand and yanked him away from the puppies, dragging him back to her car. He started yelling and kicking her ankles.

That was the last I saw of them. Her squawking, him wailing. They didn't wait for me.

I didn't want them to. I'd had enough of Bella to fill a dumpster.

I squatted down and picked up the puppies. The littlest one was stone dead. It never even got its eyes open. There was nothing to be done. I put it back in the box.

But the bigger one was alive. Just.

It looked like a blind fluffy maggot. Queenie's pup. It shivered in the wind. I smoothed the grey fluff with one finger, and the little maggot turned its nose towards my finger.

"Oh shit," I said. I stuffed the little thing under my sweat shirt next to my skin, and I tucked my sweat shirt into my jeans.

It was what Justin should've done. I told him to keep the pups warm. But did he listen? Oh no. He'd rather listen to Crystal and throw petrol on bastards she didn't like. He brought Queenie's pups out in the cold with only a cardboard box for shelter.

"Oy, you!" someone said.

I got up and saw a dirty great uniform coming straight for me. It wasn't polizei. It was a hospital security guard.

"What you got there?" he said.

"Dunno," I said. "Looks like a dead puppy."

I buttoned my jacket so he wouldn't see I had a live one under my jumper.

"Oh," he said. "Well, never mind that. There's been an attack on one of the hospital patients. Those ladies over there say you might have seen something."

I looked over, at last. But I couldn't see Stoat. There was a bunch of white coats and nurses and blankets and stuff. But thank gawd I couldn't see Stoat.

"You must've seen something," the guard said.

"Not me," I said.

"The ladies said a young hooligan threw a petrol bomb," the guard said. "You couldn't have missed that."

"I heard a bit of an explosion," I said. "And I ducked. But I never saw nothing."

"Nothing?"

"Well," I said, 'cos I had an idea. "I saw three lads running away."

"Three?" he said. "What were they like?"

"Oh you know," I said, "kids. Scruffy. Just kids."

"Okay," he said, all official. "You'd better wait till the police arrive. They're going to want to hear your description of the three boys."

"All right," I said. But I was having a hard job not laughing, because he believed me, and 'cos Queenie's little pup was nosing round my belly-button.

But as soon as the guard turned his back I walked away. I walked to the river and along the Embankment, back towards home. You think I should've stopped around to answer questions? You're barmy. Tell more lies for monkey face and Justin? Where's the satisfaction? I done my bit. It was the same old story—me doing Crystal's dirty work. If there was any satisfaction up for grabs, she grabbed it. As usual. She thought she'd fried the bastard who killed Dawn. Stupid monkey. She thought she'd had her eye for an eye, tooth for a tooth. Well, let her. I wasn't going to tell her different. At least it got her off my back. I was going home.

I wasn't following Justin and Crystal. No. When they ran away hand-in-hand they ran to the station. To Waterloo, where I first met Crystal, and Justin met the rich man the day he came to London.

I walked along in the wind with Queenie's pup tucked up under my ribs. And my heart went dum-dum-dum. And his little heart went dit-dit-dit-dit.

And I thought, I'll call you Milo. I'll call you Milo after the greatest fuckin' wrestler of all time—Milo of Croton who won the Greek Olympics five times straight.

"You better grow up big and strong," I told the pup. "Because this ain't a world to be small and weak in, believe me."

But the pup just squirmed and tickled my belly.

"You hear me, Milo?" I said. "Big and strong, or Ramses will eat you up."

I knew I'd have to keep the pup under my sweater for a long time. I'd spoken for true. Because Ramses *would* eat Milo alive if I didn't watch out for him.

But Milo would grow up big and strong. He had all the makings—a German shepherd for a mum and something huge and bull-nosed for a dad. All he had to do was learn how to fight and learn mental discipline. Like me. I learned all that, so I could teach him.

And then I thought about how much I know. And it's a lot. I know lots and lots of things. And I'm fucked if I'll let a bolly-whacker like Mr. Deeds or California Carl take it all away. I was born to fight—so I'll bleeding well fight. There's more than one promoter in the world, isn't there? Somewhere out there, there's a promoter, and he'll be *honoured* to have the London Lassassin fight on his bill. Honoured.

"You and me," I said to little Milo. "Born to fight. The bastards won't know what bit them."

If an ancient Greek could win the Olympics five times, what couldn't I do? Eh? Tell me that!